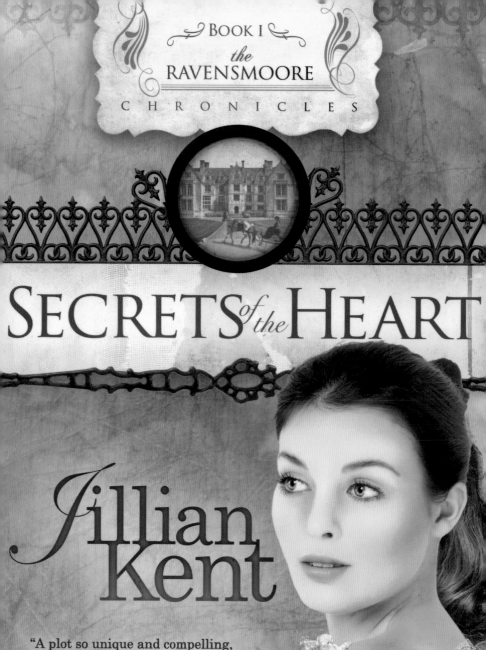

Book I

the RAVENSMOORE

CHRONICLES

SECRETS of the HEART

Jillian Kent

"A plot so unique and compelling, pages fly and sleep will be lost... and never more happily so."
—JULIE LESSMAN, award-winning author of the Daughters of Boston series

A feast for fans of historical romance, and a superb debut from Jillian Kent.

—JAMES SCOTT BELL
AUTHOR OF *TRY DARKNESS* AND *PRESUMED GUILTY*

A compelling first novel by Jillian Kent, *Secrets of the Heart* transports the reader into the mores of nineteenth-century England where thoughtfully crafted, believable characters are daring and bold, determined to live their dreams.

—MAE NUNN
AUTHOR OF *A TEXAS RANGER'S FAMILY*,
AMERICAN CHRISTIAN FICTION WRITER'S
CAROL AWARD WINNER 2010

An impressive debut for Regency romantic suspense author Jillian Kent. Fast-paced, engrossing, with thoroughly engaging characters. A compelling story of two British aristocrats who struggle against the social strictures of their class, all the while seeking their true calling—and true love. A rousing tale of romance and suspense set amidst the genteel—and some not so genteel—British upper crust.

—KATHLEEN MORGAN
AUTHOR OF *A HEART DIVIDED*

Some books are meant to be savored. Jillian Kent's *Secrets of the Heart* is one of those books. With fine writing, an admirable heroine, and vivid historical details, the novel was a joy to read. I, for one, will be anxious to read the next installment of the trilogy.

—SHELLEY SHEPARD GRAY
AUTHOR OF THE SEASONS OF SUGARCREEK SERIES

In a breathless historical debut, Jillian Kent unveils secrets of the heart and soul in Regency England amid a lush tapestry of romance, intrigue, and suspense. With vibrant prose, rich historical threads, and well-woven mystery,

Secrets of the Heart engages readers with a plot so unique and compelling, pages fly and sleep will be lost…and never more happily so.

—Julie Lessman
Author of the Daughters of Boston series

A positively brilliant debut novel by Jillian Kent! With a stirring romance, an evil villain, flawed but lovable characters, and enough intrigue and suspense to keep you turning pages long into the night, *Secrets of the Heart* sends you on an adventure you won't soon forget.

—Marylu Tyndall
Author of the Surrender to Destiny series

In *Secrets of the Heart* Jillian Kent takes the reader on a fast-paced adventure through the Regency world of 1817 Yorkshire. From the aristocratic country houses of the *ton* to the horrific interior of a lunatic asylum, Kent gives a convincing portrait of the grieving process and a very sensitive look at mental illness. The story is enhanced by a lovable cast of secondary characters who befriend the heroine in the most unlikely places. Young Lady Madeline and doctor-in-training Lord Ravensmoore overcome one obstacle after another before love can triumph. A charming and action-filled Regency romance by first-time author Jillian Kent.

—Ruth Axtell Morren
Author of *A Bride of Honor* and *To Be a Mother*

Secrets of the Heart is an amazing first book and certainly not to be Jillian Kent's last. She brings the Regency era to life with its light and dark sides for an engrossing romance tinged with danger and suspense.

—Linda Windsor
Author of *Healer, Thief,* and *Rebel,*
The Brides of Alba Arthurian trilogy

SECRETS *of the* HEART

BOOK I

the
RAVENSMOORE

C H R O N I C L E S

Jillian Kent

SECRETS *of the* HEART

BOOK I
the RAVENSMOORE
CHRONICLES

REALMS

Most CHARISMA HOUSE BOOK GROUP products are available at special quantity discounts for bulk purchase for sales promotions, premiums, fund-raising, and educational needs. For details, write Charisma House Book Group, 600 Rinehart Road, Lake Mary, Florida 32746, or telephone (407) 333-0600.

SECRETS OF THE HEART by Jillian Kent
Published by Realms
Charisma Media/Charisma House Book Group
600 Rinehart Road
Lake Mary, Florida 32746
www.charismahouse.com

All Scripture quotations are from the King James Version of the Bible.

The characters portrayed in this book are fictitious unless they are historical figures explicitly named. Otherwise, any resemblance to actual people, whether living or dead, is coincidental.

Cover design by Rachel Lopez
Design Director: Bill Johnson

Visit the author's website at www.jilliankent.com.

Library of Congress Cataloging-in-Publication Data
Kent, Jillian.
  Secrets of the heart / Jillian Kent.
      p. cm.
  ISBN 978-1-61638-185-1
  1. Aristocracy (Social class)--England--19th century--Fiction. I. Title.
PS3611.E6737S43 2011
813'.6--dc22
                                    2010053878

E-book ISBN: 978-1-61638-436-4

First Edition

11 12 13 14 15 — 9 8 7 6 5 4 3 2 1
Printed in the United States of America

This book is dedicated to everyone who has
battled the twin demons of depression and doubt.

He shall cover thee with his feathers,
and under his wings shalt thou trust: his
truth shall be thy shield and buckler.

—PSALM 91:4

ACKNOWLEDGMENTS

*D*ON'T EVER LET anyone tell you that something can't be done. I'm happy to see this book born into the world. Writing a book and getting it published really is similar to having a baby. This book greets you because of many, many helping hands. I'm grateful to all the folks at Charisma Media and Realms. Debbie Marrie, my acquisitions editor, saw a glimmer of promise in this story, and Lori Vanden Bosch, my editor, helped me mold it into the story you are sure to enjoy. Many thanks to everyone at Realms who helped make my dream a reality.

Every writer needs a mentor, so a huge thanks to James Scott Bell, mentor, teacher, and friend. I'm grateful to my awesome agent, Rachelle Gardner, who held out her hand and lifted me up when I really needed it. My thanks also go to years of studying the craft with members of the American Christian Fiction Writers and members of Romance Writers of America, including the hometown gang of the Ohio Valley RWA in Cincinnati, Ohio.

There are always those who encourage you when you just don't know what to do next, whether it's a life situation or a writing dilemma. My friends Mae Nunn, Serena B. Miller, and Vicki Cato have seen me through those times, and for that I am forever grateful to these sisters in Christ and sisters of the pen, along with critique group buddies Ginny Powers, Catherine Hershberger, and Paulette Lotspeich.

Last, but far from least, are my husband Randy Nutter, hero extraordinaire, who taught me how to laugh; my daughter Katie, who taught me the power of patience; and my daughter Meghan, who taught me the value of stepping out of my comfort zone. And then there's my mother, Edith Baroudi, a nurse, who made sure I got an education. Thanks, Mom! And thanks to my aunt, Helen Johnson, who taught me how to ride a horse, win a blue ribbon, and sparked my imagination by reading Alfred Noyes's poem "The Highwayman" to me all those years ago.

PART ONE

It is a sort of waking dream, which, though a person
be otherwise in sound health, makes him feel symptoms of every disease; and, though innocent, yet
fills his mind with the blackest horrors of guilt.
                              —WILLIAM HEBERDEN,
                    ENGLISH PHYSICIAN, 1710–1801

PROLOGUE

Yorkshire, England, 1817

"WHO'S THERE?" LADY Madeline Whittington reined her horse in and listened. She looked into the dense, wooded edge of the forest of Richfield, her family home. "Did you hear something, Shakespeare?" She petted her gelding's neck.

The horse's ears pricked forward. She studied the fading sun. Darkness would close in soon. It would be unwise to tarry over long.

The forest edges, thick with bare brambles now, would become heavy with foliage in the next few months. If she was fortunate, the blackberries would return. Last year's winter had been harsh, and she'd had to go without that succulent treat.

A shadow flitted from within, causing a branch to tremble.

"Come out." Madeline hardened her voice. "Come out at once." Papa had taught her to be firm and bold when encountering the unknown, but also cautious. She reached for the revolver in her pocket wishing she hadn't sent Donavan, their groomsman, on ahead. But she'd desperately wanted to ride alone for a few short minutes.

Two huge brown eyes in a tear-streaked and muddy face peered between parted branches held back by long slim fingers. Blood trickled from scratches on the girl's arms and hands.

"Who are you? Why did you not answer me?"

1

The eyes grew wider.

Madeline's heart softened along with her voice.

"It's safe. I won't hurt you." She tore a hunk of bread from a leather pouch strapped across her shoulder. "Are you hungry?" She offered a large portion. Crumbs fell.

The girl took a step toward her and bit her lower lip. Bruises colored the young woman's wrists and ankles, her only covering a torn chemise and ill-fitting shoes with no laces.

"What's your name? Can you understand me?"

Brown Eyes held out a hand.

"You are hungry. Of course you are. Come closer. I'm going to toss the bread to you. Is that all right?"

The pitiful creature nodded and held out both hands.

She understands me. Madeline aimed and carefully threw the bread.

The silent stranger caught it and stuffed the bounty into her mouth so fast that Madeline feared the girl might choke.

"Will you come with me?" Madeline held out her hand. "You may ride with me."

Brown Eyes stepped back.

"Don't go. It's dangerous. You cannot stay here. I won't hurt you."

The girl looked into the woods at the lowering sun and then at Madeline's outstretched hand. Brown Eyes stepped backward. One step. Two steps.

"Wait." Madeline unbuttoned her cape. "Take this. It's far too cold with only a chemise to cover you. You'll freeze to death." She threw the long, fur-lined wrap to Brown Eyes.

The girl gathered the offering and backed into the forest, keeping her eyes locked on Madeline's until she turned and ran.

"No! Wait. Please wait." Madeline searched for a way through the thicket. Not finding any, she pushed her mount farther north until she found an entry. How could she help this girl without scaring her out of her wits? She found the girl's path. Darkness chased them.

"Where are you?" Madeline shouted. "It's too dangerous."

Shakespeare's ears pricked forward, and she caught the sound of scurrying ahead and then spotted Brown Eyes. Low-hanging branches attacked Madeline, clawing her with their long-reaching arms as she herded the girl toward a nearby hunting cabin. Minutes later they broke through the trees and entered a clearing where the outline of a small cabin was silhouetted against the fast-approaching night sky.

Pulling her mount to a stop, Madeline kicked her booted foot out of the stirrup and narrowly avoided catching her skirt on the pommel as she slid to the ground.

"I won't hurt you," Madeline called. The girl hesitated and then ran again. Gathering up her skirt, Madeline chased after the girl, grabbing for the cape that trailed behind. She easily caught the girl, who fell to the ground in a heap and rolled into a ball with the cape wrapped around her.

Madeline knelt beside her and spoke gently. "Please don't run. I'm not going to take the cape from you. It's yours. A gift."

Brown Eyes panted with fear.

"It's all right. I'm not going to hurt you. I want to help." Madeline patted the girl's shoulder.

She flinched.

"I'm sorry you are afraid. I want you to stay here. See the cabin? You can stay here."

The girl peeked out from behind the cape, her ragged breathing easing from the chase through the woods. She looked at the cabin and then at Madeline.

"I know you've suffered something horrid. Come. You'll be safe here. Trust me." Madeline stood and offered a hand up.

Brown Eyes took her hand and followed her into the cabin.

CHAPTER I

Each one sees what he carries in his heart.
—Johann Wolfgang von Goethe

"Have you ever made a mistake?" Madeline settled into her saddle, avoiding her friend's probing gaze. Anxiety rippled through her as she stroked the neck of her large bay gelding while they waited for the hunting horn to sound.

"Not to my recollection." Lady Gilling gathered her reins. "I'm quite good at avoiding them."

"I shouldn't have come." Madeline's gloved hands trembled. "I hate hunting." She'd tried to avoid the ride today. She wanted to visit her brown-eyed fugitive, and she'd been unable to take food to the girl this morning because of the hunt. Mother had insisted she rejoin society *this* morning, and she'd enlisted her best friend Hally, Lady Gilling, to be certain that she rode today.

"You used to love the hunt." Hally circled her dappled gray mare around Madeline's horse, inspecting Madeline as though she were about to enter the ballroom instead of the final hunt of the season.

Madeline shook her head. "You're wrong. I love riding, not hunting."

"Perhaps. However, at one and twenty, you are far too young to give up on this world. And even though I'm only two years your elder, I've had my sorrows too, and I have found ways to battle the pain. You must do the same."

"I'm sorry, Hally." The heat of shame spiraled into her cheeks despite the sting of the cold, early spring air. She thought of her brother and sister who had died during the past two years and of Papa who had joined them last year. What could be worse—losing siblings and a parent or a beloved husband, as Hally had only two years ago?

Madeline's horse pranced in rhythm to her rising anxiety. "Easy, Shakespeare. Easy, boy." She tried to focus on the gathering outside Lord Selby's manor house where horses and riders crowded together in a flurry of anticipation. She took a deep breath to rein in her frustration and hoped her mount would settle down along with her. "Hally, you pick the most difficult of times to discuss such personal issues."

Hally edged her mount next to Madeline's horse. "I do this because you have been in hiding ever since your father died. If you refuse to mix in polite society, they will refuse you."

"Have I become a ghost?" Mist floated over the fetlocks on her horse, a dreamlike ground covering that made it seem like they waited in the clouds. "Do you not see me?" She wanted to slip away from this show of rejoining society. She wanted to check on the girl. She wanted to leave. "Does society not see me here today?"

"For the first time in a year at the hunt." Hally reached over and pushed back the netted veil that covered Madeline's face, tucking the material into her hat. "There, that's much better. Now everyone can see you."

"And that's supposed to make me feel better?" She reached up to pull the veil back into place, but Hally stopped her.

"Your mother worries, Maddie. Since your father died, you have refused to mingle, you have refused to travel, and until today you have refused to ride with the hunt. Your father would have scolded you for such behavior."

Madeline's chin trembled. "That was cruel. I enjoyed the hunt because Papa loved it when I rode with him. He's gone now. I don't have to hunt to ride."

Hally lowered her voice. "I'm sorry. I know you miss him, but society's prescribed period of mourning is quite enough. I've always believed six months far too long, and here you are six months after that. You need not suffer further isolation." She leaned closer and whispered. "For heaven's sake, Maddie, your mother is out of mourning."

"I'm afraid she thinks of allowing Lord Vale to court her." There, she'd said it aloud. "May God forgive her. She dishonors Papa's memory."

"So that is what worries you. Your mother is interested in a man."

"He's not just a man, Hally. He's Lord Vale, and there's much speculation about his actions and investments. Yet here I am, pretending all is well." Madeline lifted her chin and watched her breath dissipate like puffs of smoke on the wind.

"Pretending is a fine art." Hally smiled. "Everyone must pretend to some extent, dear, or life would be far too complicated."

"I wonder where life will lead now. Mother isn't thinking clearly and allows Vale too much time with her at Richfield. I no longer know where I belong, but certainly not in this world of gossip and gowns."

"We will discuss your fears later, my dear. But for now, your mention of gowns is a subject that warrants further consideration. I think it is time we turn our thoughts toward lighter matters, and talk of fashion will do nicely."

"Fashion?" Madeline scrunched up her nose. "Please tell me you jest."

"Fashion is always important." Hally tilted her head in thoughtful study. "Your black wool riding habit does nothing to draw attention. Green would set your hazel eyes ablaze or, at the very least, a lush russet to show off the highlights in your hair."

"Why does this matter so much to you?" For the first time that day, Madeline studied her friend in turn. A dark lavender velvet riding habit enhanced her figure. The fabric against the gray of her horse together with the soft early morning light provided Hally with an air of regal confidence, confidence Madeline envied. She was already looking forward to the end of this event.

"Because you are my friend, and melancholia does not become you."

"Nonsense. I used that emotion up long ago."

"So you say." Hally scanned the area. "The chill has bestowed you with blushing cheeks, a most charming quality that will endear you to the male population. There are some very eligible and very handsome gentlemen here today. I shall be most pleased to make an introduction."

Tentacles of panic snaked through her. "I don't believe that is required today." *Nor any other day.* The thought of an introduction to a gentleman terrified her. She'd witnessed Mother's agony when she'd lost her children and then her beloved husband. Why allow the heart such vulnerability to begin with? "Really, Hally. Do you never grow weary of your matchmaking schemes? Do you not find such things awkward?"

"My James was a rare man. I'll never stop missing him…and the children we might have enjoyed. I want you to experience that kind of love, Maddie."

Sorrow shadowed Hally's blue-green eyes. "I'm sorry. I didn't mean to be so selfish." The last thing she had wanted to do was cause more heartache.

Hally waved a dismissive hand. "It's all about love, dearest. Don't forget that."

"But love is—"

"Necessary. Not awkward. You must accept that. You missed your London season four years ago. I know many at this event. As a respectable widow I can be a great help."

Madeline didn't argue. "I appreciate your concern." She hoped to get through the hunt and the social gathering unscathed by men and their unwanted advances. The gathering after the hunt could prove to be difficult. Many men would drink, and some would drink too much, making themselves perfectly obnoxious. "Perhaps we can just ride today and think on these matters another time."

"Forgive me, dear. I'm overzealous when it comes to you. I will not speak of *opportunities* again this day. But I pray you'll think about what you are doing, think about your future, think about your life. If you continue to hide yourself away, you will not be accepted by polite society. And since your mother is ready to begin living again, should you not as well?"

The budding tree branches swayed gently in the early morning breeze and, bending toward her, seemed to hesitate on the wind, awaiting her reply. "I am in no mood to meet anyone."

"We'll speak of your moods later." Hally smiled. "Let's enjoy the present."

Bright streaks of sunlight burst through the cloudy, late March sky. Madeline contemplated her friend's advice. "You're right. It's a beautiful morning. Time to imagine the future. As for now, I'm just not certain how to proceed."

Hally reached across her mare and patted Madeline's hand. "I'll be happy to show you the way."

Lord Selby's raucous laughter roared through the crowd as he muscled his way through with his horse. Another rider crashed into her while trying to get out of Selby's way, causing Madeline's mount to lurch sideways into Hally, nearly unseating each of them.

Madeline's breath caught, but she quickly tightened her reins and gained control.

"Easy, Shakespeare. It's all right, boy." She stroked the gelding's neck to calm him and looked to see if the other rider had recovered his balance.

A pair of green eyes, wide with concern, locked on her. The beginning of a smile dimpled the man's cheeks. A strong chin, straight nose, and clean-shaven face provided him with the good looks of a gentleman in a Van Dyck portrait. She felt the heat of a sudden blush and, not trusting her voice, held her tongue.

Apology etched his handsome face. "I beg your forgiveness." He arched a single black brow. "Are either of you hurt?"

Madeline sucked in a deep breath to calm her nerves and brushed her skirt free of imaginary grime. "I am unscathed, sir," she assured him, pulling her gaze away. "Lady Gilling?"

"No injuries here." She pushed her purple plumed hat back into place.

Madeline turned back to him. The sudden urge to chuckle surprised her, but instead of laughing, she molded herself into a woman of politeness and poise. "It appears that we have survived the excitement."

"I'm afraid Lord Selby is already in his cups this fine morning." The charming stranger maneuvered his mount closer and lowered his voice. "Hippocrates here found Selby's bellowing objectionable." His smile radiated genuine warmth. "I must concur with his animal instinct."

The blare of the hunting horn filled the air. The fine gentleman tipped his hat and disappeared into the crush of riders. A twinge of disappointment tugged at Madeline's heart.

"Are you certain you are unharmed?" Hally asked as they trotted their horses out of the gate. "You look a bit pale."

"I can't help but think I've seen that man somewhere before.

Does he look familiar to you?" Madeline searched for him as they rode out.

"No. I don't believe so. Could it be that you just met a gentleman of importance with no introduction from me at all?"

"Strange. I can't recall where, but I'm almost certain."

"The hounds are on the move," Hally said. "We must discuss your newly made acquaintance later. We're off!"

The baying hounds drowned out the possibility of further discussion. A glimmer of anticipation lightened Madeline's heart. The challenge of the ride distracted her from other concerns and strengthened her spirit. *Perhaps I have been a bit melancholy of late.*

Her worries lessened with each stride of her horse and with each obstacle cleared, but flashes of the past whirred by her as swiftly as the hunting field. The horses in front of her threw clumps of dirt into the air as they pounded across the countryside in pursuit of a fox she hoped would evade them.

A pheasant burst from its nest. Startled, Shakespeare faltered as he launched toward the next stone wall. Madeline leaned far forward and gave him extra rein in an attempt to help him clear the barrier, but she knew immediately he was off stride.

The crack of rear hooves against the top of the wall thundered through her heart. Shakespeare stumbled and went down on his knees, tossing her over his head. Madeline landed with a jarring thud on her left side. She struggled to get up, but racking pain paralyzed any attempt at movement.

"Maddie!" Hally dismounted, ran to Madeline, and knelt at her side.

She rolled onto her back and groaned. *A fine mess.* "Shakespeare? Is he hurt?"

"Are *you* all right?" Hally clutched Madeline's hand in her own. "Maddie?"

She lay still, trying to assess the damage. "I believe I may have broken my arm." Tears stung her eyes. "Where's Shakespeare?" She prayed he bore no serious injuries.

A shadow fell over Madeline. "I've already looked at him. He's shaken, temporarily lame, but on his feet. He will be taken to Selby's stables to begin the healing process. Unlike your horse, young lady, I suggest you not move."

The gentleman had returned. And here she lay, flat on her back, her riding skirt disheveled, an indelicate position, indeed. She did not need a man now, especially this very interesting man.

She squeezed Hally's hand. "I'm not presentable," she whispered.

"This is hardly the time to be concerned about one's appearance," Hally whispered back, smoothing Madeline's skirt down toward her ankles, a gesture that reminded Madeline of her maid making the bed. She'd have laughed if she weren't completely mortified and on the verge of fainting. Her arm felt like glass under pressure, about to shatter.

"You took quite a tumble." He dropped to his knees. "May I be of assistance?"

Madeline tried to sit up again, determined not to appear weak. She prided herself on her independence and strength, but her body rebelled and collapsed as if she were a marionette whose strings had suddenly been severed. "Who are you, sir?"

"I'm Devlin Grayson of Ravensmoore. Where does it hurt?"

"My arm." Madeline gingerly cradled her left arm and tried to blink back the tears. "You're Lord Ravensmoore?"

He nodded.

She felt suddenly vulnerable, looking into this stranger's intense gaze. "I couldn't prevent it."

"Lie still, please."

"Everything happened so fast. It's been so long since I've been on the hunt field," Madeline said, embarrassed. "Poor Shakespeare. I hope he's not hurt. I'm such a fool."

"You are no fool. This could happen to anyone. And your horse appears to be recovering from the shock. A fine horse. And you have given him a fine name."

She gazed up into his caring green eyes. "Thank you."

"May I ask your name before I examine you? That is, if I have your permission?"

She found it difficult to concentrate. "Lady Madeline Whittington." Her head throbbed. "Examine me? Are you a doctor? No, that wouldn't be right, would it? Not if you're Ravensmoore."

"I will be soon."

Fleeting thoughts of Papa suffering in the hospital filled her mind with fear and anger. The doctors had not helped him. He had died under their care. The slightest of remembrances bubbled to the surface of her thoughts. She turned her face away from him and looked at Hally.

"Lady Madeline," Hally pleaded, glancing across at Ravensmoore. "He is offering you his medical skills."

Madeline turned back and looked him in the eye, trying to catch the elusive memory. Where had she seen him before? "Something is not right." The memories, one after another, tumbled into her consciousness and revealed themselves as they broke through her defenses and exploded into the present. "I remember you."

"Remember me?" He paused and studied her, searching her face for details, some recollection of the past.

"You were at the Guardian Gate when we took my father to the hospital." Her voice dropped to a whisper. "You killed him."

Ravensmoore paled. "What do you mean?"

"Lady Madeline! What an unkind thing to say." Hally looked at Ravensmoore. "She must have hit her head. Maddie, have you lost all reason?"

"My father, Lord Richfield, bled to death because of your ineptness." A ripple of pain burst up her arm.

"Lady Madeline—of Richfield?" he asked, turning a shade paler. "Your father? I...I do remember. I'm very sorry."

Hally gently touched Madeline's cheek and wiped away a tear. "He is only trying to help you."

"I don't want his help."

"I assure you, madam, I am not a murderer. I am most sympathetic to your loss. I promise to be gentle."

"A fine promise," she scoffed. "But I have no confidence in your abilities, sir. It is regrettable, but it is the truth."

He pressed on. "The bone might be broken."

"I do not need your attention," Madeline snapped. "It's most unnecessary."

A pulse throbbed at his temple. "You don't understand." He recovered his composure. "If you refuse to let me examine you, then I must insist on escorting you to Lord Selby's home where you can rest."

Madeline groaned in frustration. "I refuse to return to that man's home. He's drunk." The two of them outnumbered her. "I want to go home." She allowed them to assist her to a sitting position.

"She accepts your kind offer, sir," Hally put in.

"Lean against me, Lady Madeline, until we see if you can stand," Ravensmoore said.

"I appear to have little choice."

Ravensmoore put his arm around her waist and gently guided her to her feet. The strength of his body proved to be an unexpected comfort.

"That's it. Keep your left arm pressed against your side," he instructed.

The last thing she wanted to do was lean against this man who dredged up bitter memories of Papa's death. "I'm fine, really," she lied, in hope of escaping him. Her body betrayed her in a sudden burst of pain that forced her to stiffen. She repressed a moan and fought to keep her balance. Emotions from the past and present collided in a haze of confusion.

Madeline pushed away from him. "Lady Gilling will assist me." She held her hand out and stumbled. Ravensmoore caught her.

"And you will pull your friend to the ground with you."

How could she have considered this man attractive? The thought made no sense now that she had put the pieces together. Yet, he seemed kind, not at all how she remembered him, wearing that horrible blood-spattered apron. Her father's blood. She squeezed her eyes shut trying to ward off the image. "I don't want your help," she said through clenched teeth. "I can ride by myself."

"You're not strong enough. I'll take you home." Ravensmoore skillfully lifted her in his arms, careful to keep her injured arm protected. "You'll ride with me."

Madeline sat in front of Ravensmoore for the ride home. She tried not to lean against his chest for support but found the effort impossible. She'd never been so close to a man, his breath kissing her cheek. She straightened and had to smother a moan of agony when pain radiated through her arm.

When the high stone walls of Richfield came into view Madeline sighed in relief, grateful to be close to home. The great manor house spread before them, the additional wings on either side providing a sense of comfort and safety. A maze of hedges to the left of them and the soon-to-be-blooming gardens magnified the opulence of Richfield. To the right of the edifice stood stables and paddocks for the horses and housing for those who tended them.

Madeline swallowed hard. She'd just returned home with the man who'd killed her father, the man she held responsible for her father's death. Betrayal weighed heavy on her heart, for this is where Papa had loved and raised his family.

Madeline longed to be in her bed as they drew near the entrance.

She vowed to escape from this horrid day and to her room as fast as she could manage.

"Are you ready?" Ravensmoore asked.

Startled from her pain-filled thoughts she said, "Yes." But that was a lie. Madeline's head throbbed simultaneously with the beating of her pulse. She fought for control and blinked back tears when the three of them reached the steps leading into the arched entrance. She nearly crumpled when Ravensmoore dismounted, and she clung desperately to the pommel of the saddle. He reached for her. "It's all right. I'll help you."

"There is no need to coddle me, sir. I assure you, once again, that I am perfectly able."

"Excellent! Then this should not be too difficult for you."

Madeline fell into his arms, light-headed and shaky. She wobbled when her feet touched the ground. He held her, keeping her safe.

"Allow me to carry you, Lady Madeline."

Pain sliced through her arm from the jolting ride. "There's nothing wrong with my legs, sir. I *can* walk." She took two steps and swayed precariously.

"I think not." Ignoring her protests, Ravensmoore scooped her into his arms again. His warmth and scent—spice, leather, and sweat—mingled together in a balm for her pain.

Her mother, Grace, the Countess of Richfield, ran down the steps to meet them. "Madeline, you're hurt!" Her mother placed a hand on Madeline's cheek. "What happened?"

Madeline bit her lip, trying not to reveal the depth of her pain. "It's nothing, Mother. I took a spill off Shakespeare." She would not be the cause of further anguish. Mother's grief over the past two years had been more than many tolerated during a lifetime.

"She'll be fine, Countess," Hally said. "We've brought a doctor with us."

"A doctor? Thank God. Follow me, sir."

Now, beyond caring, she laid her head on his shoulder. Once again his breath whispered past her cheek as he took the stairs and delivered her safely into the embrace of her home.

"Phineas, bring some willow bark tea," Grace instructed the butler. "Bring her into the sitting room, sir." The countess continued her directions while fussing over Madeline. "The settee will do nicely. That's it, gently."

Ravensmoore's hand lingered a moment on hers as Madeline sank gratefully into the plush green velvet cushions. Surely the man would leave her in peace now.

Her mother pushed back the gold damask draperies, and muted light filled the room. A fire burned in the hearth, and Madeline shivered, perhaps from the lack of the body warmth she had shared with her rescuer on the ride home.

The butler returned with a pot of tea. He poured the hot liquid into a rose-patterned cup and cautiously handed it to her. "There you are, Lady Madeline."

"Thank you, Phineas." Steam rose from the cup. Madeline watched her mother. "Please don't worry so. It's not serious."

Ravensmoore knelt beside her. "I recommend you take a swallow of that tea as soon as you can."

"Sir, your services are no longer needed. And I will drink my tea when I am good and ready, thank you very much." Madeline spoke more curtly than she'd intended, but she longed to be alone.

"Drink the tea, young lady," Mother ordered. "The willow bark will help you relax and ease your pain. And you *will* permit the doctor to examine you. Do not argue with me on this matter."

"But Mother, you don't understand. He—"

She touched her daughter's hand and their eyes met. "I understand enough." She turned to Ravensmoore. "What can we do, sir?"

"Allow her to rest a few moments. Then remove her riding jacket so I may examine her arm. Is there a place where I might wash up?

I must have left my gloves on the field, and I don't want to cause further distress by smudging a lady's clothing."

"Of course. Phineas will show you the way."

As soon as he'd left the room, Madeline looked at her mother. "Let me explain. You must know that he"—she pointed in the direction he'd just gone with cup in hand—"was the *physician-in-training* who allowed Papa to bleed to death in York."

"I didn't recognize him." A veil of sadness shrouded her mother's eyes. "I didn't think to see any of them again." Even the worry lines that creased her mother's brow could not diminish the sculpted features of a woman who resembled a Greek goddess, though she seemed utterly unaware of her beauty. The name Grace suited her.

"He's not a doctor…yet."

Grace plucked a pair of shears from a nearby sewing basket. "You have made that perfectly clear. Now, allow Lady Gilling and me to cut away your jacket. You might have broken your arm, and there's no point in causing you any more pain."

"You still want him to examine me?"

"Of course. I must think of your welfare. The past is the past."

"But—"

"He may be able to help you. It will take a servant a long time to ride into town, locate a physician, and return with him. Let this doctor help you."

Madeline looked from one to the other, then handed Hally the teacup. "Do be careful."

"Of course we'll be careful, dear." Grace cut away the jacket in moments.

"Oh, Maddie. I'm so sorry this happened." Hally handed her the teacup again. "It's entirely my fault."

"That is not true." Madeline finished the tea. "Don't be silly." She closed her eyes and took a deep breath. "I am quite dizzy."

Ravensmoore returned, and she willed herself to open her eyes.

He looked taller. His black hair, thick and unruly, increased his appeal. A dark curl fell over his forehead when he leaned toward her. Madeline's heartbeat ricocheted in her chest, and confusion merged with pain.

"How are you feeling?" His brilliant green eyes searched hers.

"I think I should go to bed." A sudden wave of nausea attacked her. She groaned and prayed not to get sick. "Please leave."

"Lady Madeline." He sank to his knees next to her. "Does your head hurt?"

"Yes." She could no longer fight back the pain. "Dreadfully."

"A possible concussion. Is your vision blurry?" He placed his hands on both sides of her face and stared into her eyes as if he were trying to read her thoughts. An unpleasant prospect.

"Yes."

"You may indeed have a concussion. You're unstable on your feet, and your vision is blurred. In addition to that your head aches. If the pain continues beyond two days, I will want to see you again. Now...for the arm." He gently examined her arm, his fingers sliding skillfully over the silk fabric.

"I don't believe your arm is broken, although it may feel as if it is. I'm afraid the sprain is most severe."

Madeline wondered why the room tipped. She had not moved. A moan escaped her lips. Then she felt all strength drain from her body like the emptying of the soul. The cup slipped from her limp fingers and tumbled to the carpet.

CHAPTER 2

For courage mounteth with occasion.

—SHAKESPEARE,
KING JOHN, ACT II, SCENE I

*N*IGHT DESCENDED, AND only the moon lit the way. Devlin knew he must get back to the inn and prepare for the week's classes. Exhaustion, more numbing than the cold, threatened to overtake him as he rode away from Richfield. The countess requested that he return soon to check on Madeline's progress. But he knew the week would be so crowded with rounds at the hospital that he'd barely have time to breathe, let alone return to his charming and puzzling patient. Perhaps he could find a way.

Meeting Lady Madeline had been an unexpected mixture of shock and pleasure, but her harsh words had staggered him. She blamed him for her father's death, and she was partially correct. The medical crisis that had brought her father to the hospital was not one he'd soon forget.

Lord, what shall I say to her? The enchanting woman had accused him of murder!

He couldn't push the image of her from his thoughts. Tall and lithe, she had a mind of her own and didn't attempt to hide her thoughts, a flaw to some, but in his opinion an asset. She'd been devastated by her father's death and her words were harsh, but he sensed an underlying vulnerability that she guarded from further hurt. Sometimes people in pain said things they didn't mean.

When their horses collided, something sparked in those astonished hazel eyes, whether attraction or annoyance, he didn't know, but he'd thought her fascinating: the way her rich brown locks smelled of jasmine on a warm summer breeze, the way her hair loosened from its confines and tumbled across her proud shoulders, the way she leaned against him during their ride to Richfield.

The closeness of the ride with a high-spirited female ensconced between his arms had caused him to rein in thoughts of a nature he hadn't seriously considered for a very long time. Even now he yearned to bury his face in those silken tresses and feel their softness against his cheek.

"Madeline," Devlin whispered as though someone might hear the soft caress of her name on his lips. "Maddie," he breathed into the night, enjoying the intimate sound. He tried to shake off the unexpected and tender emotions. He must tame these feelings. He tried to push thoughts of her from his mind. Dr. Langford would show no mercy if he came unprepared for class because an enticing female had cast a spell over him.

Finally, he stood in the shadow of the Blue Swan Inn, where he rented a room. This had caused much gossip, but he didn't care; it suited his needs. The inn was close to the hospital, yet, if necessary, near enough to his estate to travel home in a day's ride. He'd established an arrangement with the stable boy. Whenever he returned late, there would be an additional coin for him if he'd take very good care of Hippocrates. Devlin smiled as he climbed the stairs to his room. The boy had waited up for him.

He lit a lamp and illuminated the sparsely furnished space: a couple of chairs, a table, a bed, and a wardrobe. He chose to live simply here in York. Devlin then lit the fire in the hearth and rubbed his hands together above the slow growing flames to ward off the chill that had settled in his bones.

Gathering his books and papers, Devlin tried to focus on the urgent task of study. He stared absentmindedly into the fire watching the flames dance. His elbow slipped off the edge of the table, rudely jolting him out of his reverie. He fought off fatigue and intrusive thoughts of a lady who clearly disliked him.

Ignoring his bed and a deep need for sleep, he pored over the medical books spread out on the rickety wooden table. But the image of a woman with brown silky hair continued to distract him. The scent of jasmine lingering on his clothes forced his mind further from his studies. He could understand why she blamed him. When someone died in a hospital, family members usually blamed the physician in attendance or God or both. He wondered if he could convince her otherwise.

Devlin woke with a start and squinted at the clock. "Confound it!" He shot out of his seat, every muscle in his body screaming in protest, his shoulder blades cracking aloud from too long a period hunched over his desk. "Sleeping in a chair all night...not very intelligent," he grumbled, closing his books and piling them one on top of the other.

"Langford is going to dissect me. This is just the kind of opportunity he's been waiting for."

He quickly changed his clothes, transforming himself from earl to student physician. The required cravat was coarse, not silk, the black coat simply cut and not nearly as elegant or fashionable as his usual tailor-made attire. The dark breeches were nearly worn out, and the boots remained spattered with dry blood from previous surgeries.

Devlin raced down the stairs and out the door, yearning for his landlady's cooking: fresh bread, bacon, and coffee. The aroma made his stomach growl, his mouth water, and conjured tempting images that made him want to ignore his responsibilities this one morning. *Oh, for a swallow of hot brewed coffee.* He forced the temptation from his mind and focused on what lay ahead.

Hurrying through the cobblestone streets to the Guardian Gate Hospital, he tore through the front door and then purposely slowed his steps to a respectable pace as he came to the reception area. He glanced at William, the clerk, who shook his bald head.

"You're doomed this morning, your lordship. Your absence was noted forthwith," he said, standing behind an oak desk that hid his considerable girth.

"What kind of mood is he in, Willie?"

"I don't think it's a mood you'll appreciate. God be with you, sir." Willie pointed a beefy finger toward heaven. "You'll need Him to help you this day."

Devlin winced. Dr. Langford had been difficult since the first day of Devlin's medical training in London. He'd not thought it could get worse. Apparently he'd misdiagnosed the situation.

"Thank you, Willie. You always know how to cheer me up." He dropped his books on the desk. "Hold on to these for me, won't you?"

"Of course, sir. Glad to be of service."

He rushed down the hall to catch up with the others. Rounding a corner, Devlin crashed into his adversary. Papers flew about the hallway like startled white doves. The other students scrambled to capture them.

"Ravensmoore, you're late!" Langford bellowed.

Unlike his behemoth reputation, the revered doctor and professor was a short, stout man with thick white hair and a mustache. His intimidating steel-gray glare, through wire-rimmed spectacles, pounced on any student who dared to break his sacred rules. This morning that imposing stare, directed at Devlin, could have driven daggers through his skull.

Devlin met Langford's piercing gaze without a blink. "I apologize, sir," he said.

"What a pleasure that you could join us, your lordship," Langford declared. "I'm amazed, as I'm sure your colleagues are, that you have deigned to grace us with your noble presence."

The others chuckled.

"I apologize for being late." Devlin knew that Langford would never accept the fact that he held a title. No matter that his elder brother had died, leaving Devlin responsible for the family estate. The fact that he'd hired someone to manage his assets to pursue a medical education had caused a stir amongst the *ton*. A nobleman serving as a physician? Unheard of and unnecessary. His friends had disapproved.

However, he couldn't relinquish his goal of becoming a doctor, no matter the cost to his reputation. He'd prayed for God's guidance, and this is where he'd been led. He'd trust God the rest of the way.

"This will not happen again, Dr. Langford." Devlin choked back the retort that longed to escape his lips and prayed God would grant him continued humility. There was no room for pride. Pride would eat him alive. Pride would kill his dream.

"See that it does not." Langford grabbed the wrinkled stack of papers from a student and proceeded down the hall.

As the group followed their instructor to the amphitheater, Devlin slowly let out his breath and recovered his sense of humor. Langford's gait reminded him of a mother goose leading her little ones across a busy road.

"Wipe that preposterous grin off your face, Ravensmoore," Langford demanded, "and tell us about our next patient."

Devlin peered into the amphitheater where they gathered daily to examine, diagnose, and sometimes operate on impoverished patients. Mr. Hastings lay stretched out on the examining table covered by a white sheet. Beneath the table lay a box of sawdust used to collect blood if surgery was indicated. The elderly man with the bulbous red nose glanced up at him and groaned.

"Mr. Hastings," Devlin called cheerfully and pushed ahead of the group. Langford and his retinue followed close behind.

"How are you feeling today?" He wasn't certain he wanted to know, but it was his duty to ask. Hastings had proven to be a thorn in his side for several days, and Devlin was in no mood for this patient's antics. Langford would use any sign of incompetence to get rid of him.

"I'm miserable, and ye ain't done a thing for me. I swear I'm worse today than I were yesterday. What do ye plan to do about it? I'm sick to death of yer poking me body."

"Plan, indeed," Devlin said. He searched his mind for a remedy not yet tried.

Devlin pulled back the sheet and gently examined the old man's belly through the coarse material of a hospital gown. He reached for a stethoscope, attached the wooden earpiece, and laid the horn-shaped end against the patient's abdomen. "No sound."

"Well, of course there ain't no sound," Hastings growled. "It don't talk to ye."

"On the contrary, Mr. Hastings. If we but listen to what our bodies tell us, we might learn a great deal."

"And what's me bloody gut got to say to ye?"

The other students guffawed. Dr. Langford smiled.

"Your gut says it's blocked up and in need of a purge."

"The blazes it does."

The old man's bare toes wiggled out from underneath the sheet, and Devlin frowned. "Do you mind if I take a look at your feet, Mr. Hastings?"

"Me feet! What's wrong with me feet? I suppose feet talk to ye too! Humph."

"I'm not sure yet. May I?"

"Humph." He gave a curt nod of his head.

Devlin rolled the sheet back to the patient's knees to reveal toes that were turning black and would soon be gangrenous. An ugly and inflamed pink tide crept up his ankles, accompanied by the stench of rotting flesh. The others crowded around. "Do your feet ache, sir?"

"Aye. 'Tis harder to walk each day."

"I'll discuss this problem with the others, and we'll see what can be done. You must go back to your room now."

Devlin watched two attendants transfer the old fellow to a wheel-chair prior to leaving the room. "His legs are poisoning him, are they not? Will the infection eventually kill him?"

"I'm afraid so. You were wise not to discuss that prospect in front of him." Their teacher straightened his back, tugged at his mustache, and cleared his throat uneasily. "Well, Ravensmoore. You certainly do have an unusual way of dealing with patients. The body talks, does it? And where did you get such an extraordinary idea?"

"From you, sir."

"What did I say?" Langford asked, a curious look on his face.

"You suggested that if we but pay attention to our patients, they can tell us many things, even if words are never spoken."

"How true. Glad to see you learned something after all, Ravensmoore. I might make a doctor of you yet." Langford turned to address another student.

As the words sank in, Devlin grinned.

Charles Melton, one of the younger students in the group, leaned toward Devlin as they took their seats in the crowded amphitheater, preparing for Langford's lecture on the next patient. "You saved yourself nicely, Ravensmoore. He never said such a thing." His kind, brown eyes danced in a face framed by blond hair tied back with a black ribbon. "You just fed his pride."

"Not at all. He's taught me a great deal. I'm just trying to get him to see some matters in a different light, planting a seed, so to speak, Melton. He doesn't like the fact that I'm titled, so I must present my ideas carefully. I'm really just the same as everyone else."

"Sorry, old man, but you're only fooling yourself. You can never be the same as everyone else. You're titled. That will always make you different from the rest of us. But I, for one, admire your tenacity. You have chosen a difficult path."

"But not an impossible one," Devlin said, defending his choice. "It wasn't long ago that I was in the same situation as you, Melton. The second son." Devlin's hands tightened into fists, his knuckles white with frustration. "I'm titled now, yes. That doesn't mean I can't be a good and competent physician."

"You don't have to prove it to me," Melton whispered and nodded toward Langford. "Just him…and your peers."

"I have an obligation not to sever my ties with my peers. But most of them still refuse to take my interest in medicine seriously. They believe it's a temporary amusement and only a matter of time before I come to my senses."

"Don't be discouraged. Prove them wrong. You're in a most unique situation, Ravensmoore." Melton clapped a hand on Devlin's shoulder. "You have a foot in two very different worlds."

"And it's likely I'll never be accepted in either." Devlin sat back in his seat and considered his dilemma for the hundredth time. Surely he hadn't miscalculated God's plan. Had he?

Despite the ache in her arm, after breakfast Madeline walked to the family chapel and resting place. She'd not slept well because of the pain, and her dreams had left her unsettled and restless. This was the only place she felt the presence of the beloved family that she missed so much, and the peace and quiet there were a balm to her soul.

The path to the chapel took her to the east side of the house. She followed a red brick trail leading through a garden that would bloom with roses and tulips at the right time. Perfect yellow daffodils sprouted up through the rich soil, a sign of an early spring, she hoped. Still, her breath showed itself in a steamy vapor every time she exhaled. And for some reason that made her think of God. She wondered if God was like her breath in the light morning breeze— always there but only visible under certain conditions.

She'd been filled with doubts after her father's death. Doubts that she kept to herself for fear of criticism from her mother and even Hally. Fear that her faith wasn't strong enough to be useful. Fear that she would offend God. Madeline had frequently wondered about death. What did it feel like to be dead? Would she become a spirit, or would she feel like she still had a body, only better? In the quiet solitude of prayer she'd imagined all of them together in heaven and wondered why the Lord had spared her and her mother.

Hally had recommended that she quit coming to the chapel because she descended into sadness after each visit. But without her visits she felt she might go mad. Only here was she free to indulge her questions and tears, free to cry out to the God who seemed to have shut Himself away from her.

"Why do I live? What is my purpose, Lord?" she asked aloud.

The morning light streamed through the stained-glass windows, spreading rays of gold, blue, and green through the chapel like painted ribbons of prayer. She angrily wiped the tears off her face. Madeline wrapped one hand around the spindles of the crypt's cold iron gate that separated her from those she'd lost. "Why did You take them from us?"

A length of engraved marble inscribed with each family member's name upon it indicated his or her presence in the crypt.

Madeline placed her hand on the cold marble wall, touching each name, feeling the chill of where her brother and sisters now rested with their father. The chiseled date of each death remained a vivid reminder of her loss.

Her eyes came level with the inscription in front of her. *Be not afraid.* She reached out and laid her hand on the words, trying to absorb them into her soul. *Be not afraid.*

Miriam, her baby sister, had died in infancy, after being bled by a well-intentioned doctor. Madeline shivered at the memory of the sweet babe dying in her arms. "Be not afraid, little Miriam," she whispered.

Her gaze roamed over the other names, her younger brother and sister, Timothy and Catherine, both dead from smallpox. The doctor had refused to come near them, being afraid himself of the deadly and disfiguring disease. Her mother and she had cared for them both, but they died within days of each other.

She slid to her knees, laying her head against the gate. "I don't know what to do, Lord," she wept. "Please help me. Papa always said I could do anything I wanted to do, but I cannot move forward without his strength." *If only you were still here, Papa... if only—*

A hand touched the tears on her cheek. Madeline gasped and lurched away, wrenching her sprained arm. She recognized her cape wrapped about a waif of a girl. "Brown Eyes. What are you doing here?"

The girl knelt in front of Madeline and wiped away her tears. Then she stroked Madeline's hair in a way that made Madeline aware that someone at sometime in this girl's sorrowful life must have shown kindness to her.

Brown Eyes entwined her fingers with Madeline's, laid her head on her shoulder, and sat with her. Madeline wasn't certain how long they stayed that way, but because of the sadness in their souls they developed an invisible bond of trust.

CHAPTER 3

Love looks not with the eyes, but with the mind.
—SHAKESPEARE,
A MIDSUMMER'S NIGHT DREAM,
ACT I, SCENE I

OTHER, MUST I have dinner with you and Lord Vale?" Madeline's stomach clenched at the thought of digesting food while Brown Eyes went hungry. It wasn't easy sneaking food out of the house, and she'd hoped to make one more trip to the cabin that day. Despite Vale's unfailing politeness toward her, she couldn't bear to see him take her father's place. Truth be told, she'd rather spend her time at the cabin caring for the girl. "I fail to understand why you allow him to impose upon you."

"Do you?" Grace's eyes met Madeline's. "Madeline, stop chewing your nails. It's a terrible habit." Her mother sat in front of the mirror in her bedchamber studying her own perfectly trimmed and polished nails. "You must try. Your hands tell other people about your character. You don't want tongues wagging. Before you know it, the *ton* will say you have some dreaded disease, and the gossips will be ever so glad to destroy your reputation. You can never be too careful. Appearance is everything."

Madeline wished for invisibility. *If only I could live a real life, a life built of purpose and not fluff and fashion.* Madeline pulled a finger away from her mouth. "Am I allowed no faults?"

29

"Only invisible ones, dear." Grace held a necklace of pearls in front of her and examined it as if searching for flaws in the perfect gems.

"He's so...so..." Madeline fished for a word that would not raise her growing concerns about the man or offend her mother. "...exasperating," she blurted, but she knew immediately from her mother's tight-lipped expression that it had not been the right word at all.

"Really, Madeline. You might attempt to be more gracious." Her mother tried unsuccessfully to fasten the pearl necklace. "It's not often we have a dinner guest. I find him gracious and thoughtful."

"I find him tedious."

"Madeline, how awful. Why would you say such a thing?"

"Perhaps *circumspect* is a better word," she added quickly, hoping to ease the sting of her ill-chosen statement, "but you must admit—"

"I must admit nothing. He's simply businesslike. He wants me to think carefully about some investments. He's only trying to help since our man of affairs died."

"Why not hire a new man? Someone you can trust?"

"I do trust Lord Vale. Why else would I discuss matters of business with him?"

Madeline stepped behind her mother and thought it best to let the subject drop. But still she disliked the thought of any man taking the place of her beloved father. "Let me help you with those. I may have only one good arm at the moment"—she fumbled with the clasp, laughing at her ineptness—"but together we can do this."

"You are tenacious, daughter." Grace held one side of the necklace while Madeline awkwardly fastened the pearls together.

"There you are, Mother." Madeline allowed her free hand to rest gently on her mother's shoulder for a moment while she studied their reflections in the mirror. "You look lovely."

Grace Whittington's breathtaking features made men stop and

stare. Her perfect oval face and fine high cheekbones resembled an exquisite porcelain doll.

Madeline knew she did not possess her mother's beauty, yet she had acquired her mother's cheekbones and almond-shaped eyes, for which she was most grateful. She had also inherited her father's stubborn chin and unfortunate habit of speaking her mind, a most disagreeable flaw for a young woman of breeding. She wondered what Ravensmoore thought of her appearance. Then she quickly snuffed out that unbidden thought as though it were a flaming candle.

"Thank you, darling."

Madeline bent and kissed her on the cheek. "It's been a difficult time for both of us. If only we hadn't taken Father to the hospital that day. If only I hadn't wanted to go riding."

"Please don't. *If only* will get you nowhere, Madeline. Your father is living with the Lord now. He would want you to be happy."

"Sometimes I still have nightmares." Her eyes filled with tears.

Grace stood and hugged her. "You must let go of the past, dear. Put it to rest, or the past will always haunt you." She brushed a tear from Madeline's cheek and returned to the vanity.

"I know you're right, Mother." Madeline crossed to the bedside table and arranged and rearranged the red, purple, and yellow pansies that scented the room. "I'm trying to move forward with my life." She closed her eyes and said a silent prayer, uncertain if God listened.

"Does your arm still hurt? You are blessed that it did not break and that Ravensmoore came to your rescue."

Madeline's eyes flew open. "He did not rescue me. Hally and I would have done quite nicely without his help. There were other men on the hunt field."

Grace turned away from her mirror. "You cannot blame him for your father's death, Maddie. I'm certain he did all that could be done that day. Ravensmoore could not stop the bleeding. Your father suffered a serious injury."

"He should have waited for Dr. Langford to return." She staved off the avalanche of emotions that threatened and tightly balled her fists at her sides. "He should have waited."

"Excuse me, ma'am." Agnes, her mother's personal maid, interrupted. "Lord Vale has arrived. Phineas escorted his lordship to the library."

"Thank you, Agnes. Please tell him I shall be there momentarily and offer him something to drink. We don't want to appear inhospitable, do we?" Her mother looked in the mirror, gave her hair a final pat, and dabbed perfume behind each ear.

"No, ma'am," Agnes replied stiffly and left the room.

Madeline prided herself on her powers of observation. Agnes did not care for Vale's attentions toward her mother any more than she did. However, the loyal Agnes hid her displeasure behind excessively correct behavior.

She caught her mother staring at her curiously. "I'm sorry, Mother. Did you say something?"

"You do seem preoccupied these days. I said, how do I look, dear?" She turned an elegant circle and curtsied before Madeline. "You don't think this dress is too flamboyant, do you? After all, I've only been out of mourning for a month."

Madeline appraised her mother's fashionable aquamarine gown. "You are beautiful, Mother. And your new perfume is wonderful. It smells like an exotic faraway island. "

Grace smiled at the compliment. Madeline thought she almost glowed. *Why are you so excited?* It seemed her mother had shed all memories of her father, Thurston Whittington, when she'd discarded her mourning clothes. Now she boldly entertained a male guest. Madeline thought it dispiriting that as her mother's misery lifted, her own sadness deepened. Perhaps Ravensmoore could prescribe a receipt for this dreadful malady that continued to resurrect itself.

Grace's smile slowly faded.

"What's wrong?" Madeline asked.

"You are not appropriately dressed," she complained. "Do hurry and put on something bright and cheerful, dear. I'll send Daisy in to help you."

Madeline looked in the mirror at her modest brown walking dress. Devoid of ruffles, lace, or anything one could call decoration, she thought it mirrored quite well the true essence of her being. "What's wrong with what I'm wearing?"

"It's dull." Grace lightly brushed a finger down her daughter's dark tresses. "It does nothing for this gorgeous head of hair or your beautiful hazel eyes. Please change. Why don't you wear that beautiful lilac silk gown that makes your eyes sparkle?"

"Mother! Father bought that gown in London for my birthday." Tears stung her eyes. "I want to save it for a special occasion."

"This *is* a special occasion." Grace wagged a finger. "Madeline Elizabeth Whittington, life is an adventure. Start living it."

Madeline gritted her teeth. "I *am* trying, Mother."

"Good." Grace took a deep breath. "Now, go change into something else. If you don't want to wear the lilac dress, *please* choose another. Hally can help you pick something more appropriate for the evening."

Madeline retired to her room. "Lord Vale, indeed," she muttered to herself as she jerked open her wardrobe and pulled out the black crepe funeral gown she had worn far too often in the past. "Lord Vale is a...a...horse's backside." Holding the dress in front of her, she looked at her image in the gold cheval mirror. She deemed her choice appropriate, very appropriate. She did not need anyone's help. Black suited her mood just fine.

A soft knock on the door interrupted her musings. "Who is it?" Madeline asked irritably, throwing the gown over a nearby chair.

The door creaked open. A cheerful face peered cautiously around it. "I take it this is not a good time?"

"Hally!" Madeline ran to the door, grabbed her friend by the hand, and pulled her inside. "Thank God it's you. I hoped it wasn't Mother coming after me with more advice."

Hally squeezed her hand. "What's wrong? You look as though you've been asked to dance by the shortest man at the ball."

"Just thinking, but it's unimportant." Madeline shook off the feeling of dread that kept niggling at her mind. "We'll talk later."

"Are you certain?" Hally asked.

"Yes." She took a breath and refocused her thoughts, making a conscious effort to abandon her worries. Madeline admired the yellow gown that showed off her friend's hourglass figure to perfection. "You look splendid." Hally's black hair, bound up with matching yellow ribbons, captured the light, and her sky-blue eyes brimmed with enthusiasm.

"I thought I looked a bit too much like a blooming daffodil."

"How is it you can always make me laugh when I am so far from being happy?"

Hally's eyes lit with amusement. "Maybe because laughing has nothing to do with being happy. It's a tool to help you find your way there. Pretend enough, and you may actually find you have arrived."

Sitting down on the edge of the bed, Madeline changed the subject abruptly. "What do you think of Lord Vale?"

Hally sat near her, careful not to jar Madeline's injured arm. "His presence vexes you more than I imagined it would." She looked thoughtful. "I've never met him, but I understand from the gossips that he is a respectable lord with a talent for business. I've never heard rumors of him gambling or drinking or carrying on, as some do in his position. Lord Selby, for instance. What do you think of him?"

"I don't know. I can't think of him at all without thinking of my father. I know I'm not being fair to Lord Vale or to my mother, but I simply cannot help it."

"After James died, I felt the same way," Hally said gently. "I'd lost the only man I thought I would ever love. I could not imagine anyone taking his place. Surely you remember. But time does heal all wounds, my dear, if we allow them to be healed rather than dwelling on them and allowing them to fester. I finally had to accept his loss and come to an understanding of God and the real world."

"The real world," Madeline said. "Sometimes I'd like nothing better than to slip into the pages of a book and disappear forever, leaving the real world behind."

"Don't talk like that. I'd miss you too much. Besides, the Lord is certain to have great plans for your life. Perhaps He is giving you the opportunity to explore new possibilities."

"What kind of opportunities?"

"Hmm. Let me think." Hally sat up and grinned mischievously. "Seems to me He rather conveniently provided you with a guardian angel in the guise of a physician."

"You can't be serious."

"Who happens to be titled," she continued, "and wickedly hand-some." Hally reached out and pinched Madeline's cheek. "The Lord does provide, Maddie. Open your eyes."

"Why should I believe that? He's all but wiped out my entire family. Mother and I are the only ones left." Her throat dried and painfully constricted, yet she forced the words. "I don't think God knows I'm alive. And maybe it's better that way. Maybe He'll leave me alone."

"Maddie. You don't believe that, do you?"

A sudden rap on the door interrupted their conversation.

"Come in," Madeline called, relieved to be spared an answer. She no longer knew what she believed.

The door flew open and in scurried Daisy, Agnes's daughter and Madeline's personal maid. "Pardon me, Countess." She curtsied and Madeline noticed her ill-fitting uniform. The girl simply didn't eat enough food. Then Daisy turned her attention to her mistress. "Your mother and Lord Vale are waiting dinner for you, Lady Madeline." Her eyes widened. "Why, you're not even dressed! Why didn't you ring for me?"

"Because I was thinking."

"Lollygagging if you ask me." Daisy slanted her a look of amused suspicion. "But you wouldn't be asking me, would you?" She frowned. "Countess, I beg your assistance."

"You have my help and my sympathy, Daisy." Hally crooked a finger at Madeline.

"She don't listen to me when she gets moody." The maid grabbed a hairbrush from the cluttered vanity. "Now don't be difficult, Lady Madeline. Let me arrange your hair."

"Ah, Daisy, ever the taskmaster. Hally, will you pick out a gown for me? My mother trusts your judgment, and I'm not in the mood. Anything but the lilac gown will do."

"Of course." Hally walked to the wardrobe and pulled out an elegant rust-colored gown. "Neither too pretentious nor too sedate. I believe this will do nicely. Now up you go," Hally ordered her friend. "Daisy, let's make her presentable, and quickly too. I'm famished."

Arms linked, Madeline and Hally entered the brilliantly lit dining room. Madeline grinned when her friend's stomach growled. Beeswax candles flickered above from two crystal chandeliers, casting a crystalline dance of light upon the walls. An array of candelabra illuminated the room, barring dark shadows from entry.

The smell of fresh bread and roasted chicken permeated the cool evening air, but Madeline could not find her appetite.

"There you are, my darlings." Her mother smiled pleasantly and greeted each of them with a kiss on the cheek. "Lady Hally, I am so glad you are staying with us for a while. Madeline's mood is much improved with you about. You are like one of my own."

"Thank you, Countess. You are most gracious to invite me. You know how I love to spend time here at Richfield with you and Maddie. This has always been my second home, and Maddie is like a sister to me as well as the dearest of friends."

A flicker of sadness drifted through Madeline as she thought about the two sisters and only brother she'd lost. She looked across the room for their guest and shook off a gloomy feeling of despair.

Vale stood by the window. His thick blond hair and brilliant blue eyes shining in the candlelight produced an angelic glow that caused an intake of breath. For the first time she saw what her mother saw, and it frightened her.

He quickly crossed the room to greet them. "Lady Madeline, a pleasure to see you again." He bowed low. In their previous meetings he had always been most sedate, almost boring. But tonight he seemed to crackle with some invisible energy. His presence sent a shiver of apprehension through her, and she glanced quickly at Hally. To her annoyance Hally appeared quite taken by the man.

"You must introduce me to your friend." Vale turned to Hally with a gracious smile.

"Countess, may I introduce Lord Vale, an acquaintance of my father. Lord Vale, my dear friend, the Countess of Gilling."

"It's an honor to meet such a close friend of the family, Lady Gilling." He bestowed a kiss on Hally's gloved hand. "I am most fortunate to be in such lovely company this evening."

Vale guided her mother to her seat as a footman seated Madeline and Hally. Madeline couldn't help but notice how his hand lingered on her mother's shoulder and his index finger just barely caressed the back of her neck before he moved away. Madeline also noticed a hint of a smile on her mother's face.

When Vale sat down at the opposite end of the table, Madeline realized he occupied her father's chair, a seat that had remained empty. Blood surged through her veins, and she jumped to her feet. "No! You must not sit there."

"What?" Vale jumped up and looked about as though the ghost of Lord Richfield had materialized in the chair.

"That's my father's place."

"I am so sorry." Vale stood hastily and hovered behind the chair, abashed.

"How can you be so rude, Madeline?" her mother demanded. "Apologize this instant."

Madeline looked to her mother for support, barely able to hold back the angry words she wanted to use. Her mother ignored the silent plea and turned her attention to their guest, her face flushed pink with embarrassment. "I am very sorry, Lord Vale."

Madeline opened her mouth to speak. Her mother raised the palm of her hand, demanding silence. "I know this situation is difficult for you, Madeline, but you must accept it. There is nothing else to do."

"Maddie," Hally whispered and placed a comforting hand over hers.

When Madeline turned to her friend, she imagined an invisible flag of truce in the meaningful look that passed between them. She fought for composure.

Her mother rose from her seat and went directly to her guest. "Lord Vale. As you can see, this is distressing for my daughter. May I suggest that you sit near me?"

"Certainly." Vale smiled apologetically. "I would enjoy that very much." Vale moved to a seat near her mother. "I imagine it is quite difficult for a young lady to lose her father. I never knew my own father. He died when I was very young."

Realizing the vehemence of her reaction, Madeline took her seat and lowered her eyes. *Why is this so hard, Lord? I'm acting as if my father still lives.*

"I understand you took a rather nasty fall from your horse at Lord Selby's hunt, Lady Madeline," Vale said as he shook out his napkin, "and that Ravensmoore came to your aid. Does the injury bother you overmuch?"

"I find the pain increasing this evening." She struggled to make polite conversation. "But the sling that Lord Ravensmoore fashioned for me is very helpful."

"I'm glad to hear it. I was acquainted with Ravensmoore's father and met his elder brother once. It must have been difficult when they died. No bodies to bury when a ship goes down."

"How sad." Madeline hadn't considered this. He couldn't visit the graves of his loved ones as she did. "A watery grave."

"Forgive me, ladies," Vale said. "That was insensitive to bring up in gentle company, and at dinner no less."

Grace nodded. Madeline's senses sharpened. "You are acquainted with Ravensmoore?"

"No. But I am quite certain his father would not have approved of his continued training as a physician after receiving the title. The entire *ton* snubs him. Think of it. A nobleman working at a trade. It's preposterous."

"I wouldn't be so certain of that," Hally said, after taking a sip of cider. "Lord Selby saw fit to invite him to the hunt. Not *all* of the *ton* has disapproved. I believe what he's doing is quite honorable. Unusual, but honorable. Imagine what someone of his stature might accomplish."

Madeline grappled with her thoughts, not wanting to agree with anything Vale might have to say, yet not wanting to come to

Ravensmoore's defense either. One emotion after the other followed her thoughts. "I think his choice is…is intriguing."

"You do?" Hally asked, obviously surprised. "But…I thought you—"

Madeline kicked Hally under the table. "Yes. I think more noblemen might consider the pursuit of an honorable trade," she said, looking directly at Vale. "What trade would you choose, Lord Vale?"

Vale smoothed his carefully knotted cravat. "Why, banking, to be sure," he declared. "There my experience in investments could be put to the best use. I cannot imagine anything more gruesome or grisly than the medical field. Ravensmoore must be mad to pursue such a course."

"Perhaps I am." At that moment Ravensmoore himself appeared next to the grim-faced Phineas at the entryway to the dining room. The earl wore a black tailcoat and matching breeches, spotless Hessians, a knotted silk neck cloth, and a charming smile. "But it is a most fulfilling madness."

Madeline's jaw dropped, her heart skipped a beat, and she felt her face flush crimson. She groaned silently, thinking the evening could not get much worse. Ravensmoore didn't look anything like a physician, or what she thought a physician should look like. He looked…exceptional.

Phineas stepped in front of their newly arrived guest and addressed her mother. "Lord Ravensmoore is calling to inquire about Lady Madeline's injury. Should I have him wait in the parlor, madam?"

"Heavens no. What an unexpected and pleasant surprise. You must join us for dinner, Lord Ravensmoore."

"I do not wish to impose, Countess Richfield."

"Nonsense. Cook makes enough food to feed a village. Phineas, seat Lord Ravensmoore next to Madeline."

Ravensmoore dropped smoothly into the seat next to Madeline, sending goose bumps up her spine and heat into her cheeks.

"I'm relieved to see your color coming back," he said. "A healthy sign."

Grace smiled. "I am most pleased that you have come to inquire of my daughter's health. I worry about her."

"I will do my best to relieve your fears, madam." He caught Madeline's eye again and smiled.

Madeline swallowed hard. Hally nudged her and cast a quick grin across the table. Ravensmoore's proximity made it difficult to think…to breathe. He smelled of leather and spice that she could almost taste. Masculinity laced with risk and possibilities. It made her wonder what it would be like to…

Her thoughts hurtled toward disaster.

She could not be attracted to him. She simply couldn't.

CHAPTER 4

For he knoweth the secrets of the heart.
—Psalm 44:21

DEVLIN COULD NOT take his eyes off Madeline, and the smell of her perfume, that mesmerizing scent of jasmine, nearly obliterated all else from his mind. He forced an ear to listen politely as the countess introduced him to Lord Vale.

"I heard you mention my father, sir. How is it that you knew him?"

"Primarily business dealings. I met your brother too." Vale cut into the piece of venison on the Wedgwood plate.

Devlin's gut reaction to Vale was one of mild annoyance. There was something pretentious about him. "And in what business dealings were you involved?"

Vale swallowed a bite of food, concentrating on his plate instead of maintaining eye contact with Ravensmoore. "Investments."

"Ah, yes. Which investments?" Devlin probed, curious about this man and his relationship with his father.

"The East Indies."

"I don't recall any investments regarding the East Indies. Perhaps you are mistaken."

"I am rarely mistaken in matters of business."

Her mother interrupted. "Gentlemen, you must save this talk of business for after dinner. I believe we were discussing the idea of noblemen working at a trade. Lord Ravensmoore, why have you chosen to pursue a life in medicine?"

"Do tell," Hally encouraged him.

"As the second son, I had already begun the study of medicine when my father and elder brother, Edward, died in a shipwreck. I simply chose to continue my studies along with my obligations as the heir."

"There is nothing *simple* about that, sir. Your work is most honorable," Hally said. "I've never heard of any gentleman doing such a thing. Have you, Lady Madeline?"

"No. Never." Madeline fidgeted with her fork, picked up the utensil briefly, put it back on the table, and looked everywhere but at the man next to her.

"Indeed," Vale said dryly. "What is the purpose of such an act?"

Devlin considered Vale's attitude, an attitude he'd become all too familiar with since he'd come into the title. "To help those less fortunate than myself, sir."

"A noble gesture, but quite unnecessary." Vale reached for a piece of bread and knocked over his glass. "So sorry." He tried to keep the spreading river flowing toward him from spilling over the edge of the table and ruining his clothes. A footman scrambled to clean up the mess.

Devlin caught the smile that Madeline could not contain. *She doesn't find Vale agreeable either. I wonder why?* Vale appeared to be a real dandy and possibly a skilled liar as well. Devlin knew his father never had holdings or investments in the East Indies. Yet Vale claimed otherwise. Perhaps he wished to impress Countess Richfield.

"I find that easing the pain of those who suffer is an absolute necessity," Devlin said pointedly. "If God has placed it upon my heart to become a physician, I would be unwise not to follow that path."

Madeline turned to look at him. Her piercing hazel eyes seemed to swim in a storm of emotion. "But you are of a higher social rank. It is not done, Lord Ravensmoore."

"That does not mean it shouldn't be done." Devlin searched her face expecting to see disapproval there, but instead saw only curiosity and perhaps respect.

She quickly composed herself. Her emotions vanished from her face like a turtle that suddenly disappears into its shell when danger approaches.

"I think it is wonderful," Hally said. "Bravo, Lord Ravensmoore. May God bless you and your pursuits."

Looking directly at Madeline, Devlin said, "I believe He already has."

Vale cleared his throat. "There are many ways to help those less fortunate than ourselves, Ravensmoore. For instance, it came to my attention through a business associate that the Ashcroft Lunatic Asylum was in need of financial assistance. I visited the wretched place and improved the conditions of the kitchen and the food they were providing those unfortunate souls." He shook his head. "Since this estate is near the asylum, I should alert you that one of the young women escaped from the asylum two days ago."

Devlin watched the blood drain from Madeline's face. "What's her name?"

"Amanda Quinn. She's cunning."

Madeline whispered to herself, "Amanda."

"Lady Madeline, are you all right?" Vale asked. "You look a bit pale."

She looked from Vale to Ravensmoore. "I'm fine. I was just thinking how sad it is that the poor girl is disturbed and out there somewhere in need of help."

"Never begin to think that the girl is to be pitied, Lady Madeline. She doesn't speak, but that doesn't mean she can't speak. She's chosen not to since the day she murdered her father. She's mad. The courts have said so."

Countess Richfield gasped. "How awful."

Vale turned to Grace. "Indeed. She's fortunate she didn't get the gallows. She was right where she needed to be, and now she's a danger again. I'd encourage you to have your servants on the alert in case she comes near Richfield looking for food or shelter."

Devlin noticed that Madeline twisted her napkin in her hands underneath the table.

After dinner, while the men retired to another room for port and cigars, Madeline and Hally strolled in the moonlit gardens, ripe with plants and flowers awaiting spring's call to blossom. Several grass-covered paths ran through a maze of tall hedges. Each led to a large wooden gazebo draped with ivy, an inviting, private place that Madeline loved to frequent during the summer months. With a book in one hand and a diary in the other, she would read and write and dream her time away. That was before death had plunged into their lives, hacking and pillaging its way through her family.

"What is wrong with me?" Madeline linked arms with her friend as they enjoyed the unusually warm and pleasant night. "I cannot believe my reaction when that man sat in Papa's chair. Mother was horrified, and I'm responsible. What could I have been thinking?"

Hally sighed. "I think you know but are too afraid or too angry to say the words. Your mother is allowing Lord Vale to court her. I think she hoped for your approval tonight."

How can she look at another man in the same way she did my father? "I cannot bear the thought."

"What you think is of no consequence. She is obviously interested in this man. Her eyes betray her feelings. And did you see the way he looked at her? I think the feeling is returned. Don't you believe your mother deserves another chance at happiness?"

"Of course. I'm not cruel. He's just…the wrong man. We don't even know much about him."

"I thought he was a family friend."

Madeline snorted. "Six months after Papa died Vale came to the house. He claimed to be an old acquaintance of my father, wanted to pay his respects, and wanted to know if he could be of help regarding estate details. He's knowledgeable about such things as a nobleman and knew our man of affairs had died in an accident.

"Mother refused at first, then slowly changed her mind when she got to know him better. Since she's come out of mourning, he's made a pest of himself. She's been entertaining him much too often. And then tonight she invites him to dinner."

"Maddie, what will you do if your mother decides to continue seeing him?"

"I don't know."

Hally turned off the path and led Madeline to a flat stone bench. Behind them stood a small fountain with a statue of a child pouring water from a pitcher. Its perpetual supply filled the basin, sending minute droplets of spray into the air. Madeline felt a tiny splash hit her cheek. She smiled, thinking how she used to sit here as a little girl and splash water at her father.

Hally nudged her, interrupting her thoughts. "And what about Lord Ravensmoore? You came to his defense this evening."

"I did no such thing. I merely agreed that his decision to become a physician was intriguing."

"That must be the nicest thing you've said about the gentleman since you realized he treated your father."

"Treated is not what I call it." Madeline fidgeted with her silver bracelet, turning the smooth bangle around and around on her wrist. "I find Vale irritating. I simply chose to disagree with him."

"Are you sure, Maddie? Perhaps it is time you examine your *own* heart instead of your mother's."

"Each heart has its secrets, Hally. Mine is no different." She heard footsteps and looked up.

"Ah, there you are," Ravensmoore said as he rounded the hedge and spotted them in the gazebo. "I hope I'm not interrupting, but I did want to inquire after your injury, Lady Madeline. Is now a convenient time?"

Hally replied for her. "It is the perfect time, sir." She rose from her seat. "I will begin walking back to the house while you talk. Please catch up with me soon. The countess would not want you to tarry long by yourselves. Even though you are studying to be a doctor, Lord Ravensmoore, you are very much a man." She curtsied, gave him a brilliant smile, and quickly disappeared around the hedge.

An awkward silence fell as Madeline found herself suddenly alone with this man.

"May I join you?" Ravensmoore asked. "I want to know how you are feeling. I must return to the hospital this evening and cannot remain much longer."

Madeline looked up at his towering frame, uncomfortable with her confusing emotions. Her mouth went dry when her eyes met his. She forced out the words, "Of course."

"Are you well?" Ravensmoore sat next to her. "Is the pain tolerable?"

"It has been but a day, sir." A mere inch separated them. Madeline could feel his closeness. His warmth wrapped about her like a protective cloak. "However, when I awoke this morning, it ached. I am most tired of wearing this cumbersome sling."

"I suggest a more relaxed position of the arm. It appears too tight. May I?"

"If you think it will help." Madeline's heart fluttered when Ravensmoore stood and moved behind her. "Do be careful."

"I'll be most gentle."

His fingers slid against the nape of her neck as he untied the knot of the sling. Gooseflesh covered her skin once again. Were these the hands of a butcher? She shivered, but not because she disliked his touch—the opposite.

"Let's reposition your arm and start over."

Surprised at his gentle touch and care for her feelings, a seed of guilt began to sprout as he secured the sling more comfortably about her neck. She had treated him so poorly and thought even worse of him. Could she have misjudged the gentleman? And if she had, could she have misjudged Vale as well?

"There now. How does that feel?"

She sighed with relief. "Better, thank you."

"Let's see how you fare over the next few minutes." Ravensmoore came from behind her and held out his hand. "Would you do me the honor of a short walk?"

Madeline hesitated. "I really should return to the house," she said, making excuses to escape him. The man had the dual effect of attracting her and driving her away at the same time.

His open hand awaited her answer. "Doctor's orders," he said, smiling.

Madeline accepted his hand. "You mean an *almost* doctor's orders, don't you?" His grasp, warm and gentle, comforted her. She felt oddly safe as he helped her to her feet.

"I'll be a doctor by summer's end, dear lady. Will you feel more comfortable with my position after that?" He placed his hand in the small of her back and turned her onto the path away from the house.

"Impossible, sir. You will be the only nobleman I know who is a physician. The spirit of my father forever stands between us as a reminder of what you did or didn't do." She quickened her pace.

"But—"

"Please." She stopped and glared at him. "I don't wish to be cruel. You have been kind, but I will never feel comfortable around doctors, you most of all. And Dr. Langford left you by my father's side to attend another. He also is responsible for my father's death. But you were the last one present with my father."

"I understand."

"I don't think you can. My fondest wish is to live a normal life far from death, disease—"

"And doctors."

"Yes, and doctors."

"I believe that is the feeling of most people, Lady Madeline."

"The last few years have brought nothing but pain." Grateful for the dimness of the evening light, she wondered why she had shared her personal thoughts with him.

"To live is to experience pain. Illness and death come to all of us."

"You, sir, have chosen to surround yourself with illness and have inflicted pain on others to satisfy your curiosity as you learn. And to what purpose?"

Ravensmoore stopped. "Inflicted pain on others? I imagine you are speaking of your father."

"I did not say anything about my father." Madeline walked away from him.

"You didn't have to. I understand your anger." He kept pace with her.

"You, sir, understand nothing about me. Do you fancy yourself a physician of the mind?"

He grabbed her hand. "Stop. I'm sorry that I've upset you."

Madeline faced him. "Why do you persist?"

"I only wanted to help you. As far as being a doctor of the mind,

I feel strongly that every physician must do his fair share of 'mad-doctoring,' as it is called, to take into account a patient's thoughts as well as the aches and problems of the body. Is not the brain a part of the body?"

"Of course. But I don't wish to speak of such things. My brain and my thoughts are not for you to understand. Why don't you visit Ashcroft if you wish to pursue the mad-doctoring trade?"

Ravensmoore looked as though she'd slapped him. Madeline took a step back. "I'm sorry. I didn't mean to say that. It's been a difficult day."

He nodded. "You need rest. I'll walk you to the house, and then I must be on my way." He offered her his arm.

Madeline hesitated and then put her arm through his as they continued toward the house. "What do you think of Lord Vale's impressions of the girl who escaped Ashcroft?"

"Madness is a serious affliction and not to be taken lightly. I feel sorry for the young woman, but she must be found and returned to the asylum."

"If you discovered her, would you return her to Ashcroft?"

"Yes. It's the only thing that can be done. I talked to Lord Vale about her after dinner. The keepers at the asylum are hunting for her as we speak. It's only a matter of time until she is caught, if she can survive the out-of-doors and the dangers of the forest."

"She's no better off than the fox on the hunt field. I cannot help but feel pity for her. To be locked away forever. To be hunted like a helpless animal. She has no hope of a life outside the walls of Ashcroft. It breaks my heart."

"You are most compassionate, Lady Madeline. Few women would concern themselves with such matters. It almost sounds as if you know the girl."

Madeline lowered her gaze. "Of course I don't know her." The lie hurt. She didn't want to keep the truth hidden, but she felt there was no recourse. If she told Vale or Ravensmoore, then Amanda would be sent back. "But if I did, I would consider helping her."

"And you would place yourself and perhaps others in peril."

She'd seen the bruises and the marks from what must have been shackles. Ashcroft didn't seem to be the place anyone would want to be regardless of the improvements to the kitchens and the food that Vale claimed.

"And what of compassion?" she asked. "You claim to be a compassionate man."

"What of the law? Even compassion must answer to the courts if it interferes with the law."

"We've talked too long. Countess Gilling and my mother will be concerned."

They walked out of the maze and back through the paths that led to the house. Madeline opened the French doors to the parlor anxious to rid herself of Ravensmoore and nearly collided with her mother wrapped in Lord Vale's arms and being thoroughly kissed.

CHAPTER 5

A friend loveth at all time, and a
brother is born for adversity.

—PROVERBS 17:17

*D*EVLIN AWOKE BEFORE dawn to the sound of rain splattering against the windows and the scent of Mrs. Hogarth's cooking drifting through his room. Edna Hogarth always had a tasty breakfast waiting for him. The extra coin he supplied saw to that. Sniffing the air like a hound on the trail of his dinner, Devlin's stomach growled. He realized he hadn't eaten much of the delicious meal served at Richfield. He'd found Madeline far more interesting than food.

The chill of the cold floor seeped through his thick stockings. Devlin wiggled his toes to warm them then breathed a sigh of relief; he would not be late today. Langford would just have to find someone else to criticize this morning.

Devlin lit the lamp, which cast a weak glow through the cold room, and traded his nightshirt for more suitable garments. He hurried to the small dining room where Mrs. Hogarth placed a platter of ham, poached eggs, and tomatoes on the table. His stomach rumbled.

"Good mornin', Lord Ravensmoore." Edna smiled, wiping her

gnarled hands on the clean blue apron tied around her ample waist, and offered him a quick curtsy.

"Ah, heat. A wonderful commodity," he said, sitting down at the place set for him in front of a burning fire. "Mmmm, what a delicious smell. I'm ravenous."

"Ye say that every mornin' ye have time to eat, sir."

"I think it every morning, whether I have time to eat or not. And when I don't have time to eat, I dream about your cooking on the way to the hospital."

"Such a charmer ye are, sir. I'll get yer coffee." She disappeared into the kitchen.

Devlin devoured his food and washed it down with the coffee Mrs. Hogarth served him. "You're too good to me. I should marry you," he teased, "but I don't think your husband would approve the match." He enjoyed watching her round face flush with delight.

"Yer right about that, sir. Besides, I'm a bit too old for ye." She grinned. "But I do appreciate a man with a sense of humor. Now run along, or ye'll be late and that mean old doctor will be after ye again."

"How did you know about that?" Devlin asked, both surprised and annoyed.

"Yer friend, a Mr. Melton, stopped by to cheer ye up. Said Dr. Langford had growled at ye for bein' late."

Devlin didn't approve of Melton's gossiping with the innkeeper's wife. He concealed his irritation and laughed good-naturedly, then gulped the last of the coffee. "You're right. I'd better go before Langford has reason to make an example of me again."

He plucked his black wool cloak off the hook in the hallway and darted out into the rain. So Melton had dropped by to cheer him. Very kind of him.

The April sky finally unleashed its fury that had threatened for several days. The rain beat him, stinging like tiny daggers. He thought it the perfect day to stay abed. The doors to the small, candlelit, parish church stood open and inviting against the elements, a sharp contrast to the great, stone building looming before him. Guardian Gate Hospital.

A streak of lightning illuminated the heavens. Devlin hurried past the archway of the hospital as a deafening crack of thunder chased him through the door, followed by another that shook the windows. His soggy cloak dripped puddles on the tarnished floor inside the entrance.

Familiar sounds of the hospital greeted him, making his heart race with the thrill of possibilities, possibilities of saving a life. Attendants rushed to their assignments, and the apostolic clock in the entrance hall chimed six bells. The interior of the building, well lit by multiple sconces, held warmth, a welcome relief from the elements—the life of the building, a medicinal orchestra, preparing for its most important symphony.

"Lord Ravensmoore. We're meeting in surgery in a few minutes," called one of his colleagues.

"I'll be there," Devlin said, removing his cloak. He headed to get an apron in preparation for the morning's events. The odors of herbal and mustard poultices mixed with the stench of disease and the fear of patients awaiting the unknown.

Devlin had attended Langford's lectures two years earlier in London. The doctor emphasized the need of physicians to acquaint themselves with the intricacies of surgery as well as traditional medicine, the apothecary, and obstetrics. Langford strongly believed that surgical skill was not below the physician's responsibility, as some of the medical community taught, but a necessary part of their training. One of the things that had convinced him to study with Langford was this unique opportunity to observe, learn, and practice surgical techniques.

Entering the preparatory room Devlin came face-to-face with

Melton. "Ravensmoore. Glad you're here…and on time too." Melton grinned. "Langford's got us scheduled to participate in the removal of a limb. Then we remove a bullet lodged deep in a patient's backside. Great fun, wouldn't you say?"

"If you're not the patient. I imagine they see it far differently." Devlin grabbed an apron, tying it quickly about his neck and waist. "I hear you tried to pay me a visit. Anything in particular on your mind?"

"I just wanted to see how you were getting on, that's all. After Langford's tongue lashing, I thought you might want to go to the Grey Fox Inn and relax a bit. The innkeeper's wife said you weren't available, so I went on without you. Another time, perhaps?"

"Perhaps," Devlin said, making no commitment, but pleased that at least this colleague tried to make a genuine effort to include him.

They entered the surgery room where a boy, no older than ten, lay on a wooden table fighting against two leather straps that restricted his movement. His left hand was pierced through by a jagged piece of wood and dripped blood onto the sawdust-covered floor beneath him.

The poor child writhed in pain, his pasty skin color a tribute to it. "Help me," cried the boy, his gaze jumping from one unfamiliar face to the next. His agony-laced, bloodshot eyes locked on Devlin. "Help me."

Devlin's heart shattered. He leaned close to Melton and whispered, "You didn't tell me he was a boy."

"I didn't realize." Melton turned a bit pale.

Devlin moved to the young patient's side and gently stroked the boy's hair. *Please, God, help me comfort him. Give me words to calm him.* "God is watching over you, child. It will be all right. We're going to take care of you. Soon you will feel better." Devlin hoped he could keep that promise.

The child's breathing quickened. "Don't cut off my hand!"

"We'll try to get the wood out." He ached for this small, helpless victim of the surgery.

"I'm glad to see someone has a decent bedside manner." Langford stepped forward and put a hand on the boy's sweaty brow. "What's wrong with the rest of you?" He peered from one student to the next. "Is Ravensmoore the only one who knows how to comfort a wee patient? What if that was your brother or your son lying there in pain? Next time, treat him as though he were. Bring the laudanum."

Devlin supported the boy's head and shoulders and lifted a small glass of amber liquid to his mouth. The child sputtered and coughed.

"What is your name, son?"

"Jamie, sir."

"Jamie, listen to me. You *will* be all right. I know this is hard to keep down, but you must drink as much as possible so you won't have more pain. Do you believe God can help you?"

The child nodded.

"I do too."

Jamie seemed to gather courage and sipped the liquid as best he could. Eventually his thin body quit its struggle, and he lost consciousness. Devlin breathed a sigh of relief. *Thank You, Lord.*

"Good work, Ravensmoore," Langford said. "Let's get this over with quickly and see if we can stop the bleeding." He picked up the amputation saw from the table of instruments.

"Wait!" Devlin stepped in front of Langford. "Is there no other way to save this boy's hand?"

Langford backed up a step. "Do you think I would cut off his hand if I thought we could save the limb? Look at the injury. Even if we remove the wood, we risk the chance of gangrene setting in, and then he might lose not only his hand but his life." Langford's bushy brows knitted together over his glasses. "Do you want to take that risk?"

Devlin glanced at the boy again and cast another prayer heavenward. "I think we should try."

"Then *we* shall," Langford said and laid the saw next to the other surgical necessities. "I'll guide you through this operation, Ravensmoore. The first thing you'll have to do is apply the tourniquet."

Devlin grabbed a strip of cloth and tied it around the boy's forearm. "Done."

"Now pull the wood out, understanding that it may splinter."

The other students crowded around them.

Devlin never grew tired of the intricacies of the human body. He quickly prayed and placed his hand over the boy's wrist and thumb and pulled. Nothing.

"You can't afford to be timid, Ravensmoore. If he wakes up, it will only be more difficult to achieve the outcome we want over the top of his screams and thrashing."

Devlin nodded. "Understood." He could feel the sweat forming on his brow. He suddenly remembered the wood he'd extracted from Lord Richfield's thigh and the heavy bleeding that followed. Devlin took a deep breath, placed his hand around the wood using the other hand as leverage, and pulled steadily and straight. The wood erupted from the child's hand.

"I want you to put your finger in the wound and feel for any shards of wood. The tourniquet will help staunch the flow of blood, but we don't want to waste any time in order to avoid other complications."

Devlin followed Langford's directions. The skin around the puncture gave way, and he searched for splinters. He felt them, and one stuck in his own finger. Removing each piece, Devlin slowly exhaled and turned to his instructor. The bleeding subsided, indicating that an artery had not been damaged.

"Good. Now the sutures."

Devlin stitched the hole in Jamie's hand shut, wrapped the wound, and then removed the tourniquet.

"Now, if infection doesn't set in, the child might have a chance of survival." Langford wiped his hands on his stained apron. "This, gentlemen, is one reason a physician should know how to care for such injuries. Physicians need to know how to be the best of surgeons, or patients will die. We never know what God may place in our path. We need to prepare for any eventuality. The writing of a receipt for pain or a poultice for infection would not suffice."

An attendant came to take the child. Devlin patted his patient's shoulder and whispered in his ear, "God speed, Jamie. God speed."

"We'll visit other patients while our next surgical patient is readied," Langford announced. As his entourage checked on the progress of those afflicted with gout, malaise, and pregnancy concerns, Devlin forced himself to concentrate, though he continued to think and pray for the healing of young Jamie.

Madeline awoke to the clatter of china and silverware. "Who is it?" she asked, her eyes shut tight against the morning sun.

"It's just me, which you could surely see if you'd come out from your hiding place," Daisy grumbled, a hint of a smile in her voice.

A bolt of pain shot through Madeline's head. She moaned and rolled on her stomach, pulling the pillow over her head as if to block out the hideous picture of her mother kissing Lord Vale and appearing very much like she enjoyed his attentions. Vale had backed away quickly when he saw her, murmuring apologies, but her mother just stood beside him when Madeline ran weeping up the steps to her room.

"Your mama asked me to bring you some tea. I'll be thinkin' you were a bit too upset last night, mistress. I ain't seen you like that since your papa died."

The events of the evening came crashing in on Madeline. *Mother is possessed by the weakness of her own heart.* "Oh no. I so hoped I'd had a nightmare."

"Be no wonder if you did. Cried yerself to sleep, you did." Daisy poured the tea, setting the tray on Madeline's lap. "The tea's hot, so don't go spillin' it all over you now. Eat the scone too; it'll help yer poor head."

Madeline ignored her bossy manner. "How is Mother this morning?"

"Your mama is whistlin'."

"Whistling?" Madeline carefully threw her legs over the side of the bed, ignoring the pain in her head and arm. "Where is she?"

"In the breakfast room. You'll be needin' yer robe, Lady Madeline," Daisy commanded. Madeline grabbed the robe and bolted from the room. The ideas darting through Madeline's mind made her ashamed, but she could not help it. Her mother had not whistled for a long time. Her father had always teased his wife that it wasn't ladylike to whistle, but that was Grace, and he didn't fault her for it. Madeline thought he rather enjoyed it.

She stopped before she got to the breakfast room when she heard her mother's jaunty tune drifting down the hall. "She *is* whistling," Madeline muttered irritably under her breath. Steeling herself for the worst, she entered the room.

"Madeline, dear, how are you feeling this morning?" Grace asked pleasantly.

"Don't you think the better question is, why are you whistling?"

"Whatever are you talking about?" Grace asked. "I've whistled before."

"Oh no, you haven't. Not since before Father's death at least. Are you over him so soon?" Madeline demanded.

"What kind of question is that? And how dare you ask it? It's been a year, a bit more than a year since you're counting so carefully."

Grace knocked over her teacup as she reached for the sugar. A dark stain formed on the cream-colored tablecloth and seeped across the table.

"I need to know, that's all."

Madeline followed her mother's gaze to the portrait of Thurston Whittington and stood rigidly at the end of the table. "Mother, are you listening to me? Do you have strong feelings for Lord Vale?" she asked, remembering the scene she had stumbled on the night before, a scene she would just as soon forget.

"Well, certainly not the same feelings I had for your father. Lord Vale is entertaining. I need someone to make me laugh. I miss laughing."

Madeline held her breath. "You know what I'm trying to say, Mother…" Madeline felt the heat spread up her neck and into her face. "Romantic feelings."

"Madeline! That is no concern of yours. I am very fond of Lord Vale. As I said, he makes me laugh. He was a friend of your father."

"Mother, quit dancing around the question, please. You kissed him. And how do you know, really know, he was a friend of Papa?"

"He said he was, dear, and I'm certain that your father mentioned him on more than one occasion. What possible reason could he have for lying? I think you are making too much of this. Let's talk of something else."

"I don't want to talk about something else. I want to know what you plan to do about Lord Vale. And I'll tell you why he might be lying," Madeline continued, undaunted. "He can get himself a wealthy widow…and access to everything you own."

"But he needs nothing from me. He's wealthy in his own right. And I'm not planning anything." Grace put both her hands flat on the table.

"Will you marry him if he asks you?"

Grace looked stunned. "I don't know."

"You are thinking about it though, aren't you?" Madeline continued to push. "I can see it in your face. I saw it in his eyes last night at dinner. I can see right through him, and he knows it!"

"You, my dear child, have an overactive imagination."

"Promise me you won't marry the man until you know him better. Please." Feeling defeated and tired, Madeline sank into a chair at the far end of the table.

"I can't make such a promise. It is unfair of you to ask such a thing. Someday soon you will be married and gone, and I will be here. Alone."

The cook, rosy-cheeked from the heat of the kitchen, bustled in with a platter of ham, poached eggs, and a wedge of cheese and added them to the bounty on the sideboard. "Why, you've spilled your tea, ma'am. Why didn't you ring for me? I'll go brew up some more right off."

"Never mind, Cook. I've lost my appetite," Grace said, staring at her daughter. "But I'm certain Madeline is ready for breakfast. I believe she's worked up quite an appetite. Excuse me." She pushed herself away from the table and left the room.

Hally entered the breakfast room wearing a burgundy walking dress. "What's happened? Your mother just rushed by me. I think she was crying."

"We argued about Lord Vale." The morning meal did not tempt her. She pushed the eggs around on her plate and thought about all that had happened. She didn't want to discuss Vale, so she quickly changed the subject to one that she knew would distract her friend. "Hally, I have something to confess. I have been harboring the young woman from the asylum."

Hally nearly toppled the plate of food in her hands at the sideboard as she swiveled to face Madeline. "Have you lost your mind?"

"Shh. No one else knows. Not even Mother." Madeline's head ached from worry and guilt and certainly from the fall on the hunt field. She propped an elbow on the table and held her hand across her forehead. "What am I going to do?"

The cook entered the room with a large freshly brewed pot of tea. "Good morning, Countess. I see at least you have an appetite this morning." She set the silver pot on the sideboard. "Let me pour tea for you and Lady Madeline, and then I'll be on my way."

"Thank you, Cook."

The moment the cook left the room Hally said, "You will tell me everything immediately and from the beginning."

Madeline sipped her tea and explained the details of the last few days. "So you see what a mess I've made. When Lord Vale discovers that I'm harboring the young woman from the asylum, he will think I've lost my senses, but worse than that he will make Amanda return to that dreadful place. And then when my mother finds out, it will be even worse. She'll accuse me of interfering and taking matters I ought not be taking into my own hands. This will cause a rift between her and Vale. What am I going to do?"

"First we pray. Then you are going to take me to see this girl. Perhaps I can help. And then we are going shopping. Shopping solves a multitude of worries." Hally took Madeline's hand in hers. "Lord in heaven, thank You for all that we have. Make known to us the wisdom we need for what is to come and the strength to carry out Your will. Amen."

The cabin door stood open. Madeline gasped. "I didn't lock her in. I thought she'd stay if she knew I would bring her food."

Hally held her hand up in prudent warning. "Let's not assume the worst."

"But what if she's gone? What if the keepers discovered her?"

"One step at a time, my friend."

Tethering their horses nearby, they hurried to the cabin looking for signs of danger. Madeline lifted her skirt and climbed the steps next to Hally until they reached the door.

Madeline peeked cautiously inside. "Nothing seems amiss. There is no sign of damage." She waved Hally forward.

"Amanda? Are you here? Are you all right? She's not here." Tears stung Madeline's eyes as she looked into the front room where she had last seen the girl. A chill pervaded the cabin, and the glassy eyes of mounted deer heads were the only things staring back at her. She shivered and thought she could never kill anything.

Hally joined her in the foyer of the cabin. "There has to be what—five or six bedrooms? Let's look through all of them."

They searched the lodge together, making quick work of it. Hally stopped and pointed out an upstairs window. "I think we've found her."

Madeline's eyes followed Hally's direction. "It's her! Sweet relief." She placed her hand over her heart. "She's praying. Hally, remain in the cabin. I'll bring her in after I tell her about you."

Madeline hurried outside. The girl, still on her knees, scrambled forward toward the woods.

"Amanda, it's me. Your friend, Lady Madeline. You frightened me when I couldn't find you."

The girl glanced back over her shoulder and then slowed her steps.

"Forgive me, Amanda." Madeline rushed to the girl's side. "I didn't mean to startle you and interrupt your prayers. I've brought a friend with me."

The girl looked wildly about. Her eyes wide, she seemed ready to dash away.

"She's my friend. She won't hurt you. Come with me into the cabin." Madeline held her hand out toward the girl. "Come. We've brought you food to eat."

That must have made good sense to her, for she followed Madeline into the cabin but refused to hold her hand. Madeline and Hally watched Amanda eat cucumber sandwiches until she could eat no more, drink her fill of warm milk, and enjoy a gingerbread cookie. They left the girl snuggled deep into the blankets from one of the bedrooms and returned to Richfield to embark on their shopping excursion to York.

Safely ensconced in the carriage at last, Madeline leaned back and sighed. "Hally, you are right. A trip to town is exactly what I needed. Now that I know the girl is safe, I might be able to relax and enjoy myself."

Hally looked her way. "Maddie, what do you plan to do about the girl? You can't keep her in the hunting lodge forever."

"I don't know what I'm going to do. I suppose I could be in a great deal of trouble on several levels." She closed her eyes and ticked them off in her mind as she spoke them aloud. "First, I believe it's a crime to harbor an escapee from the lunatic asylum. Second, Lord Vale has taken an interest in the girl since he is helping to support the asylum. Three, my mother believes she's in love with Vale, and when she finds out what I've done, that will only complicate her 'romance' further. Fourth, I believe—"

"Enough! I do think you are aware of the gravity of the situation. Have you—"

The carriage suddenly rocked to one side and tipped. Madeline's eyes flew open as she tumbled to the floor. To her horror the door hung open, and Hally was no longer sitting across from her. Hally was not in the carriage at all.

CHAPTER 6

Every heart hath its own ache.

—ANONYMOUS

*T*HROUGH THE CLAMOR of the patients Devlin heard the clock chime once as the morning hours disappeared into the afternoon. He grabbed a bite of lunch before heading back into surgery with Langford. A burly man lay facedown on the same table the boy had earlier occupied. Blood soaked through a well-worn sheet. An attendant stepped away from the table as they entered.

"Mr. Matthews," Langford said, "would you kindly tell us what happened to you?"

"The wife caught me in bed with her sister," he explained, eyeing the group suspiciously. "Grabbed me own gun and shot me. Ye can see where. Lucky she didn't ruin me chances o' havin' more children. But I doubt she'll be wantin' more with the likes o' me." He grimaced.

Devlin asked, "Is the pain bad?"

"No, blast it! I think me bum's gone numb, it has."

"We're going to take a look now, Mr. Matthews, and then you'll be off for your surgery." Langford exposed the wound site.

The group shuffled forward to gain a better look.

Matthews groaned. "Ye look like a herd of butchers in them blood-speckled aprons."

Devlin struggled with the image. Is that really how Lady Madeline saw him? Surgery wasn't neat or pretty, but with enough knowledge and a steady hand, he thought it would certainly save lives.

Langford removed the dressing, exposing a hole where the small ball from the weapon had entered. The black and purple skin appeared ripe with infection.

"Ravensmoore, you'll be doing this one as well," Langford said.

After the laudanum took effect, Devlin followed the attendant, who transferred the patient to the operating area. The surgery went smoothly, although it took Devlin several attempts to extract the ball deeply embedded in the patient's flesh.

Devlin wiped his hands on his apron after suturing the wound. "He won't be sitting down comfortably for a while, but under the circumstances he's fortunate his wife didn't kill him."

"Your skills as a surgeon are to be commended, Ravensmoore." Langford shook Devlin's bloodstained hand. "I couldn't have done better myself."

Devlin couldn't believe his ears. It took every muscle in his face not to allow his mouth to gape open in astonishment. The stubborn old doctor had actually complimented him twice in one morning. *A miracle indeed*, he thought with pleasure. *Thank You, Lord.*

Suddenly, the door to the amphitheater burst open, and Willie, the receptionist, shouted, "Right sorry to disturb you, Dr. Langford, but there's been an accident."

"Hally?" Madeline knelt beside her friend on the cobblestone street that had quickly filled with shopkeepers and townspeople crowding about to see what had happened. "Hally, your head is bleeding. Don't move. I've sent for assistance."

"Poppycock. I'm perfectly well. You really must let me up." Hally groaned. "This wretched street is killing my back. Besides, I detest being on display, Maddie. Just listen to everyone oohing and ahhing as if they were watching a circus performance. They act as though they've never seen a carriage accident."

"Well, at least you're not speaking nonsense. Maybe you didn't hit your head too hard. Still, it's best not to take any chances."

"Dearest Maddie, I never speak nonsense. How is that poor farmer who fell off his wagon?"

"I'm not certain. He isn't standing either." Madeline surveyed the cluttered street. The farmer's wagon and their carriage had blocked all traffic after the collision.

A pair of blood-spattered boots appeared next to Madeline. "May we be of assistance?"

Her heart skipped a beat, whether because of the voice or the horrendous look of those boots, she was not certain. She forced her gaze up into Ravensmoore's concerned eyes and sighed in frustration. "I do not believe we will be needing your assistance, Lord Ravensmoore. Look at you. You are covered with blood from one of your recent attempts at"—she lifted a brow in disdain—"butchery."

"She may not want your assistance, but I certainly do," Hally interrupted. "My stubborn friend refuses to let me get up, and now, she refuses your help. I must protest, Maddie."

Ravensmoore knelt next to Hally. "You have a nasty gash on your forehead, Countess. Since I make Lady Madeline uncomfortable with my presence, I will leave you in the capable hands of my colleague, Mr. Charles Melton." He turned to Melton. "This is the Countess Gilling. Please attend to her while I check the local farmer, who, from all appearances, is responsible for this fine mess."

Melton scrambled forward, eager to be of assistance. "I am at your service."

"Thank you, Mr. Melton," Madeline said, as she watched Ravensmoore hurry to the aid of the old farmer. "Please be careful."

"Of course, madam."

"Such a bother," Hally said. "It is nothing I assure you, sir."

"Allow me to be the judge of that, dear lady. Does anything hurt?"

"Only my pride."

Hally's voice caused Madeline to pull her eyes away from Ravensmoore and stare in surprise.

"In that case, just put your arms around my neck, Countess Gilling. I will carry you to the hospital and give you proper attention."

"Thank you, Mr. Melton. That is most kind, but I do believe I can walk with just a little assistance."

"I would not dream of letting you walk."

Hally blushed. Madeline could not believe her eyes. When was the last time she saw her friend blush? And in the arms of a man no less. "I will come with you."

"No need," Hally said. "I do believe I am in capable hands. I know how much you dislike hospitals."

Madeline smiled as she watched Melton easily carry Hally toward the entrance of the Guardian Gate Hospital. "I do believe you *are* in capable hands, dear friend." She then turned her attention to Ravensmoore.

Why did this man so irritate her? He immediately took charge of the situation and had the old farmer on his feet moments after assessing him for injuries. It appeared that Ravensmoore's current patient suffered from a slight limp but otherwise seemed well. She watched curiously as he instructed two of the shopkeepers to assist the elderly man to the hospital. As the shopkeepers passed her with the elderly man balanced between them, they suddenly stopped. "I'm right sorry fer the trouble, yer ladyship, right sorry. Is the other lady badly injured? I saw her tumble out the door when me wagon hit the carriage. Do forgive me."

Madeline's distress over the accident melted at this plea for forgiveness. "It was but an unfortunate accident, dear man. No need to worry."

"You won't be bringing charges then?" His gray eyes looked hopeful. "You forgive me?"

"Yes, I forgive you. And I will not bring charges against you."

The elderly man sighed in relief. "Thank you, yer ladyship. Yer most kind."

Ravensmoore came up behind his patient and raised an eyebrow while looking at Madeline. "I imagine her ladyship's forgiveness will do much to ease your pain, but come now, we must not tarry. I want to get a crutch for you to use and see that someone escorts you home where your wife can take proper care of you."

His words did not escape her attention, and a twinge of guilt plucked at her heart. "May I accompany you? I must see how Countess Gilling progresses."

"An honor," Ravensmoore said, falling into step beside her. "Speaking of progress, is your arm improving? You're certain the carriage accident did not worsen the injury?"

"I am well, thank you."

"I imagine the hospital is the last place you wish to visit."

Madeline stiffened. "I loathe death and disease. I want to be as far away from those twin evils as possible." She straightened her lilac bonnet and brushed the dust from the street off her matching walking dress. "Having only one good arm now has made the simplest chore frustrating."

"Forgive me for asking, especially if it opens old wounds, but have you lost someone other than your father?"

Madeline wanted him to know. She wasn't sure why, but she felt compelled to share the information with him. "My younger brother...and two sisters. Miriam, my youngest sister, died in infancy. The others contracted smallpox. It was horrible."

"I begin to understand your dislike of the medical profession.

If your family could not be saved, why should you put any trust in medicine or those who practice it?"

"Exactly."

"There is so much that needs to be discovered in order for people to combat disease. Just like Jenner's discovery of the smallpox vaccine. I vow someday I will discover a way to prevent infection. Just imagine how many lives could be saved if that were to occur."

"Imagine indeed, Lord Ravensmoore. Your imaginings seem to be quite vast. Perhaps you could write a book about your discoveries."

"Hmm. I must consider that notion." To her great annoyance, he grinned at her and opened the heavy oak door as they entered the hospital. "Now, let's see if we can locate the countess."

A burst of laughter spilled into the hallway.

"And the next thing I knew, I was lying facedown in the street, praying a horse would not step on me."

"I believe we have found her," Madeline said and smiled. She could hear Hally chattering away and knew that she was well. Very well, it seemed.

"It's a pleasure to hear the sound of laughter in this place," Ravensmoore said. "It is a rare occurrence."

They followed the sound of Hally's voice and discovered her and Melton quite engrossed in conversation.

"Melton, it sounds as if you have actually cured a patient. What will Langford think?"

Melton turned away from his patient. "That I am as good a prospect for the field of medicine as you are, I hope."

"He is quite skilled and very kind, Lord Ravensmoore," Hally said from her perch on the table in front of Melton.

"That is good to know, madam. If you will all excuse me, I must locate a crutch for our good farmer and see to his welfare. I hope you will wait until I return before taking your leave."

Madeline looked at Hally. "I don't believe we will be—"

"Of course we will wait," Hally interrupted. "Madeline, you should have Lord Ravensmoore examine your arm while we are here to be certain the accident did not cause further damage. Our carriage did receive quite a jolt."

Madeline shook her head vehemently. "Rubbish. I am perfectly well."

"Forgive me, Lady Madeline." Ravensmoore said smoothly. "I do believe the last time you made such a declaration you nearly fell to the ground. The countess is correct. I will be but a few moments, and then I will make certain you are well enough to travel home."

"Really!" Madeline glared at her friend as Ravensmoore left to see to his current patient. "Such an unnecessary fuss."

"Were you not reprimanding me just a short while ago about the exact thing, dear?"

"But you were injured, not I."

"Dear ladies," Melton broke in. "You have been through a difficult experience. It is best to ascertain any possibility of a problem to your person before allowing you to leave."

"I quite agree with you, sir," Hally said, smiling warmly at Melton. "In fact, I wonder if it would not be wise for us to remain in town. The carriage will need repair as well."

"That is a wise plan, Countess Gilling. You must take care not to overdo it."

"What's this about staying in town?" Ravensmoore asked as he rejoined them.

Madeline noticed he'd removed the bloody apron. Despite the fact that he had his white sleeves rolled up and ready for duty, a very unconventional appearance for a gentleman, Madeline could not help noticing how handsome he looked in his green vest.

"We will not be staying in town," Madeline said flatly. "I must return to Richfield tonight."

"While you two debate your plans for the remainder of the day, allow me to examine your arm, Lady Madeline."

"I assure you that it is not necessary, but if it will get us out of this horrid place any sooner"—Madeline visibly shivered—"I will permit it."

"Sit up here next to me, Maddie," Hally said, patting the examining table.

Madeline stepped onto a small step stool and carefully sat next to Hally. "Please assure me that you do not plan to operate, and I will be much relieved." She gave Ravensmoore a meaningful look.

"No surgery will be necessary. Just slip your arm from the sling very slowly. That's it," he said, as Madeline followed his directions.

She grimaced. "It hurts," she said, as he gently manipulated her arm and shoulder. "But not any worse than it has been since my fall. Are we free to go now?" Madeline put her arm back in the sling, and Ravensmoore assisted her from the table.

"I am sorry for your discomfort, Lady Madeline. As I told you when I attended your injury at Richfield, it is a most severe sprain and will take time to heal. I recommend you visit the apothecary this day if you do not return home. Where will you stay?"

"This is as good a reason as any to reopen my town house," Hally suggested, as she joined Madeline.

Madeline whispered, "Are you certain you are ready for that, Hally? The memories of you and James are bound to be everywhere."

"It is time." Hally took her friend's hand and squeezed gently. "It is past time. I will send word to your mother so that she won't worry about us and to alert the staff at my town house."

Langford interrupted the conversation. "I beg your pardon, ladies, but I have urgent need of my students. I trust you are both well?"

"Excellent, sir," Hally said. "Mr. Melton has treated me with the utmost respect and consideration. Lady Madeline can say no less of Lord Ravensmoore, can you, dear?" She lifted a slender brow.

"Of course."

Madeline studied Langford carefully, then recognition dawned. Him! It was the doctor who'd left Father with Ravensmoore when he'd been called away on another emergency. He'd left her father to bleed to death after the removal of the wood that had impaled his thigh. He should have stayed. "Let us not detain them another moment, Hally. They are obviously quite busy." Madeline held tight to Hally's hand and pulled her out through the doorway.

As they walked past the entryway and out onto the street, she prayed she would never have to enter a hospital again.

Devlin watched Madeline depart and wished he could go after her, comfort her.

Langford peered at him over his spectacles. "Tomorrow we have a unique opportunity to expand your knowledge. We will be visiting Ashcroft Asylum."

Devlin's heart raced, keeping pace with his speeding thoughts. "Ashcroft Asylum," he whispered.

"Do you have a comment, Ravensmoore?"

Devlin swallowed hard. "Yes," he said. "When we go, I prefer that you introduce me as Dr. Grayson. I'd rather not bother with the winks and whisperings of people who are wondering why an earl would visit such a place." *Nor do I want them to connect me with my mother,* he thought.

"Fair enough. Both you and Melton will accompany me. The rest of the students will care for the others here. One of the patients at the asylum is in need of medical attention."

Ashcroft Asylum. Devlin steeled his heart for what lay ahead. *They may as well send me straight to hell.*

CHAPTER 7

Canst thou not minister to a mind diseased,
Pluck from the memory a rooted sorrow,
Raze out the written troubles of the brain
And with some sweet oblivious antidote
Cleanse the stuff'd bosom of that perilous stuff
Which weighs upon the heart?
— SHAKESPEARE,
MACBETH, ACT V, SCENE III

SHCROFT INSANE ASYLUM loomed in front of Devlin like a giant bird of prey. The rain had let up considerably overnight, yet a light drizzle continued to fall. It did little to improve the appearance of the menacing gray fortress surrounded by a high stone wall. A huge, black iron gate provided the only public entrance.

Devlin tried to convince himself he had nothing to fear as they approached the building. He was not successful. Each moment he came closer to the asylum, he gave up more and more of himself to the wretched place. The asylum seemed to possess his very soul.

The memories crashed in on him as though it were yesterday. He remembered arriving home from boarding school the summer after his eleventh birthday.

"So, you have returned." His father frowned at him.

"Where is Mother?" Devlin asked, as he peered around his father to look for her. His heart beat like a drum in anticipation.

"Your mother was admitted to Ashcroft Asylum this spring. She is not herself." His father placed a hand on his shoulder. "I know this is difficult for you, but you are old enough to understand. She is gone."

"You are lying." He shook off his father's hand and took the stairs two at a time until he reached his mother's room. "She must be here," he said nervously, unwilling to accept his father's words. Tears blurred his progress. "Mother! Mother!"

Devlin tugged open the door. Instead of the pleasant smell of his mother's perfume, the musty odor of disuse assaulted him. White sheets covered the furniture like phantoms in residence.

His father entered the room. Devlin turned on him. "You did this! You never wanted her here. You never loved her. I hate you!"

"That's enough, young man. You don't understand."

"That's right. I don't understand." Tears coursed down his cheeks. Devlin glared at his father, showing him the rage he felt. "I want to see her!"

Again, his father placed a hand on Devlin's shoulder. "You cannot," he said, his voice cold. "I forbid it. Ashcroft is no place for a child."

"Ashcroft is no place for my mother!" Devlin pushed the unwanted hand away. "Let her come home," Devlin pleaded. "I want to see that she is all right. I must."

"That is not possible. She is too sick to leave." His father turned away. "You must accept it."

"I will not accept anything until I see her for myself."

The memory faded, but the anger and hurt lingered in his heart, stubbornly clinging to him, invisible cobwebs of pain. He shook his head to clear his mind, but still he saw the past looming in front of him, an unconquered demon.

Devlin had never entered the asylum to visit his mother; his father had held firm and refused. His letters went unanswered. He didn't know what her day-to-day activities had been during that time. He'd imagined all kinds of horrors. No one dared talk about it, and then she had died. Now he would come face-to-face with what he'd feared most: the reality of asylum life.

Devlin struggled to maintain an appearance of calm that he did not feel. Emotions stampeded through him, out of control. He ached to turn back.

As they approached the main gate, a guard stepped from a small shelter. He did not appear to be a friendly sort and eyed them suspiciously. "What be yer business, gentlemen?"

"We are here to see Mr. Amos Sullivan," Langford said. He gave the guard a dire look. "We are from the hospital. Sullivan wants us to take a look at one of the patients."

"He told me ye was comin'. I just like to make sure. Can't trust no one these days. The rich are always comin' up with ways to spy on 'em that's lost their wits. It amuses 'em."

Devlin spoke up. "I can assure you, we have not come here to be amused. Nor do we find others' suffering something to laugh about."

"'Tis as it should be," the guard said, pushing open the heavy iron gate. "Good luck to ye. Ye'll be needin' it when ye meet with Wiggins."

They rode through the open gate. A chill of apprehension crawled up Devlin's spine.

"What do you suppose he meant?" Melton asked. "This place gives me the shivers."

"It means," Langford said, "that we may anticipate…the unusual. I haven't been here in years. They had a doctor, but I heard he left some time ago. They will have a hard time filling the position. Always do. Here's Sullivan."

Sullivan was a tall and gangly man whose mouth sagged at the ends humorlessly. What remained of his hair scattered across his head like a spider's web. He looked more like a lunatic than any manager of an insane asylum should.

"Grayson, Melton, may I present Mr. Amos Sullivan, manager of Ashcroft Asylum. Mr. Sullivan, my students. Perhaps you can take one of them into your employ."

"So good of you to come. Let us discuss the problem in my office. The stable boy will see to your horses." He nodded to a tall, slender boy with dark circles under his eyes.

Sullivan turned and led the way through a long stone corridor. Devlin heard a great cacophony of sound muffled by the walls of the asylum: people talking, laughing, crying.

They entered Sullivan's well-lit office. Immediately struck by the spaciousness of the area, Devlin thought the man enjoyed life a bit above his position. He'd imagined it would be small, stifling, and cluttered. Instead a cozy fire burned in the hearth, and the room emanated organization and comfort.

As if reading his thoughts, Sullivan said, "I try to keep my office as hospitable as possible since this is where I meet with family members." He looked directly at Devlin. "Have a seat, gentlemen."

Langford chose a comfortable-looking wing chair, while Melton and Devlin found seats nearby. He wondered if the need for their presence had caused the commotion within or if disorder reflected normalcy for those committed.

Sullivan distanced himself behind his desk. "My most urgent need is for a patient named Andrew Wiggins. He usually keeps to himself, doesn't cause trouble. Yesterday one of the guards teased him about Amanda, the girl who escaped. Said she ran away because of him. He went berserk. Nearly beat the guard to a pulp. Took another four guards to dislodge him."

"You want us to repair the damage he caused?" Langford suggested.

"Yes, but there's a bit more to it. Wiggins is in a secluded cell, injured. We couldn't restrain him. Lucky to contain him at all. Amanda's the only one that's ever been able to calm him when he gets angry. He'll need attention. It'll take great skill and caution to deal with him."

"Why?" Melton asked.

"He's a large man and very strong," Sullivan said.

Langford frowned. "We will do what we can, but I did not bring my students here to be injured. If it is too dangerous, we will not be able to assist you. Is that clear?"

Sullivan looked disgruntled. "Certainly, Dr. Langford. Now, if you please, follow me."

The three of them followed Sullivan down a long cold corridor to a heavy oak door, the entrance to the asylum. Devlin thought about his mother. Fear washed through him. The guard opened the door as they approached. Devlin steeled himself. The voices grew louder, and the smell was a mixture of urine, stale air, and fear.

"The women's area," Sullivan said. "We have to pass through it to reach the cells."

Devlin absorbed the surroundings. Women dressed in rags and well-attired women encircled him, some dancing, some touching his cheek, and others whispering things in his ear that made him blush. Women like this walked the steps his mother had walked. These were the sights she had witnessed every day, the odors she endured. The place she took her last breath. Panic clawed up his throat. He wondered how his father had left her in this ghastly prison.

Despite his revulsion he asked, "Why are these patients dressed so differently? I imagined they would all wear something similar." Devlin studied a young woman dressed in rags curled up in a corner. Her sunken, bloodshot eyes misted with tears, and dark circles gave her the appearance of being so deeply haunted and lost that recovery might never occur.

"The families with money provide the clothes for them. The others are dependent on the charity of church folk and the like," Sullivan explained.

"Why is that woman here?" Devlin asked, nodding in the direction of a patient who watched him intently from behind a long veil of gray hair.

"Melancholy. Many of the women have melancholy.

"This way, gentlemen," Sullivan said. They continued past other patients. Sullivan stopped when they got to a large iron gate. "Open up, Henry. The doctor and his students are here to see Wiggins."

"Right away, sir." Henry opened the gate with a great rattling of keys. His beefy hands shook as he struggled. The door creaked open, as though it hadn't been used in years. "G–good l–luck," he stammered.

They filed in, and the gate clanged shut behind them. Devlin turned to find a look of relief on Melton's ashen face.

What next? Devlin's nerves turned raw with the slamming gate ringing in his ears, a never-ending echo. The procession continued through a narrow windowless corridor damp with mold. No one spoke.

Sullivan pulled out a key for another door and inserted it in the ancient lock. He turned and addressed Langford. "Wiggins is on the other side confined to his cell. I don't know how he will react to you. He doesn't get visitors."

Devlin watched apprehensively as Sullivan opened the door and allowed Langford and Melton to enter. He heard Melton gasp.

"What on earth?"

Devlin knew he must move forward, but his feet were leaden. A shove from Sullivan followed by a mumbled apology resolved the problem. Devlin stumbled into the chamber. He grabbed the bars to steady himself and immediately found his hand covered by another—a huge hand with long, dirty nails. Devlin slowly raised his head and looked up through the bars into the red-rimmed eyes of Andrew Wiggins.

His nails pressed into Devlin's hand. Devlin found it hard to breathe. The man, if he could be called a man, stood over seven feet tall, his clothes ragged, torn, and much too small for him. Wiggins's matted black hair, peppered with gray, fell below his waist. The wild mane partially covered what appeared to be features distorted by severe burns.

Devlin slowly righted himself but did not move his hand. His colleagues stood frozen. Their silence spoke their alarm.

Devlin cleared his throat. Wiggins tilted his head to one side much as a dog cocks his head when assessing someone. His long hair shifted to reveal a bulging eye. A long bloody gash sliced across his neck and disappeared into his shirt. Blood dripped from the bottom of his left sleeve and splattered large droplets onto the floor.

"Mr. Wiggins, we've come to help."

Andrew Wiggins stared at him as though he were speaking a foreign language. Devlin imagined for a brief moment that no one had ever been kind to this man. "Let us help you."

Devlin felt the pressure on his hand ease as Wiggins backed away. Trickles of blood appeared on his skin where the nails had made their deep impression. Still apprehensive, he left his hand on the bar, an attempt to reassure Wiggins.

Wiggins turned his attention to the others. Suddenly he threw himself against the bars. A growl escaped his tortured body. He raked the air, desperate to capture Sullivan in his grip.

"Get back, Wiggins." Sullivan slammed backward into the wall. "Get back, now!"

Wiggins turned and slumped down on the dirty cot, leaning against the wall, defeated. He stared at the members of the group one by one. At that moment Devlin saw a spark of intelligence in the deformed features. Andrew Wiggins assessed them one by one.

"Now what do we do?" Melton asked. He was plastered against the wall in an awkward attempt to get as far away from the patient as possible.

"An interesting question," Langford said, turning to Sullivan. "I told you I would not risk my students. It's time to leave."

"Wait." Devlin still gripped the bars. "What will happen to him?"

"He'll probably die of infection." Sullivan brushed off a cobweb from his wrinkled suit. "I know *I* won't be helping the monster."

Devlin felt a strange sense of hopelessness for Wiggins. "I have an idea, Dr. Langford."

"What would that be?" his instructor asked, an eyebrow arched in curiosity.

Devlin turned to the prisoner. "Do you want us to stay and help? I will try if you will let me."

Wiggins sat on his cot, motionless. He stared at Devlin and then at the floor.

"You must tell me what you want me to do, or we must leave. Do you want me to stay?"

Wiggins did not move. He did not speak. Devlin was certain he'd already escaped into some part of his mind where he felt safe.

"You're wasting your time," Sullivan said and turned to leave. "You can see he's in no mood to cooperate. So be it. I've done my job."

Wiggins looked up from the floor then, but not at Sullivan. He looked straight at Devlin, raised his long, bleeding arm, and pointed at him. "You...stay."

Devlin didn't know how he was going to treat this giant of a man who could easily kill him, but he knew he had to try. "I'll stay."

"Dr. Langford, will you stay?" Devlin asked.

Langford nodded his agreement.

Devlin continued, "Melton, I want you to go to the apothecary.

Mr. Sullivan will show you the way. Get everything we might need to stitch up Mr. Wiggins's injuries, including a table that will hold his weight. Then bring it all back here and leave it outside the door. I don't want anyone else inside the cell."

Melton nodded, looking relieved, and left with Sullivan.

After the door closed, Devlin again spoke to Wiggins. "Mr. Wiggins, my name is Grayson." He pointed to Langford. "This is Dr. Langford from the hospital in York. He is my instructor. I want him to help with the treatment of your wounds. Will you agree to it?"

Wiggins stood up and carefully studied the two of them. His troubled gaze landed on Devlin, and he nodded.

Devlin looked up at the very intimidating man he had just agreed to treat. *Heaven help me*, he prayed.

"When we get the medical supplies, I will give you something to put you to sleep. That way you won't feel the pain."

"No!" Wiggins stepped forward and gripped the bars.

Devlin thought it would take very little effort for the giant to bend the bars back and escape his prison.

"All right," Devlin said, trying to soothe the man's nerves. "We'll do it your way, but it will hurt like the dickens."

Devlin jumped at the knock on the door. His nerves were ready to snap. Opening the door, he saw four men carrying a huge table that barely fit in the narrow corridor. The table would hold Wiggins's weight.

Melton handed him a black medical bag. "I think you'll find everything you need in here. How do you propose not getting yourself killed?" he whispered to Devlin.

"I have no idea."

"Good luck."

Devlin looked at Sullivan. "You will have to leave this door unlocked. We won't be able to get the table in the cell. He'll have to come out."

"I will post another guard at the entrance." Sullivan looked as though he was about to say something else, then changed his mind.

"We need the key to his cell, Sullivan," Devlin said, holding out his hand.

Sullivan dug in his pocket and handed Devlin the key. "Wiggins could kill both you and Langford. What makes you think he won't?"

"Because the man's in pain. He's not an animal."

Sullivan shrugged his shoulders, turned, and walked away, followed by Melton, who cast a glance over his shoulder as if he feared this would be the last time he saw them alive.

Devlin turned to face their patient. "Mr. Wiggins," Devlin said, pretending to be quite in control of his feelings, "I am going to unlock this door. You must come out and get on the table in the hallway. Do you understand?"

Wiggins grunted in response.

Devlin felt the hairs on his neck rise when he unlocked the cell door. Wiggins rose like a giant sea monster and shuffled toward them. He pushed past Devlin and Langford.

Devlin did not know what to expect. He followed Wiggins, who went straight to the table and sat upon it. Langford stayed close to Devlin.

"You will need to remove your shirt, Mr. Wiggins," Devlin instructed. "Do you need assistance?"

Wiggins looked down at him from his perch on the table and simply ripped the shredded garment from his body.

Devlin studied the fresh wounds. It appeared a knife with a jagged edge had inflicted the deep cuts. "Who did this?"

Wiggins said nothing.

Devlin opened the medical bag, looked inside, and rummaged around. He pulled out a bottle of laudanum. "I would like to use this, Mr. Wiggins. It will make you more comfortable, and we can do a thorough job without you feeling too much pain from the suturing."

Wiggins growled and slapped the bottle out of his hand. It shattered on the hard floor, all hope of pain relief shattered with it.

"We'd better do as the man says, Grayson." Langford reached into the bag and pulled out a cloth holding several instruments. He unwrapped it and revealed the medical tools necessary to treat and suture the deep gashes.

"Of course," Devlin said, wondering how the man would ever sit still for the number of stitches it would take to sew him up. Devlin took a deep breath. "Let's get started."

Together Langford and Devlin cleaned Wiggins's injuries. He sat tall and rigid and did not flinch. As Devlin worked his way around his patient, he stopped dead when he reached his patient's back.

"Dr. Langford, take a look at this. Old wounds. It appears as though someone has whipped the skin off him more than once."

"Mr. Wiggins," Langford asked, "who did this to you?"

Wiggins shrugged.

Devlin glanced at Langford, and the two exchanged a look of concern. They continued cleaning the wounds and prepared to stitch. "This is going to hurt," Devlin said.

It took two hours with both of them stitching, and Wiggins never complained. He grunted a few times but showed no other sign of distress. How did the man do it? It wasn't human. Devlin tied off the last stitch. "You are repaired to the best of our ability, Mr. Wiggins. How do you feel? You must be exhausted."

Wiggins only grunted, his tortured body evidence that he'd endured worse than this. He had somehow learned to hide his pain. He returned to the cell naked from the waist up and lay down on the cot.

They reentered the women's quarters on the way out and were

slammed into the wall by two guards wrestling with a young woman.

"Get the chains on her. We'll teach you not to run away, you little witch!" The guards clamped manacles over her wrists and ankles.

"Stop. Stop it!" Devlin rushed to the girl's side. "This is no way to treat a human being."

Langford and Melton restrained the guards.

"What's she done that's so awful?" Devlin shouted.

"She's the one who killed her father, Dr. Grayson. Her name is Amanda, and she escaped recently. She won't be doing that again. We'll make certain she's very secure this day and every day afterward. The only reason she didn't go to the gallows was because she was found to be insane."

"And why was she declared insane?" Melton asked, still restraining the guard.

"She said the voices told her to kill him, Mr. Melton, specifically the voices of her brothers. Not what I would call normal." Sullivan's lips twisted into a bizarre grin.

"Perhaps her brothers *did* urge her to kill her father. Perhaps they're to blame as well."

"Hardly, sir. They were nowhere near the farm where she killed her father at the time. They were drunk and sleeping it off in town."

Devlin watched the woman with gray hair come to the girl and kneel on the floor where the girl curled into a ball with the chains cutting into her flesh. The old woman cooed and patted Amanda's shoulder and whispered in her ear. The girl rocked on the floor and seemed to withdraw into herself.

"Does she continue to speak to her brothers when they aren't present?" he asked, curious.

"Amanda never speaks. She has never said one word. She'll yell and scream and grunt, but she never talks."

Devlin turned to Sullivan, who then asked, "Is there anything you can do?"

"We can give her some laudanum. It will make her more comfortable and then you can remove the chains, Sullivan."

Sullivan nodded. "Give her the laudanum, but the chains remain. She's a runaway."

Devlin wondered what had caused the girl to commit such an atrocity. "Do you know why she killed her father?"

Sullivan shrugged his shoulders. "Who knows? The court decided that, not me." Sullivan looked perturbed, as though he thought Devlin was accusing him of some wrongdoing.

The three men left the asylum in silence and made their way back to York. Devlin mentally reviewed the horrific events of the morning. He was certain of only one thing. He was never going back.

CHAPTER 8

The best mirror is an old friend.

—GEORGE HERBERT

STAYING AT THE Gilling town house overnight had the exact effect on her friend that Madeline had feared, for Hally indeed spent the morning trailing about the house and sighing. The two-story stone structure simply smothered Hally with memories from the past. Over a light lunch of cucumber sandwiches and tea, Madeline decided not to allow Hally to mope her day away.

Madeline set her teacup down with a determined clank against the saucer. They would go shopping this afternoon. Shopping cured a variety of ills as nothing else could, and since their trip had been so rudely interrupted yesterday, they had not found the diversion they had sought.

"What are you plotting now?" Hally forced a smile. "I can always tell when you're plotting. You purse your lips and tap your fingers on the table."

"No, I don't." She quit tapping her fingers. "And I'm not plotting. I'm thinking."

Hally reached for her friend's hand. "You were right about this place. I thought I'd conquered all the ghosts. I barely slept, and I haven't been myself all morning."

Madeline squeezed Hally's hand. "It's no wonder after yesterday. How's your head?"

"I'm fine, really. How are you?"

"Confused." She reached for a biscuit and smothered it in honey.

"Confused about what?"

"Everything." Madeline tried to block out the wretched conversation that had occurred between her and her mother. "I so wanted us to enjoy shopping yesterday, but the accident ruined everything. I needed your company and a distraction."

The corners of Hally's mouth twitched. "I believe you were distracted. But in a different way than you'd anticipated."

Seeing Ravensmoore after the collision with the farmer's wagon had proved more than a bit disconcerting. She couldn't seem to get away from the man.

"Maddie? You're blushing. Are you well?"

"I'm most well." Madeline forced all thoughts of the man from her mind. "But I would like to finish our shopping excursion today. Do you think you can manage?"

"Perhaps."

"Good. I will send a messenger out to Richfield. Donavan and Agnes can assist us about town since we've no carriage at the moment."

"I knew you were plotting."

Madeline and Hally chatted amiably as their carriage made its way through the busy cobblestone streets of York. Donavan, Richfield's head groom, easily maneuvered the horses through the crowds. A smile tugged at Madeline's lips when she noticed that Agnes appeared to be admiring the groom's driving abilities.

The skies were clear, and the sun made a valiant effort to shine its warm April rays upon them. A light breeze kissed her cheek, and Madeline breathed in the sweetly scented spring air. Her arm felt infinitely better today. She hoped that the sling would soon be unnecessary.

York provided an array of shops, and Madeline wanted to visit several of them. While the shops didn't come close to what London had to offer, she enjoyed them just the same.

"I will do the shopping for the household," Agnes said, studying the long list she'd brought with her, "while you and Countess Gilling visit the shops."

"Very well, Agnes," Madeline said. "We'll meet you at your sister's home. Donavan will accompany you and then return for us."

"I'll enjoy the visit with Edna. I haven't seen her in a month. Time flies away so fast. Don't be surprised if she invites us all to dinner. She loves cooking, and I'm sure she'd be more than pleased if you'd consider being her guests."

"Only if she insists, Agnes. We don't want to put her out. This will do nicely, Donavan," Madeline said when they reached the dressmaker's shop. "We will meet you here after tea."

Donavan brought the horses to a stop. "Yes, yer ladyship." He assisted each of them out of the carriage. "I will help Agnes until then."

The two friends shopped the day away, stopping only long enough for tea. Madeline thought that the afternoon passed pleasantly. She thoroughly enjoyed herself, though her arm began to ache a bit. She stopped at the local apothecary for some laudanum. By tonight she might need the respite.

Standing outside the last dressmaker shop, arms filled with her purchases, Madeline said, "Hally, I think it's time we meet Agnes and Donavan."

"Agreed. One more parcel to juggle will be quite impossible."

"I'd say we had a rather productive afternoon. Thank you for helping me with some of these packages." She mentally ticked off the purchases: a lovely lavender bonnet, new material for an evening dress, a most beautiful pair of gold slippers, and a new novel. "I'm getting tired of not having the full use of this arm yet." Just then she spotted Agnes and Donavan. Agnes waved and bustled through the crowded street.

"I've ordered all the necessities for your mother, Lady Madeline, and also placed her order for the butcher." Agnes and Donavan helped Madeline and Hally secure their purchases in the carriage. Agnes turned to Madeline. "I know it's a most unusual circumstance, Lady Madeline and Lady Gilling, but my sister insists that you come take your rest and enjoy dinner at her inn before returning to Richfield."

"That sounds lovely, Agnes," Madeline said with a sigh. With a hand of assistance from Donavan she seated herself and adjusted her clothing. "Does it suit you, Countess?"

"Indeed. Let us not tarry another moment."

"Did you hear that, Donavan?" Agnes asked. "Back to Riley Street and my sister's inn. And be quick about it. She might agree to feed you if you can wipe that gloom off your face."

Donavan adopted a very pretentious grin. "I'll see what I can do for ye, Agnes."

In less than ten minutes Donavan stopped the carriage in front of a lovely building. A wooden sign, adorned with the image of a blue swan taking flight, hung over the doorway.

"This is the Blue Swan Inn, your ladyships," Agnes said proudly. "My sister's establishment. O'course she gives her husband a bit of credit for the running of it too. But make no mistake about who's in charge," she said smugly.

"Agnes, in all these years, you never told me your sister was the proprietor of such a delightful place."

"'Tis not the thing one speaks of overmuch, Lady Madeline."

Someone peeked through a curtain. Before Madeline could step out of the carriage, a younger version of Agnes came out to greet them. She was a bit taller and thinner with her hair up in a bun and rugged cheeks.

"So, Agnes, me dear, may I count on two more guests for dinner?"

"Indeed you may, and wise women they be for it. Edna, I would like you to meet Lady Madeline of Richfield and her friend, the Countess of Gilling. Your ladyships, my sister, Edna Hogarth."

"Beg pardon, I forget my manners." Edna quickly curtsied to Madeline and Hally. "Ladies, you are most welcome."

"And most appreciative," Madeline added.

Agnes beamed.

"It's a rare treat indeed when I get company the likes o' you, Lady Madeline and Lady Gilling." Edna grinned broadly, displaying a large gap between her front teeth.

"Your offer is very kind, Mrs. Hogarth."

"Come, come," Edna said, waving them out of the carriage. "Welcome to the Blue Swan Inn. I'll show ye where ye can freshen up a wee bit, if ye like. Agnes, send yer driver around back, and one of the stable lads will be out to take care o' the horse."

Agnes and Donavan carefully assisted Madeline and Hally down from the carriage. "You two must not coddle us any longer," Hally said kindly. "We are doing quite well."

"It don't hurt to be cautious, Countess," Agnes said, ushering them into her sister's home. "Ye bumped yer head just yesterday."

"Now, yer ladyships," Edna directed. "Ye can go upstairs and have a rest. It'll take me a bit o' time to prepare the meal I'll be feeding ye, but I know ye'll like it."

Madeline smiled. "Mrs. Hogarth, you are very gracious. It is extremely rude of us to impose on you."

"Bah! 'Tis no bother at all. Agnes and I will visit in the kitchen while I cook after she helps ye out o' those lovely dresses. The first room at the top o' the stairs to yer right is open and ready for company. Make yerselves comfortable."

"Thank you, Mrs. Hogarth. That sounds wonderful," Hally said.

The two friends climbed the steps with Agnes lumbering behind them to the second floor where they entered a bright, cheerful yellow room. The window was open, and the curtains puffed out from the light breeze as though friendly arms reached toward them in welcome.

"This is delightful," Madeline said.

"Now let me get both of ye out of these fine walking dresses before you take a rest. It wouldn't do to appear in public all wrinkled. I'll help ye dress when dinner's ready." Agnes swiftly completed her duties and left the room.

Madeline sat down on one of the two single beds and unlaced her shoes until she could slide out her stocking-covered feet. "Ah, that feels better," she said, rubbing her toes. "My feet were almost numb from walking."

Hally sat on the other bed, massaging her temples. "Ecstasy, it's pure ecstasy, to stretch out for even a few moments."

"Your head aches. You've been putting on a brave front for me. You shouldn't have, Hally. I'm so sorry."

"Rubbish. Nothing a few moments of rest won't cure."

"Just the same, I don't want you overdoing it on my behalf," Madeline protested. "You must rest."

"It will take time to prepare dinner for unexpected guests," Hally said, closing her eyes. "But Mrs. Hogarth seems to be up for the challenge."

"Not too long, I hope. I'm starving," Madeline said, and quickly removed her stockings.

Hally yawned. "You must be catching my appetite."

"You are a bad influence." Madeline laughed. And she too

stretched out on her bed, relishing the respite after a busy afternoon of shopping.

Devlin and Melton walked up the steps of the Blue Swan and opened the door, stepping into the entryway. The aroma of Mrs. Hogarth's cooking filled the air. "Dinner smells better than usual, and usual is excellent." Exhausted and rattled by the events at the asylum, Devlin looked forward to a nourishing, well-cooked meal.

Melton sniffed the air. "Fresh bread, beef, and roasting pheasant if I'm not mistaken. I'm ravenous."

Edna and Agnes came out of the kitchen, their arms filled with dishes and silverware. "Look what the wind's chased in, Agnes," Edna said, rushing into the dining room. "I'll wager yer stomachs are clamorin' up a storm."

"We cannot disagree," Devlin said. "It appears you are expecting more guests tonight."

"Agnes, this is Lord Ravensmoore and Mr. Melton from the hospital. Gentlemen, me sister, the widow Agnes Moss."

"Why, Lord Ravensmoore," Agnes said in surprise, dropping several pieces of silverware as she attempted to curtsy. "Wasn't ye the one who attended my Lady Madeline the day she fell at the hunt?"

"It was me, Mrs. Moss. How did you know?"

"I'm in service at Richfield. I was there the day ye brought her home."

"How is Lady Madeline?"

"Oh, she's much better, she's—" Agnes was unable to finish due to a discreet, but well-placed elbow in the ribs delivered by her sister.

Devlin caught the exchange and wondered what they were up to.

Edna picked up where Agnes had left off, albeit somewhat awkwardly. "Agnes just came from shoppin' with Lady Gilling and Lady Madeline. It would seem that both the ladies are indebted to ye again, and to Mr. Melton as well. Will Mr. Melton be stayin' for dinner?"

Melton grinned. "I'd consider it an honor. Ravensmoore constantly has my mouth watering regarding your expert culinary skills, madam."

"If it's not imposing on you and your sister's special plans for the evening," Devlin said.

"I insist," Edna said. "Yer friend is most welcome."

Melton and Devlin wearily climbed the stairs to his room to clean up after the grueling day. Devlin splashed water out of a blue flowered pitcher and into a basin and then cupped his hands to scoop the water over his face. Devlin's thoughts returned to Madeline. The idea that he might gain some information about her from Mrs. Moss made him smile in anticipation of the evening meal.

"Are you thinking about a certain woman or dinner?" Melton asked, flicking him playfully with a towel. "I'll wager it's the woman."

"And you'd win that wager, my friend. I imagine I should visit Lady Madeline and check on her."

"Not without me, you won't. Besides, I get the distinct feeling that you are interested in the woman for reasons outside the medical profession."

Devlin raised a brow but made no response. He removed his shirt and set about looking for something proper to wear for dinner.

"You'll need a clean shirt, Melton. Feel welcome to rummage around and see what you might like. Please excuse me; I will return in a moment."

Devlin discovered that he'd made a friend after their mutual experience at the asylum. Charles Melton seemed to genuinely enjoy his company. Devlin wasn't quite sure why, but he suspected Melton's status as the second son of an earl may have something to do with it. After all, it wasn't that long ago that Devlin had been in the same position.

He opened the door and headed across the hall to the privy. This was definitely one of the disadvantages of living at the Blue Swan, he thought with dismay. The plumbing at Ravensmoore was of a far better quality. Of course he could always purchase a town house, but that seemed like needless waste.

He put his hand on the doorknob of the privy when the door was suddenly flung open and the object of his thoughts stepped into the hallway, glowing with indignation and then realization.

"Lady Madeline! Forgive me. What are you doing here?"

Madeline blushed to the roots of her hair. She wrestled with the neckline of the dress apparently donned hastily. "If you must ask that question, you will not make a very good doctor. Do turn around, Lord Ravensmoore. It is most impolite to stare at a lady's bare feet."

"Of course. How thoughtless. I didn't mean…" He turned around, felt her brush past him, and then heard a door slam farther down the hall. She was gone.

Devlin stood there for a moment wondering if he'd just seen Lady Madeline. Perhaps all those long hours at the hospital were causing him to hallucinate. Then a grin spread across his face, and he chuckled. Indeed, he had seen her and her lovely feet. She was here! He didn't know how or why. It didn't matter. He knew that dinner was not going to be ordinary. Lady Madeline was many things, but ordinary was not one of them.

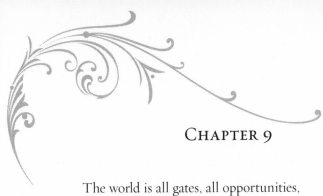

CHAPTER 9

The world is all gates, all opportunities,
strings of tension waiting to be struck.
—RALPH WALDO EMERSON

*W*HEN DEVLIN AND Melton entered the dining room, Devlin's eyes locked on Madeline's. She looked beautiful in a rose-colored walking dress. Hazel eyes flashed anger or embarrassment, or perhaps both.

"Lady Madeline, it is an unexpected and very pleasant surprise to see you here at the Blue Swan," he said, bowing low. "You have met Mr. Melton, a colleague of mine from the hospital."

Melton bowed as well. "A pleasure to see you again, Lady Madeline. And you, Countess. A pleasure indeed."

Mrs. Hogarth bustled in with a steaming platter of pheasant and vegetables. "Well, don't stand there all night gapin' at the ladies! Sit down, gentlemen. I've prepared a feast fit for the Prince Regent himself." The men seated themselves across from the women, and Mrs. Hogarth served each of them and then settled the platter on the sideboard.

"If it tastes as good as it looks, I may have to take up boarding here too, Mrs. Hogarth," Melton said. "This is far better than living above the Grey Fox Inn."

"Just let me know when you'd like to move in, Mr. Melton." Mrs.

Hogarth smiled broadly. "Now, eat up before it gets cold. I'll be right back with more victuals," she said and left the room.

"And how are you ladies this fine evening?" Devlin asked. "No ill effects from yesterday's mishap, I hope."

Madeline replied, "Lady Gilling has been fighting off an awful headache most of the day. However, she put on a brave face. I did not realize it until we arrived here."

"It is much improved since I rested," Hally assured them. "No need to fuss."

A shadow of concern passed over Melton's features. "Still, I would feel better if you would permit me to talk with you further about the pain after dinner."

"Of course, if you think it necessary, Mr. Melton. Now, let's enjoy this unexpected time together."

Madeline looked directly at Devlin. "Do you mind if I ask you a question, Lord Ravensmoore?"

"Not at all," he replied.

"How did you meet Dr. Langford?"

Devlin's heart jumped. No turning back. "He is my instructor, a very skilled physician and surgeon."

"But why is he here in York? Where does he come from?"

"He cares about the education of new doctors, so like some of his colleagues, he visits different areas of the country from time to time to teach and help those of us learn more about special areas in medicine. He actually spends most of his time between London and York. He has a home in York and a town house in London when he is there for teaching purposes at the Royal College of Physicians."

"I see."

Madeline seemed to be thinking something through, and Devlin was afraid he knew what that something was. *Why did Langford leave me alone with her father?*

Silence grew.

"Do you have other family, Lord Ravensmoore?" Hally asked.

Grateful for the question, he gathered his jumbled thoughts. "I have two younger sisters at home, Countess. My parents are deceased, and my brother, Edward, died in a shipwreck along with my father, leaving me as heir."

"I am so sorry," Hally said.

"Why did you return to your studies, sir?" Madeline asked, a frown creasing her forehead. "It must be very difficult with your many responsibilities."

Melton grinned mischievously, raised a brow, and looked at Devlin. "Ravensmoore is a gentleman of many talents. One being to challenge our teacher whenever the opportunity presents itself."

Devlin explained, "Dr. Langford does not approve of my desire to practice medicine. He would prefer I use my funds to help the college in the training of new physicians. As a man of science, he does not understand the calling that God has placed in my heart."

"Why do you persist?" Madeline asked, then took a sip of her tea.

"I believe the good Lord put us on this earth to fulfill a purpose, Lady Madeline, a mission of sorts. And although I'm painfully aware that most of my peers disagree vehemently with my plans to be a physician, I believe being born into wealth is no excuse to ignore my calling."

She studied him silently. He wondered if she laughed at him from behind her composed expression.

"It must be very difficult for you to be snubbed by your peers," Madeline said.

Her remark surprised him. "You grow used to it, eventually."

He watched a shadow of sadness pass over her face. Devlin hoped the subject had not caused her undue stress. He feared at any moment that she might ask him questions about Langford and about her father's death.

Agnes entered the room with hot bread and a platter of beef.

Devlin was grateful for the interruption, enticing them into other subjects of a less volatile nature. Mrs. Hogarth followed with another pot of tea.

"This pot of tea is for ye, Countess. 'Tis willow bark and will help the ache in yer head."

"Would you agree with that, Mr. Melton?" Hally said, lifting the cup to her lips.

"It certainly cannot hurt. Many teas are medicinal. We probably don't know the extent of their abilities yet."

Agnes disappeared into the kitchen and returned with an overflowing bowl of boiled potatoes. "I told ye she was a grand cook," Agnes said proudly.

Mrs. Hogarth glowed with appreciation. "I don't believe in coincidences. 'Tis fate what brought us together this night. Ye mark my words, this is not the last night ye four young people will be together. Enjoy yerselves, now. I'll come check on ye shortly."

The sisters returned to the kitchen, but just before the door shut they all heard Mrs. Hogarth say, "What handsome couples they make."

An embarrassed silence filled the room, and then Melton burst out laughing. "Does anyone else think those two are up to some matchmaking scheme?"

"It couldn't be more obvious," Hally said in agreement. "What should we do?"

"Nothing," Madeline said. "I'll have a serious discussion with Agnes. I had no idea her sister was so bold. She's gone a bit too far."

"I think the two of them have good intentions," Devlin said. He raised his glass. "Let's have a toast. May the Lord bless us all and those less fortunate with health and happiness."

The others echoed his words and raised their glasses. He noticed that Madeline's smile did not extend to her eyes.

The dinner continued with pleasant conversation. Devlin

convinced himself he was under some kind of spell that made it impossible not to stare at Madeline. Never before had a woman fascinated him as she did, charming one moment and suspicious the next. A complex female.

Agnes and Edna appeared with a delicious-looking apple pie and a bowl of clotted cream. "I hope each of ye enjoyed yer dinner," Edna said.

There was a chorus of cheers, applause, and good wishes. A blush rose in Edna's cheeks, and both women glowed with pleasure.

"I told ye she was a wonderful cook," Agnes repeated with pride. "We've been havin' a grand visit, but I suppose we should be leavin' soon."

"Nonsense. What's the difficulty in staying for pie and a brief stroll in the moonlight?" Devlin asked. He studied Madeline's reaction to his suggestion.

"It's already dark." Madeline stood up and looked about like a hunted deer desperate for escape. "We really must go. Wouldn't you agree, Lady Gilling?"

Hally stared at Charles Melton as if he might disappear at any moment. "I believe we have time for a short walk before we return to Richfield."

Madeline nodded reluctantly and sat down. "A very short walk."

Agnes sliced up the pie while Edna served her guests. The sweets disappeared quickly.

"That walk sounds like a splendid idea, Ravensmoore," Melton said. "It's not good for a body to sit around after a big meal. Waste of energy. Wouldn't you agree?"

"For once, I agree with you completely," Devlin joked good-naturedly and rose to his feet. "Lady Madeline, Countess, your company would be most welcome."

"And just where do ye think ye are goin' without a chaperone?" Agnes said as she entered the room and began to clear the table.

"Ye are both eligible and unmarried females," she announced, as though it were a great secret. "I suggest ye wait for Edna and me."

"I am a widow, Mrs. Moss. I hardly need a chaperone and can certainly serve as Madeline's. But please join us."

"Of course," Madeline said. "I would never leave without you, Agnes."

Devlin didn't miss the plea in her eyes as she spoke to Agnes.

"We'll wait outside," Devlin assured her. "The evenings have been quite chilly. You will need your wraps."

Agnes nodded. "We'll be right out." She returned to the kitchen.

Devlin assisted Madeline with her pelisse. Once outside he offered her his arm.

She hesitated for a moment, as if weighing her decision carefully. "I am not comfortable with this situation, sir," she whispered. "If the countess weren't so smitten with Mr. Melton, I would not find myself in such a dilemma."

"As you wish, Lady Madeline. We will simply walk next to each other." He watched Melton offer his arm to Hally. She immediately accepted as though she'd been doing it all her life. Envy tangled his emotions like weeds in a garden.

"The stars are beautiful tonight, are they not?" Madeline said, avoiding his eyes.

"The stars are beautiful, but I do believe you outshine them," Devlin declared, his voice carefully modulated so as not to betray the depth of his feelings.

"You are too bold, sir. They will hear you," Madeline said urgently.

"The important thing is that you heard me." He turned slightly. "They appear far too interested in each other to bother with us."

"Well, *they* certainly are getting along. I never thought to see Hally so taken with a gentleman again." Hally and Melton were engaged in an intimate conversation of their own, oblivious to all else.

"Melton is a charming fellow, with more strength of character than one might suspect on first acquaintance," Devlin said.

Madeline glanced at him askance. "He is trustworthy, then?"

"As far as I know." The door opened behind them. "Ah, here are our chaperones." He couldn't prevent a twinge of regret from creeping into his voice as Edna and Agnes joined them.

Devlin and Madeline took the lead, walking in front of Hally and Melton. Devlin hoped to put a little distance between them and the others. The two sisters followed the couples down the cobblestone street.

Devlin longed to take Madeline's hand and nestle it into his elbow. But he knew she just barely tolerated his presence, much less his touch. "How have you have been feeling since the accident yesterday? Did your arm give you any difficulty today?"

"As your patient, I must tell you that I am doing very well...most of the time."

"Most of the time?" Devlin frowned. "What exactly does that mean?"

Madeline looked straight ahead. "I have difficulty sleeping, and my arm sometimes hurts at night. I stopped in at the apothecary today for more laudanum, but I was hoping not to use it."

"Don't hesitate to use it, if necessary. However, you must be cautious. I think I should visit soon and discuss this further. Would that be acceptable?"

Madeline was silent.

"Do you dislike me that much?" he asked, keeping his tone light so as not to reveal his hurt.

"No, Lord Ravensmoore. I do not dislike you. I just do not think your visit would be a good idea."

"Why not? You're angry and blame me for your father's death. We must talk about it."

"Talking about it would serve no purpose. My father is dead. It would only make things worse."

"What things?"

"Things you do not understand. You cannot understand."

"Perhaps I could if you would give me a chance."

"I cannot do that."

"But *why* can't you talk about it?" Devlin pressed.

Madeline stopped walking and turned to him with pain-filled eyes. "Because it hurts too much."

The eyes were nearly his undoing. He stepped closer, instinctively reaching for her hands to pull him to her and comfort her, but she sent him a pain-filled glance of confusion and pulled away. Defeated, he dropped his hands. "Shall we continue our walk?" he asked politely, woodenly.

She nodded.

He tried to think of other things to talk about to break the tension of the silence and to take his mind off his own pained thoughts. "You might be interested to know that the young woman from the asylum has been found."

"What?" Madeline turned to him with fear in her eyes. "When?"

"This morning. She returned with two of the keepers. Are you all right? You look as though you've seen a ghost." He tucked her hand into his elbow to steady her.

"I'm just concerned for the girl. Is she safe?"

The pressure from her grip on his arm increased. "I was there when they brought her back. We were called in to care for another patient at the asylum."

"How did they find her?"

"I don't know. Unfortunately, they put her in manacles. Langford dosed her with laudanum to help her relax."

Madeline gasped. "How cruel. Why would they treat her so dreadfully?"

"I agree, it's cruel. But the courts have confined her to Ashcroft because she's been found to be criminally insane. There is nothing to be done."

Madeline stopped and turned to Devlin. "There is *always* something that can be done. All one must do is try." The vehemence in her voice told him that she still blamed him for her father's death. How could he convince her that it wasn't his fault?

They returned to the inn in silence.

CHAPTER 10

Nothing is so burdensome as a secret.

—FRENCH PROVERB

*T*HAT NIGHT MADELINE tossed and turned in her bed at Richfield. She could not stop thinking of Ravensmoore. "He seems to be interested in me," she murmured, "and, God forgive me, I am attracted to him."

Her thoughts clung to the wave of confusing emotions that besieged her. "I cannot care about him," she said aloud. "He is the enemy. What am I going to do now? The only man I ever trusted was my father."

Madeline sat on the edge of her bed and reached for the bottle of laudanum. She swallowed the bitter-tasting medicine and prayed it would help her sleep. She padded to the window in her bare feet. "Oh, Papa, I'm scared. I miss you so much. If I could only talk to you. Mother is not thinking rationally, and I cannot talk to her."

She wiped a tear away. "God, why do You torture me? My heart aches. I cannot care for this man. I cannot forgive him. Yet my unforgiveness eats away at my soul. Help me, Lord. I feel I'm losing my mind."

Chilled to the bone, she crept back to her bed and under the covers. Nosey cuddled next to her as though he felt her pain. Madeline slipped her hand around the cat and pulled him close.

In the morning she was wakened by a quick rap on the door. Agnes entered the room, a broad grin on her face.

Nosey scrambled off the bed, and Madeline pulled the pillow over her head.

"Well, that's a fine welcome." Agnes put her hands on her hips. "Daisy's not feeling well, so I've come to help ye dress. I imagine your head's spinning with thoughts of Lord Ravensmoore this morning."

"My head is spinning. I'll grant you that."

"It's much too difficult to interpret yer words when they are caught under a pillow. Come on out, dearie, and greet the day."

"I'd really rather not, Agnes. I have a dreadful headache. The light hurts my eyes."

"I hope you're not too angry with Edna and me for playing the matchmakers last evening," she prattled on, ignoring Madeline's plea. "A blind man could sense that ye were taken with each other right off. And Lady Gilling and Mr. Melton. Another grand couple to be sure." Agnes continued, oblivious to Madeline's mortification.

Madeline forced herself to peek from under her pillow, blinking against the sunshine. "I would prefer you not talk about last night, Agnes. It is finished."

Agnes froze in her duties and stared at her mistress, aghast. "What's this? Ye can't mean it. Edna believes Ravensmoore most smitten, and though we frequently disagree, I believe she's right this time."

Madeline finally rebelled and sat up a bit too fast. Pressing her palms to her temples, she said, "He may be smitten, but I most certainly am not. He's smitten with his work as a physician, possibly obsessed. The man is not normal. It's a wonder he finds time to care for his estate."

Agnes walked over to the chair where Madeline's robe lay and picked it up. "He goes home to be certain all is well with his lands, according to Edna, and tends to the business of a gentleman, but he always returns to study in York whenever Langford comes to teach. I'm so happy ye have an admirer, dear."

"He may be an admirer, Agnes, but he's not a beau."

"A very handsome admirer, I must say," Agnes continued, as if Madeline hadn't spoken a word.

Madeline slammed the bed with her fists. "Do you forget who he is, Agnes? He let my father bleed to death. I cannot forgive him!"

Agnes carefully laid the robe on the bed. "Eventually ye must forgive those things ye do not understand."

"I understand perfectly. You needn't concern yourself, Agnes. I'm all grown up. I can take care of myself." Madeline said, uncertain if she struggled to convince Agnes or herself.

"Even grown girls need someone to look after them now and then, Lady Madeline. Take yer mother, for instance. She fancies herself taken with Lord Vale. He's not what she needs, but it's not my place to say anything."

"You mean you've noticed it too?" Madeline didn't know if she should be alarmed or relieved. She scooted to the edge of the bed and threw her legs over the side. The cat appeared from beneath the bed and pounced on her cold, naked feet. "Nosey. You bad kitty." She picked the feline up and gently set him on the bed where he chased his tail with determination. "What do you know, Agnes?"

"She's happy again."

"Has Mother shared her feelings with you?"

"No. She doesn't have to. It shows in her face." Agnes poured water into a basin. "It would be hard not to notice." She continued, "Come sit at your dressing table. I'll brush yer hair. Ye'll feel better."

"I feel fine." Ever since Papa died, everything had changed between Mother and herself. He'd been the glue. Without Papa true happiness always seemed just out of reach.

Madeline tried to shake off the gloomy feelings that attacked her.

She donned her robe and sat down at the dressing table to let Agnes brush her hair. "Work your magic, Agnes."

"I haven't done this for ye in years." Agnes untangled the mass of dark curls. "Ye still have the most beautiful head of hair, even more beautiful than yer mother's."

Nosey jumped onto Madeline's lap. She stroked the cat as Agnes brushed. Hypnotic movements eased the tension in her muscles. Madeline stared sightlessly into the mirror. "I wish I were a little girl again, Agnes. Everything seemed easy then. Why does life have to be so hard?"

"Sometimes…" Agnes began, and then stopped, as though choosing her words very carefully. "Sometimes we make life harder than it need be."

After several minutes Madeline took the brush from Agnes. "Thank you, Agnes. That felt wonderful. I think I'd like to go for a ride this morning. Will you help me dress now?"

"Of course." Agnes looked worried. "I hope I didn't speak out of turn."

"No, not at all. I need to go for a ride. I want some time to myself to think."

"Very well."

Agnes dressed her mistress in a brown velvet riding habit. "Are ye quite certain ye are all right?"

Madeline saw the concern in the old woman's eyes. "I am well, really I am. I just need a bit of fresh air."

"Don't forget to eat breakfast." Agnes brightened. "You'd best be on your way."

Madeline skipped breakfast and headed straight to the stables. The blend of hay, oats, and leather mingled with that of each animal to produce a scent that any horse lover could appreciate. She inhaled a deep breath and smiled a warm greeting at the groom, who tipped his hat to greet her.

"Good morning, Donavan. Would you saddle Shakespeare when I've finished grooming him?"

"Yes, yer ladyship. But allow me to ready him."

"I want to groom him, Donavan. I've missed him."

"'Tis not proper," the groom mumbled under his breath. "And what would yer father be thinking?"

Madeline ignored the remark. Donavan meant well. He'd adored her father. She headed for the stall, still expecting to see Papa walk through the stable door to go riding with her.

"Good morning, Shakespeare. I've brought you a treat." She held out a purloined carrot from the kitchen, loving the feel of the animal's soft muzzle against her hand as he munched the offering.

Madeline grabbed a currycomb and brush and made quick work of cleaning him up. She loved caring for her own horse, and she enjoyed doing what others would only consider fit for a groom or stable boy. She sneezed. The hair and dust flew about the stable, sparkling in the rays of the morning sun.

"Bless ye," Donavan said as he approached her. "Would ye like company this fine morning?" Donavan opened the stall door.

"Thank you, Donavan. I prefer to go by myself."

"But ye have only one good arm."

"Now, Donavan. My arm is out of the sling now. I'm much better. You know Shakespeare as well as I do. He's a safe ride, and his injuries are healed, are they not?"

Donavan nodded. "No galloping yet though. Only walking."

"We will enjoy a gentle walk. I have no doubt we will both be fine."

"Still..." Donavan said, rubbing the stubble on his chin and looking thoughtful. "I don't think ye should go alone."

Voices of one of the stable boys and a visitor filtered into the barn. She recognized the other voice.

"She won't be alone." The deep male timbre intruded into the conversation.

Her thoughts scrambled about like chickens pecking at feed in the stable yard, but she quickly pulled herself together. "Lord Ravensmoore. What an unexpected surprise. You do seem to make a habit of showing up at the most inopportune times. What brings you here?"

"Trying to keep you in one piece. It sounds like you're trying to break your neck riding off with no escort and an injury that's not completely mended."

"My lord." Donavan bowed awkwardly. "Humph. Exactly what I been trying to tell her meself, sir. Seems ye pull more weight."

"Your groom is a wise man. You should heed his words. I simply came to check on my patient. I believe I told you I'd visit as soon as possible. I'd be happy to ride out with you."

"No. That is not necessary." Madeline turned and brushed out Shakespeare's tail.

Donavan said, "Now there's a fine idea. His lordship's a doctor. I should think ye couldn't be in better hands. I'll tack up Shakespeare for ye now."

"I am honored to be of service, Lady Madeline." Ravensmoore smiled at her as the groom slipped a bridle over the horse's head and quickly saddled Shakespeare.

She frowned at her escort. "So it would appear."

Madeline led Shakespeare from the stable, and Ravensmoore retrieved his mount from the stable boy. "Shakespeare seems much improved. It appears you are both on the mend."

"Yes. I thank you for your help the day of the accident. I've been told I can be quite stubborn, and I'm afraid you received the brunt of my distress that day."

"It was a difficult time. Allow me to give you a leg up."

He easily boosted her into the saddle and gave her time to arrange her skirt. As they rode across an open expanse of meadow at a leisurely pace, the smell of spring danced in the air, a mixture of nature's perfumes blended into a glorious outdoor bouquet.

Madeline struggled with her thoughts, what to say. Finally she said what she was thinking. "I thought we agreed that it was not a good idea for us to meet."

"*You* thought it wasn't a good idea. I didn't agree." Devlin moved his horse closer to her. "Actually, I received an unexpected reprieve from Dr. Langford."

Madeline cast him a suspicious glance. "How nice." She maneuvered Shakespeare away to a safe distance. His closeness and the rich smell of spices he wore created a jumble of emotions, emotions that warned of feelings she couldn't accept or condone.

"Fortuitous, really. I barely slept last night. Lack of sleep can be dangerous in medicine."

"I should think you're accustomed to it." Madeline brushed an annoying tree branch away from her face as the trail narrowed.

"Unfortunately, lack of sleep is something I will never get used to."

An awkward silence punctuated the early morning mist. They crested a hill and stopped the horses at a beautiful pool of water. The sun glinted over ripples that lapped gently onto the ridge of the pond. Two blue birds fluttered over the water in a mating dance.

"Why did you come here?" Madeline asked again. She did not want to discuss anything of importance with him. She didn't trust him, and she didn't trust herself.

"Since I attended your injury, and you shared that sometimes your arm pains you in the evening, I thought I should check in on you. Did you use the laudanum last night?"

"Yes, I did. A nasty concoction. Left me a bit muddleheaded this morning. But it did help ease the ache."

"I'm glad of that. Not the muddleheaded part, of course. I meant the relief of pain."

Madeline noticed the twinkle in his eye and a slight blush to his credit as well. "I understand your meaning, Lord Ravensmoore. I do appreciate your concern, but there really is no longer a need for it. I am certain all will be well."

They moved on in silence for several minutes. Madeline watched him now and then from the corner of her eye. What was it about him that intrigued her so? Granted he was good-looking, but handsome looks alone would never be intrinsically important to her. And her father...she would never forget. So how could there be any attraction?

"Should you ever need anything...anything at all, I would be most happy to be of assistance. Last evening I suggested that we should talk about your father—"

"And I told you that I do not wish to talk about him. Not with you. I know I must sound dreadful, but I miss my father more than you could ever understand. When he died at the Guardian Gate, I thought I would die as well. And not to be with him as he breathed his last breath... At least if we'd taken him home he could have died in his own bed and been surrounded by those who loved him. It was a mistake."

"It's only natural that you should feel that way—"

"Natural?" Madeline went rigid. "There is nothing *natural* about it. Death is a horrid, wicked thing that robs those left behind of happiness and robs the one that dies of a future. It leaves a gaping hole in the soul that is constantly looking to be filled. What, sir, is so natural about that?" Madeline wiped angrily at the tears she could not prevent.

"I am sorry." He took a silk handkerchief from his pocket. "Please, take this."

Despite her anger and humiliation Madeline accepted the handkerchief and dabbed at her tears. "Thank you."

"I do know something of loss. My mother died. A long time ago. I loved her very much."

Madeline's heart hammered in annoyance. She did not want to hear about his pain. She was the one who ached because of what he had done to her father. "Anyone who mutilates bodies surely cannot appreciate God's gift of life. You cannot possibly understand."

He sighed. "I don't know how to make you grasp the importance of it all." His frustration showed ever so slightly in his glance. "Surgery is not mutilation. It is an attempt to heal when the body rebels against itself." He frowned. "There's much to learn, much to be understood in the field of medicine. Until then we must live with the inevitable. Death comes to us all. And even the best medicine cannot prevent it."

She couldn't help asking, "How...how did you come to live with it, accept it?"

"My mother had a strong faith in God."

"How did that make it easier for you to accept her death?"

"She always used to quote Scripture. I remember her saying that God would never leave us nor forsake us. That gave me comfort when she died. And I know it gave her comfort as well."

"And you have the same strong faith as she?"

"I have faith, not yet as strong as hers. I still struggle. Death is so final. So quiet, so unchangeable."

She nodded. *Perhaps he did understand more than she thought he did.* "Thank you for telling me about your mother. I can tell you miss her. I guess that's why it's so important for me to protect my mother. She's my last surviving relation. And she wants to change our lives by marrying a man who"— she shook her head— "may not be a good choice."

"Sometimes we cannot control the choices that other people make. No matter how much we love them."

"Stop a moment," Madeline asked. She could see a coach and four leaving Richfield from their vantage point on the hillside. "I believe that's Lord Vale's coach. I wonder why he is visiting so early this morning."

Ravensmoore tilted his head toward her. "It will turn out well. Your mother is an intelligent woman."

Madeline looked into his eyes. She'd never really studied those forest green windows of his soul. They were honest eyes filled with compassion. Yet she couldn't allow her heart to feel the compassion she observed therein for it would cause her much distress. "Yes. My mother is an intelligent woman, but her heart rules her head. Loneliness fuels her heart. Love is blind indeed."

"Why not speak to her?"

"I did so a few days ago. That is why I chose to go for a ride. To clear my head." She nudged her horse with her heel. "Let's return. I do not want to overexert Shakespeare, and perhaps you are right. Maybe I should talk to Mother again."

When they approached the path to the stables, Madeline could see that Agnes awaited them. Anguish etched her face. Madeline pushed Shakespeare into a trot. "What's happened?"

"Your mother's gone. She's left with Lord Vale."

CHAPTER 11

Man, while he loves, is never quite depraved.
—CHARLES LAMB

*S*HE DID WHAT?" Madeline asked, incredulous.

Agnes sobbed into her already soaked apron. "She left with Lord Vale, taking her best gowns and saying they would return within a fortnight. She asked me to look after ye."

Ravensmoore stood next to Madeline in the stable. "It seems none of you are happy concerning the countess's relationship with Lord Vale. What are you going to do when they return as a married couple?"

"Married! You think they are going to be wed?" Madeline asked, feeling weak in the knees.

He frowned. "It certainly appears that way. No gentleman would arrive so openly with his coach to leave for a fortnight with his mistress. Especially not someone like your mother. They are going to Gretna Green. I'd wager my future in medicine upon it."

"I have to stop them," Madeline said. "Mother cannot marry. It's far too soon."

"How do you plan to stop them?" he asked. "They are able to do this if both are willing, and it sounds like your mother has made her decision."

"She's confused. How could she think to marry so soon after coming out of mourning?"

Agnes nodded. "Beg pardon, Lady Madeline. She's not so much confused as lonely. She's left ye a note in your room."

"Donavan, please see that the horses have water. Then saddle my father's stallion." Madeline straightened her shoulders. "I'm going after my mother."

"Just like that?" Ravensmoore shook his head. "You are recuperating from a severe sprain and think you can go tearing about the countryside on a stallion? If you manage the ride, what do you plan to do when you catch them?"

"I don't know. I'll work that out as I ride." She left them and headed toward the house.

He grabbed her hand. "Wait! There's nothing to be done."

"My mother's lost her reasoning."

"I don't think she has, Lady Madeline." He covered her hand with both of his. "She's made a decision to love again."

"Well then, she's made the wrong decision. I know my mother. She is not rash. In fact, she is painstakingly cautious. That man must have done something to muddle her reasoning." She pulled her hand away and determinedly walked to the house.

"Foolhardy as it is, I'm going with you. Someone has to look after you." Ravensmoore caught up to her. "And you are my patient."

"If you're serious about coming with me," Madeline replied, "I would be grateful for the company." She entered the grand hallway, then turned and ran up the stairs.

She opened the door to her room and grabbed the note on her dressing table. There, scrawled in her mother's handwriting, was proof indeed that her mother planned to wed Lord Vale.

Dear Madeline,
    Forgive me. I know you disapprove of my relationship

with Lord Vale. But life is short and I must have hope. We've left for Gretna Green. Wish me happiness.

Love,

Mother

She rummaged in a drawer next to her bed. "Where is it?" she grumbled in frustration. Reaching to the very back of the drawer, she felt the hard, cold object, then withdrew the small pistol and placed it in her beaded reticule.

Ravensmoore waited for her in the hallway. The most patient man she'd ever met, and she'd ordered him about like a common house servant. "We must hurry. You were right. They are traveling to Gretna."

"We'll catch up with them, Lady Madeline. They are riding in a traveling coach. A horse and rider will always be faster. You might want to think about what you plan to do when we overtake them."

Madeline brushed past him and out the door where Donavan held her father's dappled gray stallion and one of the stable boys held Devlin's horse, Hippocrates. Agnes continued sniffling into her handkerchief.

"I will stop her," Madeline told Agnes confidently and gently squeezed the old woman's hand. "I must."

They traveled the Great North Road, rough from the recent rains, but easier for them than for Vale's coach. Still, Madeline had seen it worse, and other coaches and riders traversed the road with them. She found it comforting to ride her father's horse, Samson, and though she would never admit it to Ravensmoore, she needed all her strength to manage the horse.

"He's a big brute." Ravensmoore rode beside her.

"He's almost seventeen hands." Madeline hoped she wouldn't end up in the mud. It was a long way to the ground, and she'd surely break her neck.

"A handsome gray. Still I'd have preferred you'd chosen an easier horse. Your arms must ache by now. It's been half an hour."

"I'm fine," Madeline lied. It seemed every time she was with Ravensmoore she found herself lying about one thing or another. Her arm weakened. Then thinking of self-preservation she said, "I suppose we should walk for a while and allow ourselves and the horses a bit of rest."

He slowed. "A sensible decision. Perhaps we can enjoy a few moments."

She glanced at him. Mud caked his boots and spattered his breeches—and even spotted his face. The sight amused her. "You, my lord, are covered with mud."

"If that beast you're riding was closer to the ground, you'd have had a similar experience."

She couldn't help but laugh. It felt good. Riding always cleared Madeline's head, and this had been no different. But what would she do when she caught up with them? Her mother would be angry, and Lord Vale was certain to be furious. But she had to try and stop them. She needed to speak to her mother before this went further.

Madeline studied the road ahead. "No sign of them."

"It's just a matter of time."

And it was. They spotted the coach within the next hour.

"Whoa," called the driver when he saw Devlin wave him over. "Whoa."

Vale glared out the open coach window. "So, you've brought reinforcements with you, Lady Madeline. Why could you not have just let us be?"

Madeline ignored him. "Mother, I must speak with you."

"What is the meaning of this?" Grace protested. "And why are you on Samson? He's too strong for you."

"Shakespeare is not yet up to such a long ride. I just need to speak to you, Mother. Please."

Vale opened the coach door, grudgingly handed her mother out, and stood beside her. "You may ask her your questions from there." He kept her hand firmly in his own. "No need to come closer with those filthy horses."

Grace stepped toward her daughter. "I'm so sorry, Madeline. I know I should have talked to you about our plans, but we decided that wasn't a good idea. You haven't been able to understand."

"We?" Madeline asked. She looked at her mother and then at Vale. Anger and fear swallowed her. "Why are you doing this, Mother? Why run away to wed?" *God in heaven. If You are there, please stop this.*

Grace looked ashamed. "I'm sorry, Madeline, but I couldn't bear your disapproval. Lord Vale understands how lonely I've been. His wife died two years ago. We just want to be happy."

"Mother, don't do this. It's too soon. It won't work."

Vale intervened. "You don't seem to understand, Lady Madeline. Your mother and I have already discussed this. We've made our decision. We'd both hoped for your acceptance and your blessing, but you cannot let go of the past. And we want to move on with our lives."

"Give this decision more time." Madeline wanted to force her mother to come home, but she had no way to do so.

"We did this for you, Madeline." Her mother turned to Vale. "Didn't we, my lord?"

"Indeed." Vale slipped his arm through her mother's arm. "You're upset, my dear. Let's be on our way."

Ravensmoore moved his horse forward a few steps. "What harm could be caused by waiting, Countess Richfield?" he asked. "Perhaps more time would allow your daughter to accept your marriage."

"This is none of your affair!" Vale stepped away from Grace and strode angrily toward Madeline, stopping just short of Samson's nose. "Whether you accept it or not is *your* problem, Lady Madeline, not ours." He reached up to grab Samson's bridle.

Devlin quickly put his horse between Madeline and Vale. "I wouldn't try that again."

"You have no authority here. Who do you think you are to intervene?"

"I am Lady Madeline's physician. I'm here to see to her welfare."

"Perhaps you should give her a calming draught to settle her nerves. She's a bit high-spirited."

"Please, Mother." Madeline started to dismount, but Devlin reached over and stopped her. She realized he was trying to protect her, but someone had to do something. She prayed for wisdom, but she could hear nothing but blood rushing to her head. She had to act.

Vale backed off. "Come, my dear. We are leaving at once. There is nothing they can do."

"But shouldn't we try to explain?" Her mother, obviously upset about the exchange of harsh words, placed her hand on Vale's arm.

"There's nothing to explain."

Madeline reached into her reticule and pulled out the pistol. "Stop right there, Lord Vale." She aimed the pistol at him with careful precision.

Vale, his face white, stepped in front of Grace. "Get in the coach, my dear. Your daughter has lost her wits."

Grace pleaded, "Sir, she is overwrought. Give her but a moment."

"She may shoot me in that moment, madam," Vale said dryly.

"This will solve nothing," Ravensmoore murmured urgently. "You might hurt your mother." He snatched the gun out of her hand.

"What are you doing? He must be stopped."

"Not like this."

Vale took advantage of the opportunity and followed her mother into the coach, then yelled at the driver, "Get moving. We've wasted enough time here." As the carriage rocked forward and passed them, Vale leaned out of the coach window. "Your patient should be locked away."

"Look what you've done!" She swallowed back her tears as the coach continued its journey toward Gretna Green. "What am I to do now?"

"Follow them."

"Follow them?" She was not certain if he was teasing her or not. "Then what?"

"We'll know when we get there. But be absolutely certain of one thing," he said. "The pistol remains with me." He pocketed the weapon.

Madeline nodded, surprised that he was willing to accompany her and shocked at her own behavior. "I don't know why I did that."

"Desperation, I imagine."

"I imagine," she echoed his words.

"And one more thing." He touched her hand. "Your mother has not been taken against her will. She has a mind of her own."

"Her mind is not working logically."

"She appears perfectly in control of the situation."

Madeline mentally wrestled with the words. "Unlike me?"

"I didn't say that."

Her mind instantly filled with thoughts of Ravensmoore and their morning ride in the meadow. He always seemed to be there for her. "Why are you helping me?" she asked.

"I agree with you. I think you and your mother need the opportunity to talk before they wed."

"Perhaps I can still change her mind."

"I don't think that outcome likely."

The trip had proved to be more difficult than Madeline had imagined. They'd had to leave their horses at one of the inns along the way. Ravensmoore paid for the use of a coach and four and the care of their horses until they could return. Madeline's arm ached from her stubborn decision to ride Samson. In the coach she had the leisure to think about what she would say to her mother when they reached their destination.

By the time they reached Gretna Green, the full moon gleamed in the star-filled sky, a brilliant jewel guiding their way. Madeline forced herself to concentrate when she saw the look of total astonishment on Vale's face when he and her mother quit the coach.

"What are *you* doing here?" Vale asked. "This is too much."

"Madeline, really." Her mother looked at her daughter as if she had just committed an unthinkable act. "I cannot believe you followed us. What can you be thinking?"

"I am thinking only of your welfare." Madeline knew her mother. Although she protested, there was a measure of relief in her tired blue eyes. "If you insist on getting married, I am going to be here."

Grace's face lit with joy. "Did you hear that, my lord? She is not opposing the marriage any longer." The countess went to her daughter while the stable boys tended to the horses. "I am so *very* glad you are here, my dear." Grace kissed Madeline's cheek and wrapped her in a hug.

"It is too late to be wed this night," Ravensmoore said. "We will just have to get some rooms and wait until morning. I will share a room with Vale, and you and your mother share another. That will give you more time to talk."

Vale came face-to-face with Ravensmoore. "I have no intention of sharing a room with you, sir. I can certainly understand the countess wishing to spend the night with her daughter. Lady Madeline is overwrought. Everyone knows she's never recovered from the death of her father. She's going to try and convince her mother not to marry."

Grace intervened. "Nonsense, my lord. I am most tired. Madeline and I will speak plainly tonight, and tomorrow all will be as it should."

Vale bristled, "But—"

"If you and the countess are in love," Ravensmoore said, "I am certain there is nothing Lady Madeline can do to change that. Now let's find our rooms and get some rest."

"A splendid idea. It has been a very long day." Grace linked arms with Madeline, and together they entered the Welcoming Maiden Inn.

Ravensmoore arranged for a room for Madeline and her mother. "Since you refuse to share a room with me, Vale, I shall leave you to make your own arrangements. Pleasant dreams."

"Bah." Vale shook his head. "This was completely unnecessary. Goodnight, sir."

Ravensmoore accompanied the women to their room. "Goodnight, Countess. Goodnight, Lady Madeline." He bowed formally. "I trust you will sleep well."

"Thank you," Madeline said, grateful that she'd actually been able to stop the wedding thus far. She knew she would not have been able to do it without his help. "Sleep well."

His eyes lingered on her. "I doubt I will sleep at all." He touched her hand gently, then briefly raised it in his own.

Madeline swayed forward and for a brief beat in time thought he would kiss her hand. Instead he smiled gently and walked away. A shadow of disappointment crept into her heart.

She softly closed the door after watching Ravensmoore disappear into his room. She felt secure knowing he was close.

Turning, she confronted her mother, who stood watching her with a warning look in her eye. "I know what you are going to say, dear, and though it may appear that I don't know my own mind, I do plan to marry Lord Vale on the morrow." Grace removed her bonnet and gloves and laid them carefully on the bed.

"I thought you would give the notion of marriage to him more than a night's sleep." Madeline paced the room. "What can you be thinking? He's not right for you, Mother. Can you not see that?"

"Hush now," Grace ordered. Her shoulders straightened with determination.

Madeline must have made that same precise movement a hundred times herself when she was determined to have her own way. Now what was she going to do?

"Why?" she asked, refusing to give up. "Why are you so determined to marry this man so quickly? Why not announce your intentions and marry in the church? With a special license from the Archbishop of Canterbury's Office you need not wait. Or better yet, purchase a regular license and have the banns read."

"Madeline, there are some things that a young woman like yourself cannot understand. It is more than loneliness. It is the need to connect with another human being on a level that surpasses everything else."

"Are you saying you desire him?" Desire. Isn't that what she'd thought about Ravensmoore earlier that day? Did she desire him?

"Of course I desire him. I wouldn't marry him if I didn't, but I love him too. That's what marriage is all about. Desire without love is simply lust. My feelings for Lord Vale go beyond that." She sat down on the side of the huge poster bed and sighed. "You don't understand, dear. You've never been in love."

Madeline thought of her father and what a grand couple her parents made. She thought of what loving someone meant, of what losing someone meant. She had never lost a husband or been in love. But she'd seen what Mother and Hally had suffered. "I imagine you are lonely at times."

"Very."

She wondered what tomorrow would bring. "If only Father—"

"Stop it, Madeline. That will do no good. You know he's not coming back. He's dead, and there's nothing any of us can do about that."

Madeline nodded silently, feeling numb. Her shoulders drooped. Tears stung her eyes. "I do know that Father's dead and that he's not coming back. I'm not insane. But I am heartbroken. I don't understand how you can fall in love with someone else so easily."

"I've told you my intentions, dear." Her mother rose and went behind Madeline to massage her shoulders. "You really mustn't worry. Nothing will change for you. If that is what's on your mind, put it to rest. Now, do try to be happy for me. Please."

"You will be leaving Richfield to live on his estate, and you say nothing will change? Everything will change."

"No, dear, you don't understand. We won't be living at his home. We will be living at Richfield. That is the way I want it. Lord Vale has agreed to it." She came around to face Madeline. "I want you to be happy too."

Madeline cringed inwardly at the thought of Vale living with them at Richfield. *Nothing will change?* Love must be blind if her mother refused to acknowledge that *everything* was changing and was spinning madly out of control.

"I would prefer that you take more time to think this through," Madeline continued, hoping her mother would come to her senses. "We really don't know enough about Vale. Have you ever been to his home?"

Grace pursed her lips. "It is not necessary, Madeline. I trust him."

"If he really makes you happy, then I will *try* to be happy for you." She stood and embraced her mother but couldn't stop feeling as though she were losing her mother, her last remnant of family, and there was nothing she could do to prevent it.

"Thank you, dear. You'll see. Everything will work out beautifully."

The following morning dawned dark and drear, a reflection of Madeline's inner turmoil and mood. She'd tossed and turned most of the night dreaming of Ravensmoore and of her mother's decision. If she allowed herself to feel any emotions, she might become as vulnerable as her mother.

Madeline helped her mother dress in a beautiful red silk gown. "You are stunning," Madeline said with admiration.

Grace kissed her daughter's cheek, then stood back as if closely evaluating her. "How did you sleep last night, darling? You look tired."

"I'm fine, Mother, really. I wish I could fit into one of your gowns. I'm afraid this riding habit isn't well suited for a wedding."

A rap on the door startled her. She opened it to find Ravensmoore standing in front of her. He was impeccably dressed in black with a white cravat knotted perfectly at the neck. And in his arms was draped a lovely green dress, her favorite color, with a matching but dark shade of green pelisse. "Good morning, Lady Madeline." He bowed formally. "I thought you may want to change. I apologize for being late, but it took a bit longer than I imagined finding the shopkeeper."

The man positively oozed genius, and that annoyed her. She dipped into a deep curtsy. "How wonderful. It's very kind of you, Lord Ravensmoore. More than kind, actually." She decided to pretend she was in control of her emotions and the situation. Nothing was further from the truth. "I'll change quickly."

When Ravensmoore returned, she opened the door.

He scanned her figure, seeming to approve as much of her as her dress. "I have exquisite taste," he pronounced.

Madeline blushed. "You, sir, are a rogue."

He ignored her charge and looked past her. "I must say, Countess, that you are a picture of beauty itself. I hope Vale realizes how lucky he is to have captured your heart."

"Thank you, sir. That is most kind."

"It is merely the truth. Lord Vale is waiting downstairs. I have come to escort you." He held out his arm to Grace, who accepted it graciously.

Madeline found herself jealous of her own mother. She followed them downstairs and couldn't help wishing it was she herself getting married this morning. That a dashing gentleman had whisked her off to Gretna Green and that they would be sharing their lives together. She shook off a sense of loss.

The remainder of the morning rushed by as she watched her mother and Vale exchange their wedding vows with one another. No church nor minister was needed. Only a pledge and a kiss in the tradition of hurried weddings at Scotland's Gretna Green in the presence of two witnesses. To Madeline's chagrin, she had to admit that Grace and Vale made a striking couple. Her mother's alabaster complexion glowed against her red wedding gown, and Lord Vale's blond magnetism stood out against his black clothes and tightly knotted cravat.

"I hope you will be very happy, Mother." Madeline hugged her. "I will miss you."

"Madeline, everything will be wonderful. I will see you in a fortnight." Her mother hugged her tight and kissed her on the cheek once again. "I am very glad that Lord Ravensmoore will see you safely home."

Vale stepped up to Madeline. "You are a beautiful stepdaughter. I've always wanted a daughter." Then he stepped in closer and whispered in her ear, "Now I have you."

Something in his tone and the glint in his eye made her shiver. She blinked her eyes as if trying to clear her thoughts. Perhaps she was overwrought and just imagined his tone of voice.

As she and Ravensmoore departed the Welcoming Maiden Inn, a sense of foreboding anchored heavily in Madeline's heart. "I hope she will be happy." She looked at Ravensmoore sitting across from her. "Thank you for coming with me. I couldn't have done it without you."

"I was pleased to be of service." He removed his hat and laid it on the seat next to him. "I hope you don't mind, but I'm a bit warm." Then he unknotted his cravat, allowing it to hang down the front of his coat. "I wonder what you would have done with this revolver"—he withdrew it from inside his coat pocket—"if I hadn't been with you?"

Madeline squirmed uncomfortably beneath his gaze. "I always carry a pistol when I'm alone and riding. My father taught me how to use one."

"And were you planning on using this pistol on Vale?"

Madeline looked away and pretended to study the scenery outside her window. "I meant only to scare him."

"I wonder if you thought at all when you pulled the gun. Emotional rages have killed before: a jealous husband, a scorned woman, dare I say an angry daughter?"

She listened to his words and wondered if she'd indeed lost control of her emotions. She didn't want to admit that, but perhaps, for just that moment, she had lost control.

Madeline looked at him. His steady gaze unnerved her. "Rage is a powerful force," she mused. "I think I can understand more and more how someone like Amanda could be pushed over the edge into insanity. It's a fragile, dark line."

"You are beginning to sound like someone in the mad-doctoring trade. A doctor of the mind, as you've said in the past. An appropriate designation. Didn't you accuse me of that after dinner at your home?"

"I was angry…and confused." The swaying of the coach relaxed

Madeline. "I still am." She watched the trees pass by outside the coach and listened to the sound of the horses' hooves on the road. "What's the difference, my lord, between Ashcroft Asylum and a prison?"

"Very little, I'm afraid. I wish reforms would happen faster, but it's a slow process. Those who suffer from severe melancholy, delusions, hallucinations, and such need a lot of help and better understanding. Unfortunately, there are many, even in Parliament, who believe that demon possession is responsible for this kind of ailment."

"And you don't?"

"No more or less than I believe that any sickness of the body is from the evil one. Why should illnesses that affect the brain be due solely to the devil, but illnesses that affect other parts of the body be simply happenstance, neglect, or bad luck?"

"An interesting thought, my lord. And one that makes a great deal of sense. Why are you interested in mad-doctoring at all? Why not simply do what physicians have done for years without getting so preoccupied with the workings of the mind?"

"Because, dear lady, I don't believe you can separate the mind from the rest of the body. There are secrets to uncover that will make medicine better. Look what they do to our own King George. He's blistered and bled and even chained, and it makes no difference. Sometimes I think the treatment more hazardous than the ailment."

"But what else is to be done?" Madeline asked, her interest piqued. "Society can't have lunatics running around causing mayhem."

Devlin sighed. "I've read Samuel Tuke's works. He's the grandson of William Tuke, a Quaker who believed that patients in asylums should be treated humanely and not like animals. He called this moral treatment."

"That is what Amanda needs. Or at the very least to be treated like a human being. I worry about her. I believe they starved that poor girl. I find it hard to believe she killed her father."

"And that brings us back to asylums being no better than prison. Ashcroft is Amanda's prison. She will never get out. It is a sad thing."

Madeline shut her eyes, trying to hold back the tears. "It's horrible." She took a deep breath to quell the overwhelming emotions that choked her, but the tears betrayed the extent of her anguish.

Suddenly he was next to her. "Let the tears come. It's all right." He put an arm around her and held her close.

Beyond the worry of appearances and social regard, she lay her head on his chest and sobbed her anguish. All the strain of the past few days, along with the grief of the last few years, coursed through her.

When at last her crying subsided, she found herself too exhausted to lift her head. Her eyes closed, and she slept.

The rocking of the coach eventually woke her, and for just a moment she didn't remember where she was. Then she heard the beating of his heart. Devlin's heart. She gasped and sat up.

"Lady Madeline. Are you all right?"

He looked at her, and she noticed a softness in his green eyes that she'd never allowed herself to see before this day. Her hands went to her cheeks that burned. "I'm so embarrassed. Forgive me."

"There is nothing to forgive. You were exhausted. Do you feel better?"

She smoothed her dress and patted her hair into place. "I'm not sure what to feel." She turned to him and could no longer deny the attraction. Whether the closeness of him within the carriage or the relief of all she'd held within, something within her lightened.

He placed his hand on her cheek and traced her bottom lip with his thumb. Tempest green eyes searched hers, and in that moment all else disappeared. Mere inches apart, Madeline longed to feel something again, something other than sadness. Instinctively she moved closer, and when his lips touched hers, she closed her eyes, reveling in the gentleness of his lips, the subtle smell of leather and spice on his skin.

The driver pounded on the roof, startling her out of his embrace. They had arrived at the inn where they would claim their horses.

Madeline pushed away from him. "We must both be mad." She blushed and moved to the other side of the carriage.

"Madeline."

"Ravensmoore." She swallowed hard and looked into his eyes.

Ravensmoore grinned. "I cannot find it in myself to apologize. I do believe we may have just discovered true sanity."

"This only proves why it is necessary for a single woman to be in the company of a chaperone when a man is present," she replied tartly. He chuckled but followed her out of the carriage without further comment.

Madeline enjoyed the ride on Samson to Richfield. His strength and speed invigorated her, and the weather brightened with her mood. Ravensmoore did not try to press his intimacies but kept the conversation bright and cheerful. And she was grateful, for she needed time to think away from this man who produced nothing but chaos in her head and her heart.

They arrived at Richfield before dark. Madeline looked forward to a warm bath and sleep. The footman appeared to take their horses.

"Would you like to come in and rest before you ride to the Blue Swan?" she asked. "You must be exhausted. You are welcome to stay the night. Phineas could avail himself to act as your valet. And then you could get an early start tomorrow."

Ravensmoore sighed. "I appreciate your kind offer, but I can stay only long enough to have Hippocrates here fed and watered. I want to meet with Dr. Langford early. He won't be happy about my absence." He dismounted and allowed the footman to take care of his horse while he stretched his legs.

He reached up and helped her dismount. Regret crossed his face as he held her gloved hand lightly, looking down at her. "Because I am nearing the end of my training, I will be working nonstop for the next few weeks, and it is unlikely that I will be able to escape my duties to visit you. I hope you'll understand."

"Of course." Disappointment flitted at the edges of her thoughts, but she paid them no heed. "Thank you again for your help, Ravensmoore. I owe you a great deal."

"All you owe me is a promise to take care of yourself." His voice was low, his tone gentle.

"I will. Good night." Unable to cope with the storm of newly awakened emotions, she turned away from him and walked into the house.

When she slid beneath the covers a short time later, she fell asleep thinking of how safe she'd felt in his arms. A safety, she sensed, that could shatter all too easily.

PART TWO

For God hath not given us the spirit of fear; but
of power, and of love, and of a sound mind.

—2 TIMOTHY 1:7

CHAPTER 12

Our doubts are traitors
And make us lose the good we oft might win
By fearing to attempt.

—SHAKESPEARE,
MEASURE FOR MEASURE,
ACT I, SCENE IV

TRUE TO HER word, Grace returned from her wedding trip within a fortnight. As the days went by, Madeline watched Vale take control of Richfield...and her mother. He charmed his way into her mother's soul and played her emotions better than Madeline could ever hope to play the pianoforte. But despite her mother's pleading glances, Madeline remained cool and skeptical toward her new husband.

Madeline spent every waking moment riding, gardening, or doing anything to get out of the house and away from the newlyweds. Hoping to gain a fresh perspective, she took a long walk in the gardens. It was a sunny morning in mid-April and no clouds threatened, but her mood grew darker. She did not know how long she could bear living in the same house as Vale. And as he'd warned, there had been no visits from Ravensmoore, only letters. In a time like this, the written word was cold comfort. She felt neglected and abandoned.

Hearing voices, she looked up. Lord Vale and another man were approaching her from the direction of the stables. Vale waved. She hoped he wouldn't detain her long.

"Lady Madeline, I would like to introduce Amos Sullivan. He is the manager at Ashcroft Insane Asylum. He's got a problem on his hands, and I thought you might be able to offer support."

Sullivan removed his hat and bowed. "Lady Madeline. A pleasure."

But Madeline didn't see this as a pleasure at all. "Mr. Sullivan. What could I possibly do at Ashcroft?" She immediately thought of Amanda.

"As you know," Vale said, "I am a benefactor of the asylum. Naturally, Sullivan thought I might have some way of remedying the current situation."

"And that would be?" Madeline looked toward the house hoping her mother would join them, but she was nowhere to be seen.

"Twin boys, eleven years of age, have been dropped on the asylum's doorstep. Their aunt who was caring for them died, and now they await transport to the Royal Military Asylum. Their father died in the war, and that allows them an opportunity for a decent life, but first they must be examined by a physician who will attest to their health."

Madeline frowned. "And how can I help?"

"The children are a bit unruly. We would like you to teach the boys their manners and other subjects until arrangements can be made for them to leave. Dr. Langford insists on seeing them but can't make time to come to Ashcroft for several days. Would you consider teaching the boys some lessons in preparation for their new home? It would keep them out of the cook's hair, and I thought you might enjoy it."

Madeline thought of Amanda. This would be her chance to see the poor girl again and to find out how she faired. Madeline nodded. "I could help the boys. When would you like me to come?"

"Tomorrow, at your convenience." Sullivan bowed, and Vale smiled.

Madeline nodded curtly then turned on her heel, eager to escape their presence.

Madeline met the boys for the first time the day following her conversation with Lord Vale. This was her third day of teaching, and she found she looked forward to seeing the twins. Something about them had touched her. Their joking and cheerful spirits coaxed her out of her gloom and even revived her long-lost sense of humor.

As she pushed open the door of the barn where they liked to play, she heard a string of colorful words that followed the sound of hoof meeting pail. "Jenny? Is that you?" She wandered toward the milking stalls, looking for the milkmaid.

"Whad'ya want?" An angry, grime-smeared face jutted around the corner. "Oh, it's you, my lady. Beg pardon."

Madeline nearly collapsed into the pile of hay behind her. "Jenny. Could you please not do that! You frightened me nearly into a swoon."

"Beggin' yer pardon, my lady, but the door squeak'n had Glory kick the milk pail over."

"I am sorry, Jenny. I'll try to be more careful. Could you gather the boys for me?"

Jenny put her fingers to her lips and let out with an ear-splitting whistle that upset the livestock far more than Madeline's creaking of the barn door.

Madeline looked around. The hay piled next to her shivered, and a pair of wide, dark eyes in a dirt-streaked face sparkled mischievously amongst the strands of straw.

"Danny, is that you?" Madeline smiled.

Jenny stuck out her tongue at the boy in the haystack and went back to her milking, unaware that the child returned the affectionate gesture.

"Ye lookin' for me, Lady Majesty?"

"Yes, I am looking for you. It is time for your studies. And what have I told you is the proper way to address me?"

"Lady Madeline." He scampered up, spitting pieces of hay out of his mouth and dusting off his head of red curls. "I don't need no studies."

"What would you like to be when you are grown?"

"Dunno. Do mad folk get to be somethin' when they's growed up, Lady Majesty?"

"Danny, you are strong-minded. You are not mad."

"Sure am. Mr. Sullivan says I'm batty more than most my age."

"I'll have a talk with Mr. Sullivan. You are as normal as any boy your age. Just because you have no parents does not make you mad."

"You sure?"

"I'm sure."

"Good. Then I'll be…a pickpocket."

"Danny!" Madeline took a deep breath and sighed. "You will not be a pickpocket."

A serious expression covered his face. "Lady Majesty, I promise I'll be a good one."

Madeline burst out laughing. "I am sure you will be the best. You must be anxious for your studies to begin. I don't believe I have ever seen you come so quickly. Excellent. That is the sign of a curious student."

"I just don't wanna do work is all." He grinned, a mouth full of missing or decayed teeth marring his freckled face. He shuffled from one foot to the other, a nervous gesture that emerged whenever addressed by an adult.

"And where is Jack?" The hay shivered again and birthed another redhead.

"Jack!" Danny flung a fistful of hay at his eleven-year-old twin. "Gotcha, string head!"

Jack immediately pounced on his brother. "I'll get you, bushy head!" A blur of arms and legs stirred the dust on the barn floor into a small whirlwind.

"I hope you are finished playing your games so we may get some work done today," Madeline chided, trying to sound stern, but then had a fit of coughing from the dust swirling about her. "Now, follow me to our classroom."

Madeline led the way to a corner of the barn padded in hay. The boys plopped down and sprawled out in comfort. They watched Madeline set her overly large reticule on a barrel, open it, and pull out several pieces of chocolate. Eyes grew wide with grins to match.

"Dr. Langford will be here tomorrow to make certain you are healthy enough to leave for the Royal Military Asylum in London. He will give you a thorough going-over, and then as soon as transport can be arranged, you will be off on a new adventure."

"Do we have to go?" Jack asked. "We like it here."

Madeline settled herself on a bale of hay. "It's an opportunity to get your education so you can grow up to be more than pickpockets. Since both your poor parents are dead, and now you've lost your aunt, God rest their souls, the Duke of York has provided a place where children like yourselves can learn and grow together."

"Will there be girls at this school?" Danny asked.

"Yes, I believe there are." Madeline pulled out her Bible and a book of poetry.

"Then we ain't going." Jack crossed his arms and shook his head. "And why on earth not?"

"Because girls are dim," Danny said and crossed his arms too.

"Some year in the not too distant future you will change your minds about that. But until then I thought you might enjoy a sweet. Who can recite a line of Scripture that we memorized yesterday?"

Danny shouted "I can!" a moment before Jack did, and the talk of dim girls was forgotten.

"All right, Danny. Go ahead."

"Blessed are the poor..." Danny scratched his head in thought. "...'cause they'll get rich."

Jack hooted.

"Danny, you're almost right," Madeline praised him and handed him a piece of candy.

He popped it in his mouth faster than a barn cat chasing a rat.

"'Blessed are the poor in spirit, for they will inherit the kingdom of heaven.'"

Danny defended himself. "Yeah, that's what I said."

"Which of you can recite something from this book?" She held up a book of poetry.

Jack jumped up. "Something is rotten in...in...hemlock!"

Madeline could not help smiling. Danny laughed aloud.

"Can I have my candy, Lady Madeline?"

"You are getting much better, but you have some thinking to do. The answer is 'Something is rotten in the state of Denmark.'"

Just then movement caught her eye, and she looked out a grimy window and stared in astonishment as Lord Vale entered Sullivan's office with Amanda in tow.

The boys followed her gaze. "Amanda's in trouble again." Jack ran to the window. "The keepers made her cry yesterday. I don't like them keepers."

Madeline thought of the first time she'd seen Amanda. "What do you mean, they made her cry?"

"They wouldn't give her no food. That's what Cook said."

Madeline pursed her lips, then made a quick decision. "Boys, I want you to memorize this scripture. 'Ye shall not fear them: for the LORD your God he shall fight for you. Deuteronomy 3:22.' I'll be back in a few minutes. I want to speak to Mr. Sullivan." Madeline touched each of their heads as she departed, knowing they were not likely to memorize Scripture in her absence. But she could not sit there knowing that Amanda could be suffering at the hands of Mr. Sullivan.

Madeline hurried through the yard to the office. She could hear Amanda crying, and instead of stopping to knock she hurried inside unannounced. Amanda lay in a heap on the floor unmoving.

Madeline whirled on Sullivan. "What are you doing to this girl?" she demanded.

"We haven't decided yet." Sullivan drawled, reaching for his pipe.

She glared at Vale. "How could you permit this outrage?"

Madeline rushed to Amanda and took her hand. The smell of her nearly made Madeline vomit. Barely able to hold her head up, Amanda looked at her. Those big brown eyes made Madeline want to weep. Dark circles were under her eyes, and her right eye was bruised and swollen. "Who hit her? Was it you?" She looked at Sullivan.

He packed his pipe with tobacco. "The patients frequently fight, my lady." He lit his pipe as though nothing of importance was being discussed.

"You are not to interfere with the management of the patients, Lady Madeline," Lord Vale snapped. He sat in a chair across from Sullivan, who was behind his desk.

"When was the last time this patient had a bath? When did she have the opportunity to wash her hair? She's emaciated, and the boys said that you, Mr. Sullivan, were refusing to let her eat. You are treating her worse than an abused animal." Madeline entwined her fingers with Amanda. "What is the meaning of this?"

Sullivan stood behind his desk. "This is that runaway, the murderous Amanda. She tried to run again last night. She must be trained not to attempt that behavior again, or she will be placed in solitary confinement."

Madeline bristled. "If you treated her well, perhaps she would not want to run away. And you say 'train her' as if she's not human." She looked from Sullivan to Vale, barely able to contain her disdain for both of them. "Lord Vale, how can you approve such actions as a benefactor of this asylum?"

"There are things you cannot comprehend at your age and having lived a life of privilege, Lady Madeline. Certain measures are necessary to maintain order in an institution like this."

"You cannot approve of such ill treatment, Lord Vale." Madeline feared that Amanda might die if she didn't get some food. "I want you to have Cook bring some food. I will help her bathe."

She watched the interactions between the two men. Vale shrugged.

Sullivan said, "Very well. You will see that I am a compassionate man and not the monster you believe me to be. I will send for food, and then you may assist her in her toilet." Sullivan left the three of them alone.

Madeline turned on Vale. "How can you have business dealings with such a man? He's awful, and he's treating this poor girl dreadfully. I hesitate to think what else is going on behind the closed doors of this place."

"You misunderstand, Lady Madeline. This is not a business. I merely help support the place because of my concern for those less fortunate. The same thing that your friend, Ravensmoore, boasts about."

"He is nothing like you." She laid Amanda's head on her lap where they sat upon the floor. "How do I know that she will not be abused when I leave?" Madeline demanded. "How can you overlook such cruelty?"

Vale came to stand over them, sending a shiver through Amanda that Madeline absorbed.

"Sullivan's actions are based solely on the actions of the patients.

If they do as they are told and don't make trouble, then they have nothing to regret with the exception of what their tormented minds tell them to regret."

A keeper arrived to carry Amanda to a room off the kitchen that was toasty warm. Madeline followed behind, ordering that a bath be drawn and fresh clothing provided. While she waited for the water to heat, Madeline spooned chicken soup into Amanda and hot tea with lots of sugar. Amanda revived enough to climb into the tub of warm water, groaning in what Madeline imagined must be sheer relief. Madeline let her soak and then washed her hair and clothed her in new garments provided by the local parish.

Madeline returned to the office. This time she knocked before entering.

Lord Vale stood in front of the fireplace, his hands clasped behind his back. "Is she well?" he asked and turned to face Madeline.

"She is very sick." Madeline searched his eyes but could detect no emotion hidden there—neither hatred nor approval. "I want to take her to Richfield until she's better."

"I think you know what the answer to that is." He took a few steps closer to Madeline. "Absolutely not. Have you not been listening?"

"Will you give me your word that you will talk to Sullivan and allow Amanda to go to the kitchen and eat with Cook every day?"

"I will ask him. Now, as you know, the boys are to see Langford tomorrow and then be on their way to the Royal Military Asylum in London. There is no need for you to return. In fact, I will speak to your mother, and together we will forbid you to return. I will not be able to be here to see to your welfare, and I have business that must be attended to for both Richfield and my estate at Vale House."

Madeline struggled to keep her voice even. "Will you also have Sullivan consider keeping a physician on these grounds to attend to the needs of the sick?"

"I will discuss it with Sullivan, but it is very unlikely that any physician would want to take up residence here at Ashcroft."

"Time will tell, Lord Vale. I will say good-bye to the twins and be ready to return home within the hour."

Vale nodded. "Very well."

Once back home Madeline went for a long walk in the gardens and spoke to God. She could make no sense of why the Lord allowed such misery to exist.

"A penny for your thoughts."

Madeline's hand flew to her throat as she turned toward her friend. "Oh, Hally. You gave me a fright."

"Agnes told me you'd gone walking in the gardens." Hally reached for her friend's hand and squeezed tight. "You don't look well, Maddie. I can tell from the circles under your eyes that you are not sleeping."

Madeline blinked back the tears. "I'm lost, Hally. Mother appears happy with Vale. I do not understand what she sees in him."

Hally steered her toward a small bench where they sat down. "You are adjusting to your mother's marriage. It must be so hard for you."

"Harder than even I imagined," Madeline said. "I should not be so miserable. My mother is happy. Yet I know Vale is hiding something." She told Hally everything that had transpired at Ashcroft. "I cannot detect any flagrant sign of evil in him, but neither do I find true compassion. It worries me that Mother could marry someone so skilled at hiding his emotions."

Hally hugged Madeline to her. "I cannot claim to know how an asylum is to be run, dear Maddie, but I do know that you are full of compassion for all living things. Even the fox that all the farmers hate. Perhaps you need to get away from the asylum now and not return. It only makes you melancholic, and my goal from the beginning was to have you happily ensconced within society once again."

"It's not society that I detest, Hally. It's what they do to each other. So much gossip and slander. You'd think they had nothing more to concern themselves with than the next juicy scandal."

Hally took Madeline's hands in her own. "I dare say you are bordering on the brink of a great melancholy. Therefore I plan to distract you with other thoughts if only for a brief while. Did I tell you that Lord Ravensmoore and Mr. Melton are working ridiculously hard? Dr. Langford has them performing surgery or tending the sick night and day. He's been very demanding ever since Ravensmoore returned late from your adventure to Gretna Green. He has been in touch, has he not?"

"Yes. He's written me the same things that Mr. Melton has told you." Madeline fished out her handkerchief and blew her nose. "But that makes no difference. He is unimportant in my life."

"Have you prayed about this?"

"About what?"

"About your feelings for Ravensmoore?"

"I have no feelings for him. And I do not think God hears my prayers about anything."

"Rubbish. He hears everyone's prayers. Perhaps you haven't been listening to Him. You should take a holiday and get away from Richfield for a while. Why don't we go somewhere together? Just the two of us."

Madeline brightened at the prospect. "A holiday? Where?"

"I don't know. Anywhere. Where would you like to go?"

"The sea. I love the water." Madeline felt the first burst of hope and the possibility that maybe she would feel better again. "I need to get away from this place; it's making me sick," she said sadly.

"Let's plan it then." Hally clapped her hands together. "Down to the last detail."

"Let's go to Scarborough." Madeline was suddenly taken with the notion. "It's not too far and exactly what I need."

"Then Scarborough it is." Hally stood, pulling Madeline up with her. "Let's walk and make our plans. It will be such fun!"

CHAPTER 13

Have mercy upon me, O LORD, for I am
in trouble: mine eye is consumed with
grief, yea, my soul and my belly.

—PSALM 31:9

*D*EVLIN RUBBED HIS hands over his face, attempting to ward off the exhaustion that had settled deep in his bones. Langford seemed determined to siphon every bit of work out of his students that he could. The old physician continued to preach his own personal doctrine.

"You are all inept! I am going to make good physicians and surgeons of you if it's the last thing I do. It's my reputation on the line. You're not butchers. You're both physician and surgeon. Even though some people think a horse doctor will serve them just as well, it is our duty to prove them wrong."

Splashing cold water on his face, Devlin prepared for rounds. He would never quit. Langford had no mercy for those who could not maintain his standards. And reputation and experience were everything to his future.

One thing that really irked him was his inability to get away to visit Lady Madeline. He'd taken to dreaming of her often, and those dreams were no longer satisfactory. He needed to see her. He needed to touch her face, hold her hand, and look into those hazel eyes that turned alternately greener, or a deeper brown, depending on her mood.

Melton burst through the door of the preparatory room. "Ravensmoore, Langford's looking for you, and he's angry as a hornet." Melton's shirtsleeves were rolled to his elbows, and his hair had partially escaped its black ribbon, giving him the disheveled, terror-stricken look of a child about to receive punishment from a sturdy rod. "He says one of your patients is failing and shouldn't be. He wants to know what you plan to do about it. Now!"

"Which patient?" Ravensmoore asked, his brow furrowing with concern. "Everyone has been doing exceptionally well."

Melton leaned against the door and closed his eyes. "I don't know, he didn't say, but he's as cranky as an old man with gout. I think he's trying to kill us off. One by one. The man's heartless."

"He's only concerned for the patient." Devlin yawned. "Let's find out what the problem is. He'll eventually ease up on us."

Opening his eyes Melton said, "I won't hold my breath."

The two of them rushed to the room where a young woman was crying and clutching her stomach. "I'm goin' to have me babe. Please help me. 'Tis comin'. I can feel it."

Devlin rushed to the young woman's side. "Mrs. Brown, calm yourself. You are all right. Don't you remember?" he asked, gently taking her hand in his.

"Remember?" Mrs. Brown looked at him perplexed.

"The baby. The baby we took from you last night." Something was terribly wrong. A claw of dread inched its way up his spine.

Mrs. Brown twisted in agony. "I'm havin' me babe now, doctor. Can't ye help?"

Devlin looked to Melton for support and then saw Dr. Langford standing in the doorway observing his actions. He turned his full attention back to his patient, deciding to ignore whatever Langford might be thinking.

"I'm going to help you, Mrs. Brown." He tucked back a piece of damp hair from the young woman's face. "Get me some laudanum," he ordered the attendant in the room. "Hurry!"

"I don't want no potions," she cried hysterically. "I want to hold me babe."

Not knowing what else to do for his patient, he prayed for wisdom and opted for the truth. Holding the young woman's hand tightly in his own, he said, "Mrs. Brown, look at me."

She thrashed about in the bed and clutched her belly.

"Look at me! You had your baby last night. He...he died shortly after birth."

"Yer lyin'. Yer lyin'! He's 'ere in me belly." Tears flowed down her flushed cheeks. "He's 'ere." She whimpered and clutched her abdomen with both hands as if it were full of life.

Devlin ached for the tiny woman who had no children. *God forgive me. I don't know what else to do.* Reaching for the blanket that hid her empty womb, he quickly snatched away the covering. Though the hospital garments fully covered her body, the truth was evident.

"No!" She shuddered at the revelation of what Ravensmoore had exposed. She looked at her sunken, lifeless belly, horrified. "He's gone? Me babe's gone!" She broke into new waves of sobbing.

"I'm sorry, Mrs. Brown. I'm sorry you lost your baby." He knew that she was just beginning to accept the fact that her child had died. It was something he had to force her to acknowledge, force her to understand; otherwise she might be lost to the world of madness. Lost, as his mother had been lost, and lost as the girl Amanda was now. He said a silent prayer that the young woman would recover and perhaps someday be able to birth another child.

Devlin squeezed her hand and whispered in her ear, "Grieve and cling to hope."

Devlin left his patient in the care of a competent attendant with strict instructions not to leave her alone lest she hurt herself in a moment of grief. He sent an aide to bring the vicar.

Langford awaited him in the corridor. "Nicely done, Ravensmoore. I believe you may actually become a good physician," he said, his expression serious. "You, on the other hand," he said as Melton approached, "may need further training." Turning sharply he left them.

Melton groaned and looked at Ravensmoore. "It becomes increasingly difficult to remain your friend. You must stop showing me up. The idea of further training with Langford is enough to push one to the brink of despair."

"Don't despair, Melton." He repressed a grin and slapped his friend on the back. "I won't leave you behind. It would be unconscionable. Let's get a cup of tea. It's going to be another long day."

Willie, the receptionist, approached them as they sat enjoying their refreshment. "Good mornin', gentlemen. And a jolly good mornin' it is to be sure. It would seem that Dr. Langford has a soft side after all and has granted you a reprieve and given you both two days' holiday."

Melton looked over his steaming cup. "It's not nice to play jokes on us, Willie. Be careful, or we might decide to practice medicine on you and fix that bent nose of yours."

Willie felt the tip of his nose. "But I'm not jestin'. He gave me instructions to search you out. Yer free for two days. After all, it is May Day," he reminded them.

"Holiday!" Devlin stood up with one thing on his mind. Madeline. "Let's get out of here before he changes his mind, Melton."

"Wait for me." Surprised at the sudden turn of events, Melton rocked back on his chair and tipped over, sending hot tea splashing across the floor. He lay sprawled at Devlin's feet.

Devlin stared at his friend. "Come on, man, don't you wish to see Lady Gilling today? She's still at Richfield, is she not?"

Melton scrambled to his feet. "Lady Gilling is indeed at Richfield."

Devlin grabbed him by the arm to steady him. "Do pull yourself together, Melton. Time's a fleeting."

They rode to Richfield together, but Devlin's thoughts were private. *What must she think of me for staying away so long? What if she doesn't understand? What if she doesn't care for me?* His thoughts were such a confused jumble, he barely noticed the blossoming apple trees or the fresh green of the meadows. But when the huge stone manor of Richfield came into view, Devlin's intelligence snapped into place, cautioning him to be wise.

Since the trip to Gretna Green, he and Madeline had written brief notes to each other. Nothing he could interpret as interest from her, but he held out hope that God might make a way for him to enter her life as more than a physician. He reminded himself that she had let the walls down for a short time while in the carriage.

Melton interrupted his thoughts. "Do you suppose they will be pleased to see us?"

"Let's hope so. Doesn't absence make the heart grow fonder?"

"Perhaps." Melton stretched his legs out of the stirrups.

At the manor two footmen appeared to care for their horses. Devlin and Melton took the steps two at a time. Phineas, the butler, answered the door.

Devlin stepped forward. "Kindly tell Lady Madeline that Lord Ravensmoore is here to see her, and that Mr. Melton is here to call upon Lady Gilling."

Phineas carefully examined the two with a critical eye. "Yes, my lord. Follow me." He directed them to the library.

A blur of pink fabric whirled past Devlin several moments later. Lady Gilling nearly ran him over in her haste to reach Melton.

"Mr. Melton." Hally held out her hands in welcome. "How grand of you to come."

"Countess. I must say, you look exquisite." He took her hands in his and then offered her his arm. "Shall we take a turn about the gardens in celebration of May Day?"

"That would be lovely." As they were about to exit the room, Countess Gilling turned. "Lord Ravensmoore." She blushed and gave him a quick curtsy. "Do forgive me. I didn't see you."

Devlin bowed. "It is obvious your mind was elsewhere, madam." He smiled as the pair departed for the gardens.

"They make a sweet couple, don't you think?" Madeline said, entering the room, glowing in a golden gown. Her maid took a seat outside the room. "If absence makes the heart grow fonder, they should be quite smitten with each other, wouldn't you agree?"

"So it appears." Devlin bowed deeply. "Happy May Day, Lady Madeline."

"Happy May Day, Lord Ravensmoore." She curtsied. "Do sit down."

He settled on the settee near the unlit fireplace, hoping she would join him. He would have preferred to walk with her, but she seemed distant, preoccupied. Had he simply imagined that she might care for him? Doubt began to gnaw away at the edges of his mind.

"How is your mother? I trust the first few weeks of marriage have suited her."

"She seems quite happy, thank you." She walked past him and pulled a cord. The butler entered the room. "Please bring sandwiches and drinks, and perhaps some strong tea for Lord Ravensmoore, Phineas."

"At once, my lady." He left the room after a curt bow.

Madeline deliberately seated herself across from him, rather than beside him, and Devlin chafed at the distance. "Lady Madeline, I fear I've offended you with my neglect of late."

"Have you?" she said coolly, giving away nothing.

Annoyance collided with desire. "You know I could not leave the hospital. I told you that when we returned from Gretna. That is why I wrote to you. Langford has been demanding."

"And you are *Lord Ravensmoore*," she said coldly. "Why must you pursue this profession with such passion and put up with that awful doctor? It is beneath you. It is he who should serve you."

Phineas returned with cucumber finger sandwiches, lemonade, and a pot of tea. Devlin ignored the refreshments. He could not take his eyes off Madeline. But she avoided his gaze.

"What is on your mind, Lady Madeline?" he asked gently.

She shrugged. "I don't wish to burden you with my concerns."

"I would not feel listening to your concerns a burden."

She looked at him as if to gauge his sincerity, then the words came with a rush. "I don't know where to start. There is so much. There's Vale. I don't trust him." She told him everything that had happened at Ashcroft.

"I think you are right not to trust him. What you describe at Ashcroft are abuses that must be reported. I will speak to Langford. He'll know what to do. It's not right. It's not right at all, and I worry about you being there. You put yourself at risk."

"I'm just so worried about Amanda. Someone must help her. I'm afraid she might die."

"I promise you that I will convey your concerns to Dr. Langford. It will be investigated further."

"And then there's my father."

"Do you want to talk about your father?" He studied the look in her eyes and made a decision. "Your father was severely injured when he came to the Guardian Gate."

"I know." She stood and walked to the mantel, placing a hand upon it as she gazed into the cold fireplace. "But you were there."

"You don't understand." Devlin felt panic strike and begin to crumble the walls of his heart. "I did everything in my power to stop the bleeding."

She turned to face him, eyes blazing. "Did you?"

"Your father fought hard to live. I did everything I knew to stop the bleeding, but it was impossible. His life just slipped away in a matter of moments."

She took a step toward him. "Is there anything you can think of that you should have done and didn't?"

"I'm sorry. I didn't mean to upset you. But the branch that skewered your father's leg hit an artery in the thigh. When Langford left to attend another patient, we thought the bleeding was under control. Your father complained of the pain and asked me to loosen the tourniquet. I didn't do it because it was far too dangerous, and as I attended another patient nearby, he loosened the tourniquet. I couldn't stop the bleeding then."

Tears glistened in her eyes. "Leave now."

"Lady Madeline, he was in pain and did what he thought would relieve that pain. He couldn't make a reasonable decision. He was barely conscious. But I did turn my back for a few minutes to attend another. Maybe—"

"Don't say anymore." Madeline reached out and braced herself against a chair.

Devlin held out his hand. "Let me help you."

"I believe you've done enough. I've decided to take a holiday with Lady Gilling. I need to get away from here. I must get away."

"I'm sorry. I wanted you to understand."

"Don't." She sank into the chair, her hands shaking in her lap.

"I'd hoped you'd understand." He saw the confusion in her eyes. "I'm so sorry. I couldn't save him."

"I do not want to see you again."

"You mean you don't want to be with me." Devlin studied her carefully. "I thought you had feelings for me." He knelt next to her. "You are building a wall, my lady. A wall to separate us. Why? I thought we'd developed an affection for one another. A starting place at least."

He watched her intake of breath.

"I'm afraid."

"Afraid of what?"

He saw the answer in her eyes, read it in her situation. Her father had been so strong. If he hadn't removed the tourniquet, would he have lived? If Devlin had discovered the blood loss quicker, would it have made a difference? She needed to blame someone.

"I am not your father," he said, trying to keep his emotions under control, "and I am not Vale. I care for you, Lady Madeline. I will never betray your trust, but I am not perfect and will not pretend to be so. Can you forgive me for any mistakes you believe I may have made?" He covered her hands in his own. "Don't run from me."

"I'm not running from you. I just explained."

Devlin thought he knew what she was trying to say. All his insecurities resurfaced. "It's because of my decision to practice medicine, isn't it? It's all too much for you."

"The memories would always be there. I want to live a normal life. I want to have children. What kind of life would it be for them? Reminded each day of sickness and sorrow and suffering?"

"It is not all that! It is a life of kindness, of service." His hands clenched into fists. "What about your needs? What do you desire?"

"You don't understand, Ravensmoore."

He continued as though he hadn't heard her. "Then there are my peers. The *ton* does not understand, but I thought you might. It would be difficult to explain though, wouldn't it?" He stood and walked toward the doorway.

Madeline rose from the chair. "Wait. There is so much happening in my life. It's not just you."

Devlin turned back to her. "All evidence to the contrary, my dear. It is who I was, who I am, and what I'm called to be." He couldn't think clearly anymore, and he couldn't listen further. He knew what she must be feeling. He doubted his decision to be a physician at times himself.

God, what am I to do? Choose between Madeline and medicine? "You've made yourself clear, Lady Madeline. Good day." He turned away, nearly colliding with the butler, who quickly sidestepped him.

"Tell Mr. Melton when he returns that I was called away," he told Phineas. Without waiting for an answer, he strode out of the manor.

Devlin collected his mount, then recklessly galloped across the countryside in the direction of York. Concern for Hippocrates finally made him pull up and dismount near a creek, where the animal could drink and rest.

"What in blazes was that all about?" he yelled to the heavens. He kicked a rock out of his path like a small boy having a temper tantrum. Hippocrates looked up from the creek, then returned to quenching his thirst.

Devlin sat on the ground and raked both hands through his hair. *Maybe I'm going mad. I carry the blood of madness in my veins, and Madeline wants to have children. The children I dare not dream about.* "God, help me to know what to do."

CHAPTER 14

Hell is wherever heaven is not.
—SEVENTEENTH-CENTURY PROVERB

*D*EVLIN RETCHED INTO the basin Mrs. Hogarth held.

"I hope yer visit to the Grey Fox Inn will teach ye a lesson, Lord Ravensmoore."

"Shhh." Devlin squinted up at Mrs. Hogarth. She stood over him, looking like she'd just discovered her husband in bed with another woman.

"Humph, I bet ye had a row with Lady Madeline. Why is it, every time a gent has a quarrel with his lady he can't think proper? Believes drink will solve the problem." She dumped the contents of the basin into a bucket.

"It seemed a good idea at the time." He lay on his back and shaded his eyes with his arm. "Can't you shut out that infernal light? It's about to do me in."

"Appears to me ye already did yerself in. But because yer sufferin' in grand style, I'll have mercy on ye, though I know not why." She laid a cool damp cloth across his forehead.

"Ah. Sweet relief."

Mrs. Hogarth continued unabated. "Yer old enough to know better, and a doctor ta boot. I'm surprised a person of yer caliber would indulge so deeply in the devil's brew."

"I wasn't in the mood to consider the consequences." Devlin heard Mrs. Hogarth shuffle about the room. The light dimmed a bit. Tempting fate, he cautiously opened one eye. "Have mercy."

"Oh no, not again." She ran and held the basin for him as he vomited what little contents remained in his stomach.

"Arrrgh."

"Arrrgh is right," Mrs. Hogarth growled. "I'm not a nursemaid."

Devlin groaned and rolled over, pulling his pillow over his head. "Leave me to die in peace."

"I'm leavin'. But I'll be bringin' ye back a remedy of me own."

Devlin's gut clenched at the thought of swallowing anything. He prayed death would come quickly and drifted back to sleep.

True to her word, Mrs. Hogarth returned all too soon.

"Do you have to be so loud in your comings and goings?" Devlin complained.

"I'm quiet as a mouse. 'Tis the bangin' in yer head and the moanin' in yer gut. Here, drink this down," she ordered.

"What is it?" he turned his head, and bolts of pain streaked through his brain. His stomach churned again. He tried to focus on her offering.

"It's good for what ails ye. Now, be a good patient and drink it down."

Devlin forced himself up on his elbows and stared suspiciously at the thick yellow liquid tinged with red. His stomach lurched.

"Hurry and drink it down," directed Mrs. Hogarth, "and hold yer nose while yer at it."

"Why?" He eyed the concoction suspiciously.

"Because it don't hold the odor of roses, that's why."

Devlin pushed himself up to the side of the bed and accepted his landlady's largess. Holding his nose with one hand, he gulped the drink.

"Yer turnin' an interesting shade of green," she said, unable to contain a giggle.

Devlin felt as though he'd retch again. "Remind me to teach you something about bedside comportment," he said, trying not to gag.

"Why? Yer sick by yer own fool hand. Ye don't think I'd treat a truly sick man like this, do ye?"

Devlin gave her a lopsided grin despite his condition. "You're a hard woman at times, Mrs. Hogarth. You're right." He scrunched his face up at the sour taste that remained in his mouth after swallowing the tonic. "What did I just drink?"

"Yer better off not knowin', but I promise, ye'll be feelin' better in no time at all. Now, just rest a bit more, and I'll bring ye somethin' to eat later." Mrs. Hogarth wiped her hands on her apron, took the glass from Devlin, and bustled out of the room.

"I don't think I'll be eating much today," he called after her, too weak to be certain she'd heard him. He took her advice though and slowly laid his head on the pillow.

Much to his surprise, he awoke later to the sounds of someone in his room. He popped open one eye and spied a young boy filling a tub with hot water. "Who are you?" Devlin asked, hoarsely.

"James, sir," he said smiling. "Me uncle's Edward Hogarth. He's taken me under his wing."

Devlin gingerly sat up on the side of the bed, inspecting the lad. "And why is that?"

"Me mum says I'm gettin' too big for me britches, and he should help do somethin' about it since me pa's dead." James headed to the door. He turned and looked at Devlin. "I'll be bringin' another bucket, and then you can have yerself a nice warm bath."

Devlin smiled, thinking James reminded him of someone, himself perhaps. Or maybe it was just that all young boys got into trouble sooner or later; it was just sooner for James.

The interruption of the boy filling the tub had temporarily

distracted Devlin from himself and his sad state. Reevaluating his physical being, he realized Mrs. Hogarth was right. He did feel better.

Devlin slowly stood, his hands pressed to both temples, and focused on the tub to prevent the room from spinning. He tested the water with one hand. The temperature was so inviting that he quickly stripped out of his clothes and stepped into the tub, sinking low, with his knees above the water. A satisfied groan slipped from his throat.

The door creaked open after a quick rap of warning. "I see yer better," Mrs. Hogarth said from the doorway, hands on hips and a wide grin on her face. "James is on his way, but said ye was still in bed. I thought I best check."

Devlin slouched down as far as he could in the small tub. "Mrs. Hogarth, I would appreciate you turning your back. I'm not used to bathing in front of women. Have you lost your delicate senses?"

"I apologize to ye, Lord Ravensmoore. I lost me delicate senses years ago. It's good to see ye still have yers." She chortled and turned her back. "I'll bring up a tray for ye when yer done bathin'."

"Just have young James bring the tray, Mrs. Hogarth. That way I won't surprise you, or *my* delicate senses."

She quickly left the room, a wake of laughter floating on the air. Left alone, Devlin's thoughts drifted to Madeline.

Now that he felt better, he wondered what he could have done or said differently. *It's hard to think when someone is stepping on your heart. Perhaps I reacted without thinking things through. I allowed my heart instead of my head to rule the conversation.*

Another rap on the door. Devlin steeled himself for the reappearance of Mrs. Hogarth. "It better be a member of the male species, or I'm moving out," he barked.

"I never knew you to have anything against women,

Ravensmoore." Melton entered the room with a large tray of food and a prankish grin on his face.

"Melton. I didn't expect to see you until tomorrow. Don't tell me you and the countess had a falling-out as well."

Melton set the tray of food on the cluttered desk, picked up a sandwich, and took a huge bite. "Mmmm, good," he muttered, chewing away and shaking his head at the same time.

"Well. Why did you return? Not because of me, I hope. I wouldn't want to be responsible for coming between the happy couple," Devlin said dryly.

Melton swallowed. "I would not be here of my own accord, no matter how fond I am of you." He grinned, a piece of lettuce stuck between his front teeth. "I was having an enjoyable time with Lady Gilling, most enjoyable."

"Then what on earth are you doing here?" Devlin asked, arching a brow. He had a feeling he was not going to like what Melton had to say.

His friend took another bite of the sandwich and continued talking while he ate. "The countess and I came back to fetch you and Lady Madeline and discovered you had quarreled."

"Is that what she called it?" Devlin muttered under his breath. "And we call them the gentler sex."

Melton sat down in a chair close to the table. "We have to return to the hospital tomorrow. God knows when we'll be free of Langford again. What are you going to do?"

"Nothing," Devlin said. "I'm going to do nothing."

Melton picked up yet another sandwich. "The countess says Lady Madeline is upset."

"*She's* upset? *She's* upset?" he repeated in disbelief. "*She rejected me.*" He hit the surface of the water with his fist, splashing Melton.

Melton jumped up. "I don't need a bath!" He took a nearby towel and wiped at his waistcoat. "So you're just going to let her go. I thought you liked a challenge. I think you'll be an incredible doctor, but when it comes to women…you have a lot to learn." Melton sat down and continued eating.

"I suppose you, on the other hand, are an expert?"

Melton snorted.

The door creaked open, and James entered the room struggling with a bucket of hot water that sloshed all over the floor. "I'll be heatin' yer bath, yer lordship." He stopped to catch his breath. "Though I fear the water's coolin' fast."

"Don't just sit there stuffing your face. Help the boy," Devlin ordered, splashing water at Melton.

Picking up the bucket, Melton tested the water with his finger, went to the tub, and poured the contents over Devlin's head. "Is this what you were waiting for, your majesty?"

The boy and Melton burst out laughing.

"That's not exactly what I had in mind." Devlin wiped the water from his eyes with the towel Melton tossed to him. "But it will do."

Melton refused to let go of the subject. "So, just what do you plan to do?"

"I'm returning to my estate. I'm leaving medicine."

James, who'd been mopping up the water, suddenly froze.

Melton nearly choked on his sandwich. "You've lost your mind."

"On the contrary."

"But why?" Melton stumbled over his words. "I thought you were committed for more than earthly reasons."

"I've got my reasons." Devlin picked up his soap, ready to scrub, and happened to spot James's expression of horror. "What's wrong, boy? Don't you feel well?"

James stared at him. "Don't go. Yer a good doctor."

"And how would you know that?" Devlin studied the boy more closely. "Are you all right?"

James showed Devlin the palm of his hand

Devlin grabbed the sides of the tub. "You're Jamie! You're the boy I operated on in the surgery. Why didn't you tell me?" The boy rushed from the room. Confused and ashamed, Devlin stared after him. "Melton. Bring him back here. I must apologize."

Moments later Melton returned with the boy. "Here he is. I suggest you curb your enthusiasm for leaving medicine."

Devlin donned a towel. "Come here, Jamie. Or is it James?"

"Me uncle calls me Jamie, but me aunt calls me James." Head down, he shuffled toward Devlin.

"I'm sorry if I upset you. May I see your hand?" He held his hand out toward Jamie.

He opened his hand to show the scar. "It's all better, yer lordship."

Melton hovered over the boy. "Does it ever hurt?"

"Sometimes I get a stitch, but it goes away."

Devlin rubbed his thumb over the scar. "Can you use it?"

"Yes, yer lordship." Jamie wiggled his fingers, and they laughed.

"That does my heart good this day, Jamie. I'm glad that whatever you choose to do with your life, you'll be doing it with both hands."

"You're a fine doctor, yer lordship. I would have lost me hand without ye, says Dr. Langford. Me aunt Edna wanted to surprise ye, and that's why she didn't tell ye who I was. Said she thought ye were still too drunk to notice."

Devlin winced. "I'm sorry, Jamie. Let this be a lesson to you about the danger of drink. Now go get your aunt so I can apologize to her as well."

Devlin stood outside the church doors two days later. He longed to make peace with God and repent of his drunken self-indulgence that had done nothing to resolve his problems except to give him a roaring hangover and loss of esteem from his landlady, who heretofore thought him fairly flawless for a member of the male species.

Gathering storm clouds and a flash of lightning in the distance fit perfectly with his inner thoughts and sense of encroaching ruin. He hesitantly opened the door and entered the stone building.

No one sat in the pews, and the stained-glass church windows didn't shine or cast its sparkling colors throughout God's house. His remorseful soul aligned within this atmosphere, and the full weight of what he'd done crashed upon him like waves on a stormy sea.

"Forgive me." He walked toward the front of the church and knelt at the altar. "Forgive me, Lord, for my thoughtless act of wallowing in drink. I have disappointed You, I have disappointed those who thought me trustworthy and decent, and I have disappointed myself. A model of what a man should be, I wasn't, for the lad Jamie who attended me and thought so highly of me since his operation. All I can do is beg Your forgiveness. Give me strength to lean on You and not drink to solve my troubles."

A wave rolled toward Madeline, climbing higher until it crested and collapsed into miniature waves at her feet. She chased the ripples back into the sea, water and sand squishing between her toes.

"Isn't this simply wonderful?" she yelled over the roar of the surf. She spread her arms wide pretending to fly with the seagulls, swooping and swaying. Hally mimicked Madeline's actions, following close behind. Their black bathing garments flapped in the heavy ocean breeze, giving them the appearance of earthbound birds.

Madeline and Hally laughed and collapsed in the sand just above the waves. "I'm so glad we came to Scarborough, even if it is too cold to swim." Madeline stretched out on her back, enjoying the surprisingly warm day despite the cool wind coming off the water. "I feel like an entirely different being. The sea is a tonic for me. Just breathe in the freshness of it, Hally."

"We've been here for two weeks, and every day you say the same thing." Hally touched her arm. "It's good to see you smile again, Maddie. You haven't been this happy for a very long time. We should have come sooner."

"I got caught up in memories of my father and couldn't find my way out of the past." Madeline sat up and started digging in the sand with her fingers, enjoying the cool, damp feel of it. "I still can't find my way in some matters," she said, but she refused to let the pain surface, choosing to concentrate on pleasant activities. Hally joined in Madeline's sand play, and soon they were engrossed in the task of building a castle.

They returned to the Watersprite Inn for a delicious evening meal of potato leek soup, salmon, and asparagus. Later they joined other guests in the parlor for a game of whist. This nightly ritual began the evening they arrived and continued with whoever wished to play.

"I am surprised," Lady Darby said, "that two lovely, young ladies like yourselves haven't been followed by some besotted beaus." She studied her cards.

Madeline watched the old woman carefully. Lady Darby, a widow for many years, flaunted a double chin, a keen eye, and a tongue for gossip.

"After all," she continued, "there is little to do here so close to the sea *after* the sun goes down. Wouldn't you agree, Mr. Smithe?" she asked her card partner.

"That would depend on what one has in mind of an evening." He winked at Madeline.

Lady Darby peeked over her spectacles, her owlish eyes bestowing a knowing look on first Madeline and then Hally.

Hally giggled and blushed. "They are far too busy to be following us, Lady Darby."

"So you are spoken for," Lady Darby said. "How intriguing. Do tell."

Madeline thought the woman too obvious, trying to worm her way into their confidences. She gently kicked Hally under the table in warning. "We are not spoken for, Lady Darby. I'm afraid Countess Gilling is giving you the wrong impression."

"They are studying under the tutelage of Dr. Langford from London. They will soon be physicians," Hally blurted out. "Lord Ravensmoore saved Madeline's life on the hunt field."

Madeline booted Hally under the table again, not so gently this time, and sent her a warning glance. Hally ignored her, declaring, "He's a courageous soul."

Lady Darby frowned. "No self-respecting gentleman would lower himself to work as a physician, dear. You must be mistaken."

Mr. Smithe cleared his throat and fidgeted with his cards.

"I am not mistaken." Hally slapped her cards on the table.

"Your mother will forbid it, Lady Madeline. I am quite certain she will not allow you to marry beneath your station. But once you do marry"—she looked about and lowered her voice—"you can always be discreet with your physician friend."

Madeline turned beet red and dropped her cards. "What a horrible thing to say."

"You go too far, Lady Darby," Mr. Smithe said, folding his cards. "There's no need—"

"I think we should excuse ourselves for the evening, Lady Darby," Hally interposed hastily. "I am quite tired from our day's activity."

"Just one moment." Lady Darby looked puzzled, then her countenance turned to dread. "Oh dear, now I remember."

Lady Darby's tone held Madeline captive in her seat.

"It is said that Countess Ravensmoore went mad when your physician-earl was only a boy. She died at Ashcroft Asylum. The Ravensmoore seed is tainted. But I daresay he did not tell you that."

Madeline shot to her feet. "What a horrible thing to say." Angry tears sprang to her eyes, and she fled the room, not wanting to make a further spectacle of herself.

She rushed out of the inn toward the cliffs above the sea. *He would have told me such an important fact. He said he would never betray my trust. But how well do I know him, really?* Thickening clouds and a brisk wind warned of an approaching storm, but Madeline took no heed. She ran toward the cliffs, her thoughts a whirlwind of confusion and rage.

"Oh God in heaven, it can't be true. It mustn't be true. Was I right to send him away after all? Is he like Vale and not to be trusted?"

Lightning streaked across the sky, briefly illuminating her path. The sea crashed against the rocks below. The rain soaked through her yellow muslin gown, and she shivered. Lady Darby's spiteful words stung like the sudden pelting rain that mixed with her angry tears.

"God, why do You punish me? You have taken away everyone I have ever loved," she shouted to the cloud-swept heavens. "I have fought the attraction I feel for Lord Ravensmoore. I have sent him away, not knowing if I could trust him, and yet even now, knowing of his mother, I feel like I've committed some grave error in judgment. Why do You turn Your back on me? You truly do not care for me…and once…a long time ago…I thought You loved me." She dropped her head in her hands and sobbed.

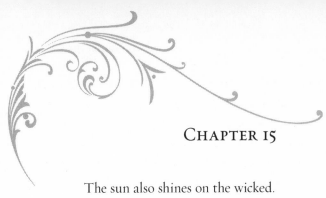

CHAPTER 15

The sun also shines on the wicked.

—SENECA,
ROMAN PHILOSOPHER,
MID-FIRST CENTURY

ON THE JOURNEY back home Madeline sank into melancholia. The weather did not help her mood with its slow, seeping, drizzle of rain. A thunderstorm or downpour would have been a welcome change from the incessant weeping of the clouds. Even Hally, usually a bright spot in Madeline's life, couldn't rouse her, so she took refuge in naps while Madeline stared, sleepless, out the carriage window.

After two long days of travel, the coach dropped Hally at Gilling, then entered the road to Richfield just before the afternoon meal. Madeline, relishing the idea of a hot bath, closed her eyes and breathed deep. It had finally quit raining.

The butler opened the door. "Welcome back, Lady Madeline."

"Good afternoon, Phineas. Would you have the footman take my trunk to my room and fill a warm bath for me?"

He took her cape and hat. "Immediately."

She passed through the elegant foyer and entered her mother's library. Mother had always loved this little hideaway. Her escape from the world, as she liked to call it. A place to keep her books and correspondence. Madeline knocked on the door and entered without waiting for permission. "Mother, I—"

Strange. Mother always enjoyed reading here this time of day. Madeline looked about and noticed the drapes were drawn. "How strange," she murmured. The drapes were rarely closed; Mother loved them open. Since it had finally stopped raining, perhaps her mother had decided to sit out in the garden. Madeline stepped out on the terrace leading to the gardens but did not see her mother anywhere.

Perhaps she and Lord Vale were out. But Phineas would have mentioned that to her. She ran up the stairs to her room, where the footmen were pouring water into a large tub. "Daisy? Are you in here?" she asked, looking about. "Have either of you seen Daisy?"

"Folding linens, I believe, yer ladyship. Shall I fetch her?" asked the taller of the two.

"Please." After they departed her quarters, Madeline removed her gloves and unpinned her hair, which fell about her shoulders in tangled disarray. Wiggling her fingers in the water of the tub, she judged the temperature near perfect.

"My lady." Daisy inched into the room, her arms full of bed linens and towels. "I didn't expect ye." She offered a small smile and set her load on the bed. "There now. Did ye have a nice holiday?"

"It left much to be desired, although the beach was lovely. I love the smell of the sea."

"Let me help ye out of your travel clothes." Daisy made quick work of discarding Madeline's dress and underclothes and helped her into the tub.

"Ahh. Heavenly. Daisy, would you scent the water with my jasmine?"

Daisy picked up a glass container from Madeline's vanity and poured a small amount of the perfume into the bathwater.

Madeline waved her hands under the water to disperse the

jasmine. "Now, dear Daisy. Sit down and tell me where Mother is and what's been going on since I left. You are being far too quiet, and I never even knew you possessed the ability."

Daisy looked away. "I really must go, my lady. There is much to do, and I wouldn't want to fall behind in my duties." The maid placed the towels and linens in the appropriate drawers.

"*I* am your duty, Daisy. Why don't you tell me what's going on around here while you wash my hair? You haven't looked me in the eye once since you entered my chambers, and you've never been shy about gossiping in my presence."

Daisy lathered Madeline's hair and rinsed it out. Madeline enjoyed this ritual so much that she nearly fell asleep as Daisy repeated the process. "You are not talking. That in itself tells me something is amiss. Out with it."

"Now don't go gettin' yerself all ruffled. I'm sure it's nothin' too serious. Your mother is a bit ill, but I'm sure she'll be up and about in no time at all."

"What kind of illness? Nothing serious I hope."

"She's overly tired. My mother has been takin' good care of her. You can go see her after yer bath."

"I believe my bath is finished. Grab my dressing gown and slippers, Daisy. Where is Lord Vale?"

"I'm not sure where he is, my lady." She held the rose-colored dressing gown out for Madeline, who slipped into it after drying off. "I'm going to see my mother right now. Pick out a suitable gown, Daisy, and I'll be back shortly."

Daisy nodded.

Madeline padded through two hallways that opened into an expansive atrium that led to her mother's suite of rooms. She knocked and, hearing no response, walked in. Taking in the scene, she tried to control the panic that threatened to overtake her. "Mother?"

"Oh, Maddie dear. I'm so glad you are home." She ran to Madeline and flung her arms around Madeline's neck and cried.

"Mother? What's wrong? Let me look at you." Madeline immediately noticed dark circles under her mother's eyes and a look of one lost. Not her mother at all. The drapes were drawn in this room as well. "Let's get some light in here." Madeline reached to draw back the drapes.

"No. Please don't, darling. The sun hurts my eyes, and I have an awful headache. I think I'll lie down for a while." She crawled into her bed and reached for a bottle at the bedside. "My medicine will help." She picked up a spoon.

"What medicine? What are you taking?" Madeline rushed to the bedside and grabbed the bottle from her hand. "What is this?"

"Laudanum. Now let me take my medicine so I can sleep for a while, Maddie."

Not knowing whether she should or shouldn't allow this, she slipped the bottle into the pocket of her robe. "I must speak to Vale first."

Madeline raced back to her room where Daisy waited. "Help me dress quickly, Daisy. How long has Mother been like this? Why didn't you tell me?"

Daisy looked at the ground. "Lord Vale told me not to. He's been different since ye left."

"I'll take care of Lord Vale," Madeline said, anger burning up her spine. "And where is Agnes? Where is your mother?"

"Fixin' some food for the countess. She won't even let Cook do it."

Madeline didn't bother putting her shoes on or asking Daisy to fix her hair. As soon as the last button popped into place she grabbed the bottle and went looking for Vale, finally finding him in the library.

"What have you done to Mother?" Madeline demanded.

Vale leaned back in the leather chair that her father used to occupy. "Welcome home, Lady Madeline. I see that your journey did nothing to improve your temperament."

"Mother is not herself. She's unsettled and restless. There are dark circles under her eyes, and she wanted to take this." She held out the bottle of laudanum.

"Yes. Grace has been having headaches, so I obtained the laudanum from the apothecary. She has improved only slightly and has been talking out of her head. I'm making temporary arrangements for her to stay at Ashcroft until she gets better." Vale closed the book that lay open before him.

"Ashcroft? Whatever for? It's a lunatic asylum! She's not insane. She suffers from laudanum poisoning, I suspect. If you believe I will let her go, you are mad and can take yourself off to Ashcroft."

"Be reasonable, Lady Madeline. I've done nothing to your mother." Vale placed his hands on her shoulders.

She shrugged him off and stepped back.

"We cannot care for her here. She needs the kind of treatment that Ashcroft offers. Perhaps they can bring her out of this stupor. Don't you see, you would be helping her to get well, not remain like she is."

Madeline pushed away from him when he dared step closer. "I don't care what you say; I will take care of my mother. I will make certain she gets well. If you love her, you will not speak of Ashcroft." Angry tears threatened. She wished that her mother had never married this dreadful man.

"I do love her. That is why I must insist that you do what is right." He poured a glass of port.

Madeline studied him. "You insist? Has a physician seen her?"

"I know what she needs. I spoke to the apothecary in York. I have everything under control."

Searching his expression, she found what she was looking for.

Arrogance. "How dare you." Losing control, she slapped him. "You're a monster! Leave this house at once!"

Vale remained amazingly calm and sipped his port. "You don't know me very well, *Lady* Madeline, if you think I would leave Richfield."

Unperturbed, he continued. "You have a lesson to learn, and I am just the man to teach you. Richfield is my home now."

Madeline stormed from the room. *I must be careful. I must use my common sense, or he will take it out on Mother. He is so devious no one would ever know what a fiend lurks behind his handsome face. Please, God, protect us from this evil.*

Agnes wiped the tears from her eyes when Madeline entered her mother's rooms.

"She sleeps again. She remains the same," Agnes said, bitterly.

"The same as what? What happened while I was in Scarborough?"

"I'm not sure. I thought it a fever at first or the beginnin' of a serious illness. She became weaker and weaker with each passin' day. Talkin' out of her head and then not talkin' at all. Sleepin' and then restlessly pacin'."

Madeline sat down on the side of the bed and tenderly laced her fingers through those of her mother—a morning ritual they'd shared many years ago when her mother would wake her. "Mama, can you hear me?"

No response.

"No matter what happens, I will not leave you." She squeezed her mother's limp hand, then raised it to gently touch her cheek. "I will not let you go."

No response.

Her mind searched wildly for answers. What to do? Ravensmoore. No. Perhaps. He offered the obvious advantage. His medical expertise, plus the added benefit of being on her side and willing to do anything to help her. The trip to Gretna Green had told her that much. She'd lost her father, and Ravensmoore had been unable to save him, but did she have any choice but to trust him now that Mother's life was at risk? He knew her mother, he understood her situation, and he might be able to help her.

"Agnes, send word to Ravensmoore that he is needed immediately."

"An excellent plan, Lady Madeline."

"Be careful that Vale does not know. Send Donavan."

Madeline climbed into bed with her mother and cuddled close. She began singing a lullaby, one her mother used to sing to her and her siblings at night. Only it wasn't meant to rock her mother to sleep. It was meant to reach that place deep inside of her, where she would hear, hold on, and know she wasn't alone.

"Don't be afraid, Mama. Don't be afraid. I've sent for Ravensmoore."

She fell asleep praying, *Lord, save my mother. Vale must not succeed.*

Madeline woke with a start as the door banged open and Vale entered his wife's room. Upon seeing Madeline, he stopped short.

Agnes edged her way into the room. Vale turned to her. "Agnes, I want you to prepare a trunk for Lady Madeline and then ready her for a short trip." He touched his wife's forehead.

Madeline slapped his hand away. "What are you talking about?"

"I plan to escort you to Ashcroft Asylum, where you will get the treatment you deserve. It is quite evident that the seashore was not enough to cure your melancholia."

Madeline wanted to scream her outrage, but she forced herself to maintain control. "Lord Vale, what do you think you are doing? You cannot send me to Ashcroft. You have no reason to have me committed, and you have no authority."

"Ah, but you're wrong. You're my stepdaughter, and I do so hate to see that you've diminished mentally since the death of your father." He flicked a fly off his cravat. "I've decided you are right. I am going to keep a very close eye on my wife. But you are dangerous, Lady Madeline. You are dangerous to others, and that cannot be tolerated. You attacked me upon your return yesterday and slapped me, to say nothing of pulling a pistol on me when Grace and I eloped. I think that should keep you in Ashcroft long enough. Others have been committed for lesser offenses."

A knot tightened in Madeline's stomach. She thought of Amanda and how abused she'd been at the hands of the keepers, and perhaps even by Vale. "You are mad. I've done nothing to deserve admittance to Ashcroft. I've sent for Lord Ravensmoore. He will help us. You cannot deny Mother a physician."

Ignoring Madeline, Vale turned on Agnes. "What are you waiting for, woman? Did I not tell you to get her packed? She's lucky I'm being so generous. I should just take her as is, and she can be admitted as a pauper."

Agnes took a step back and looked to Madeline for direction.

Vale's hand clamped over Agnes's upper arm. "I give the orders around here. Now do it," he hissed.

Agnes winced, and Madeline capitulated. "Go, Agnes. Do as he says."

Agnes sent her a look of warning to be careful and left the room.

"Don't take all day about it," he growled. "I've things to do. And Ravensmoore will not be coming to your aid. I intercepted the message." He held the letter out for her to see, then ripped it to pieces.

"Where is Donavan? He carried the letter."

"I interrupted Donavan's delivery. He's in the stables where he belongs. No one is going to help you."

Madeline seethed and pointed a finger at him. "You *will not* interfere with the care Mother needs, and you are not to hurt or abuse anyone in this household."

Vale looked at her nonplussed. "What do I care? You mean nothing to me. I will go where I want, do as I please, and use or misuse as much of Richfield's money and her people as I wish. As long as Grace is under my care, I will have complete control over you."

"You will never have control over me, you evil snake."

"Ah, but I already do. You see, my dear, I will tell Mr. Sullivan to take great care of you. However, if you cause trouble, your mother will suffer for your misdeeds. Am I clear?"

Madeline looked from her unconscious mother to Vale. Fear invaded every pore and paralyzed her ability to pray. "You cannot do this."

"Now you will cooperate and get yourself to the waiting coach or"—his hand reached out and touched her mother's index finger, bending it backward just enough that Grace flinched—"I will break her finger."

Madeline gasped. "Don't! I'll go with you."

"I thought you might be persuaded. Now say your good-byes."

Madeline kissed her mother on the forehead and whispered in her ear, "I'll find a way, Mother. Somehow I *will* find a way." She hadn't felt so helpless and angry since her father had died, but that had been different. That was an accident, and for the first time a door of understanding opened in her heart for Ravensmoore. He had tried to save her father. Vale was intent on controlling Mother to get what he wanted. Would he go so far as to kill?

She left the room and took one backward look to see Mother in the deep sleep of laudanum. *Lord, surround this house with Your mercy and protection. Don't let Vale hurt anyone.* She wished she still possessed the pistol that Ravensmoore claimed when she'd pointed it at Vale.

Vale took her by the arm and walked her downstairs where Agnes, Daisy, and Phineas waited in the foyer. "Now tell them to behave themselves, or you and your mother will suffer the consequences."

Madeline hugged Agnes and then Daisy. With tears in their eyes she stepped back and looked at the three of them. "I must ask you all to keep this in confidence. Not for my safety but for Mother. I know that you will listen to what Lord Vale says no matter how much you may want to do otherwise. We must all keep my mother, your countess, safe. Is that understood?"

They nodded. "God speed, Lady Madeline," Phineas said. "We will pray for you."

"The coach awaits." Vale guided Madeline outside.

The footman opened the door and Madeline climbed inside to come face-to-face with Mr. Sullivan. Taking a chance, she pleaded, "You cannot condone this act! It is criminal!"

"I take my orders from Lord Vale, my lady." He reached in his pocket and pulled out a flask. "Drink up. A special brew for the occasion. We find it easier to transition patients into the asylum with a little help."

Vale entered the coach and sat next to her with Sullivan opposite. He took the flask from Sullivan and tipped it to Madeline's lips. "Cheers, my dear."

CHAPTER 16

'Tisn't life that matters!
'Tis the courage you bring to it.
—SIR HUGH WALPOLE,
FORTITUDE

*D*EVLIN SAT IN the massive library at Ravensmoore contemplating, for the thousandth time, his decision to leave medicine. Only weeks away from completing his education and he'd quit. That's what it came down to. He missed medicine. Misery had befriended him.

"You have visitors, sir," announced Hummel, the butler. "A Dr. Melton and Countess Gilling. They appear most anxious to see you."

"Most anxious, indeed." Melton stood in the doorway. "We must talk with you at once, Ravensmoore." Melton gently pulled Hally in after him as Hummel quietly withdrew.

Devlin rose to his feet, bowing graciously to his guests. "This is an unexpected surprise. I'm happy to see you, but from the stricken look on your faces I know this is not a social visit. Come, sit down and tell me what is wrong."

Devlin showed them to a cozy arrangement of chairs. "Now, what is it?"

Melton looked at Hally. "I think Lady Gilling should explain. Tell him all of it."

"Madeline told you that she and I were going on holiday in Scarborough," Hally began, nervously fidgeting with her reticule.

"Yes, she mentioned it the last time I saw her. Has something happened to her?" He leaned forward in his chair.

"Yes, I'm afraid so." Hally went on to explain the devastating outcome of their trip, the evening Lady Darby told Madeline about the Ravensmoore legacy of madness.

"That's what you've come to tell me?" His heart raced. "And now you know as well." Devlin stood and walked to his desk. "I suppose she was quite horrified. However, I don't understand why you felt compelled to come in person. Why not simply send a messenger?"

"There's more," Melton said ominously. He nodded at Hally. The look that passed between them increased Devlin's anxiety tenfold.

Hally drew a deep breath. "Yesterday Vale committed Madeline to Ashcroft Asylum. Last night Agnes sent word to me through Donavan, and I immediately contacted Charles." She sent a grateful gaze his way. "By then it was too late to see you, so we rode out first thing this morning to tell you ourselves."

His heart squeezed in agony. "Vale—that devil!" Devlin stood raking both hands through his hair. "I must go to her."

"I am so afraid for her." Hally wiped at tears slipping down her cheeks. "Agnes is desperate and reports that Countess Vale is ill as well. Something must be done. We will do anything to help."

"The first thing to be done is to get her out of the asylum." Devlin hit the desk with his fist. "Then I'll deal with Vale."

Hummel entered the room with a pot of tea, an assortment of breads and cheeses, and a pitcher of lemonade balanced on a silver tray. He placed the tray on the table between them. "Will there be anything else, sir?"

"It appears I will be leaving, Hummel. Please pack."

"Yes, sir." Hummel's expression was one of surprise, but he said nothing and left the room after serving them.

"So you're leaving me again." A young woman in a wheelchair entered the room, pushed by another close to her age. "Forgive me for interrupting. I could not help but overhear."

Melton was instantly on his feet.

"You mean you couldn't help eavesdropping, don't you, Snoop?" Devlin said.

"I never eavesdrop," she said, smiling charmingly.

"We'll discuss that later, dear sister." He stood and placed a quick kiss on the forehead of each girl. "I've no time for pleasantries, I'm afraid."

"She's bored again," the younger girl said, smiling.

"So it would seem."

"Snoop." Devlin cleared his throat. "I mean, Victoria. I would like you to meet my friends, the Countess Gilling and Dr. Melton." He turned to his guests. "My sister, the Lady Victoria, and our youngest sister, Lady Mercy."

Melton bowed. "Ravensmoore, you said you had sisters, but you never mentioned how charming they are."

"I'm surprised he mentioned us at all. We are well-kept secrets," Victoria said. "And is this your lady, Dr. Melton?"

"Indeed," Melton said, and gently reached for Hally's hand.

Victoria studied Hally carefully. "My, you certainly are beautiful. Do sit down, Dr. Melton. We didn't mean to cause a stir. It's just when I heard that our brother is leaving…well, I couldn't help myself."

Devlin quickly informed his sisters about what had happened and why he must leave. "Victoria and Mercy, please show the countess where she may freshen up while I discuss this situation with Dr. Melton."

"Getting rid of us, are you, brother?" Victoria patted Devlin's cheek. "Perhaps we can all visit longer at another time. Come with us, Countess; we will leave the men to discuss their plans." The three exited the room as the men regained their seats.

Devlin gathered his thoughts, struggling to keep his fear for Madeline under control. Nothing had prepared him for the blow that Lady Gilling had delivered.

Melton said politely, "How long has Lady Victoria been confined to a wheelchair?"

"She's been sick since childhood with few respites between bouts of illness. She grows weak frequently. Although bloodletting is advised, I've decided to try other remedies of my own making and hope that God will smile on my efforts and heal my sister. Victoria finds it easier to get about in the chair with Mercy's help. She says it gives her more independence." He frowned. "Better than lying about all day. It's hard to see her like this though. She longs to be self-sufficient." Changing the subject, he said, "Now, let's talk of the crisis at hand."

"Langford told me that Ashcroft was still looking for a capable physician." Melton looked at Devlin with meaning.

"I'm following you. It's the best way for me to enter Ashcroft. I'll locate Lady Madeline and get her out as fast as possible."

"I'll come with you."

"No, you won't. It will appear suspicious."

"Then what? You cannot expect me to abandon you. You may need help."

"This is my problem. I appreciate your bringing Countess Gilling here and informing me of Madeline's dilemma, but I must enter the asylum alone, as Dr. Grayson, not Ravensmoore."

"Agreed. Tell me, why did you leave York? I believe old Langford was actually disappointed. I know I was."

"I had a fool notion in my head that Lady Madeline might be displeased that I was pursuing medicine instead of her. I decided to postpone my studies and return home to think this through, pray, and make certain I am not being selfish. I knew I had to tell her about my mother, but I didn't dare broach the subject of my mother's illness for fear that she would never understand."

"I don't think you give the woman credit. I believe she admires you because you were following your heart regarding medicine and not taking the easy road. You had her respect."

"I'm not certain I would call it respect, Melton. She still struggles with the memories of her father. I do not think she can love me. She rejected me. What am I to make of that?"

"Only Lady Madeline will be able to tell you, but only if you can rescue her from Ashcroft. You have a difficult task ahead of you, Ravensmoore. Let me know how I can help."

He and Melton stayed up half the night planning a strategy. Devlin left before dawn and traveled east from Ravensmoore to Ashcroft. He'd left Melton and Countess Gilling in Victoria's capable hands, with the understanding that he would send word to Melton in York as soon as possible.

The driver banged on the roof of the traveling coach. After Devlin had traveled all day, stopping only briefly for dinner, Ashcroft was near. Peering out the window through the deepening twilight, Devlin again assessed the building and the vast brick wall that surrounded the asylum. Blocking out the pain of their last meeting, he prayed for her safety.

He prepared himself mentally for any questions that Sullivan might ask, hoping the manager was too self-absorbed to ask for his paperwork. He needed to get Madeline safely away and as quick as possible. It was imperative that Sullivan not discover the real reason he'd returned to Ashcroft. If the man uncovered the truth, it would put Madeline and her mother in further danger. And then how to protect Countess Vale from her dangerous husband would become the next obstacle. *Lord, I'm going to need a miracle.*

A guard stopped the coach at the entrance. "State yer business."

Devlin leaned out the coach window. "I've come to see Mr. Sullivan. I am Dr. Grayson."

The heavyset guard recognized him. "'Bout time." The guard shifted from one foot to the other. "Hope yer plannin' on stayin' awhile."

"Why is that?" Devlin asked.

"Ye'll be seein' soon enough. Best be gettin' on with ye." He waved them through the gate.

He imagined that Wiggins or some other patient had become violent. Devlin had the distinct feeling he should turn and leave while he still could. But if Madeline was here, he had no choice but to aid her.

The moment he entered the asylum, he knew he would not be leaving anytime soon.

Something is not right. People stare at me, and I know not why. So far away. Yet I know they are not. I wish they were. I wish they were, far, far away. Sleep. That's what I need. Sleep will make them go away and leave me in peace and the nightmare will be over.

Separated from reality by a misty curtain, Madeline observed her surroundings like a play upon the stage. She watched others shuffle past her. She couldn't speak; she couldn't open her mouth; she couldn't remember how. All was bedlam.

When she first arrived at the asylum yesterday—or was that the day before?—she'd wanted to run. She'd lost track of time. Entering an asylum as a patient committed for an underdetermined amount of time terrified her. But Vale knew she wouldn't do anything to jeopardize Mother's safety, and he'd enforced that with the drugs he'd forced down her throat.

Upon entrance to the women's quarters she gasped at the sight of the patients. Elderly and young women pointed at her. A gray-haired woman who looked to be in her forties walked about nodding her head and saying, "The king is coming. He's coming to see me. We'll have tea, and then we'll see." A woman about her own age raged and tried to get a manacle off her neck screaming, "I can't breathe! Help me!" She scratched at the iron until her neck bled. Madeline covered her ears and thought she'd go mad with the sights.

She looked for Amanda but couldn't find her. Instead she saw one tortured soul after another—some beaten and rocking to and fro on the floor, others chained and embracing each other for warmth. Madeline prayed she would awake from this nightmare and be safe at home in her bed with Nosey curling up around her feet. And then a manacle clamped around Madeline's neck.

"Welcome to hell, my lady."

Madeline grabbed at the fetter around her neck. Another manacle clamped around one ankle, and she found herself trapped with the other "unfortunates."

She'd lost track of time with more drugs forced upon her. Rough hands lifted her by each arm and dragged her into the cold-water treatment room. The skin on her bare toes was raw and sore, her dress ripped and dirty. A man's gruff voice broke into her cocooned thoughts. "We'll be needin' ye to do some work 'round here. Maybe the tank will wake ye from yer stupor."

Shoved under water she struggled and twisted, but two pair of hands held her fast…no escape. Frigid suffocation. Terror claimed her mind. Lungs burned. *God help me.*

Brutal fingers tangled in her hair and yanked her above the icy water. Madeline sucked in air and was again plunged under the wave. Cruel, muted laughter stung her ears. Panic rose. She pushed against unrelenting hands, aching for breath. *Please help me.* She crested the surface and gulped more air, preparing for the worst.

"The opium's made ye daft but docile enough." Two men imprisoned her in steel grips and hauled her to the side of the bath, laughing and telling crude jokes. "Ye still livin'?"

Madeline gasped and choked.

"We thought that would wake ye, but we better be sure. Seems ye lost yer tongue." The smaller man grabbed her hair and held her under until she nearly lost consciousness then pulled her up close to him. "A hard bit of baggage ye've been to control." His stinking breath wafted over her face.

As she gulped in air, her lungs ached with the effort. "Let me go." She coughed.

"'Tis going to be a full moon tonight, *my lady,*" the larger man said, then yanked her away from his friend and pulled her tight against his chest. "You know mad folk bay at the moon, don't ye?"

Mind-numbing awareness battered its way toward consciousness. "Stop it! I'm not mad!"

"Yer in Ashcroft, darlin'. Ashcroft Insane Asylum. That makes ye mad. Can't be doin' no bay'n inside; 'tis not polite. I think ye ought to sleep outside tonight. Maybe I'll come visit ye later." He laughed, then whispered in her ear, "You'll be wantin' a body to keep ye warm."

She gasped at the intimate suggestion. They dragged her onto a small balcony and chained her to a wall by one wrist. Even if she'd had the strength to try, there was no hope of escape. Her cheek against the hard, cold stone she moaned, "God help me," and shivered in the chilly air. Water pooled around her still form. Her burgundy walking dress clung to her, a frigid shroud of death.

"God help me. Devlin," she whispered.

Chaos surrounded him. Devlin recognized the symptoms: fever, chills, backaches, headaches, and blister-like pustules. Smallpox! He'd walked straight into a wretched smallpox epidemic. Blast the scourge.

Looking up from the woman he'd just examined, he knew she was in the stage that offered temporary relief. The rash covered her. Within a matter of days the disease would progress. He grabbed a nearby attendant. "Where's Sullivan?"

"Probably hidin' out in his office, the squeamish worm. He's not set foot in here since the outbreak."

"We must plan to prevent further spreading of the disease. When did it begin?" Devlin asked.

"About ten days ago."

Devlin looked at the attendant in astonishment. "Ten days! Why wasn't a doctor sent for earlier?"

The man shrugged and hurried on his way.

Rage swelled in Devlin. Madeline was here in this epidemic. He went in search of Sullivan. The manager sat in his office, surrounded by everyday luxuries, while the poor souls inside the asylum had very little to comfort them.

"Why in the name of heaven haven't you sent for help?" Devlin grabbed Sullivan by his lapels, yanking him to his feet. The smell of liquor, pungent. "You're drunk. Where is Lady Madeline Whittington? What have you done with her?" He threw the man back in his chair.

"She's here…somewhere," Sullivan mumbled, groping for his glasses.

Devlin slammed his fist down on the desk. "Where?"

Sullivan cowered. "I don't know. There are more than a hundred patients here. I can't keep track of all of them. You'll have to send some of the attendants to look for her."

"Tell me you haven't allowed anyone to leave the asylum, Sullivan. You have an epidemic here."

"You passed the guard, didn't you? He knew we could use someone like you. Other guards are posted to be certain no one leaves and no one enters."

"You're going to help me." Devlin grabbed Sullivan by the collar and ushered him out of the office and toward the locked door of the asylum.

"No!" Sullivan pushed away from him. "I can't go in there. I haven't had the vaccine either," he whimpered. "I haven't had the vaccine!"

Devlin let him drop to the floor in a heap. "How many of the patients and staff have been vaccinated?"

"Not sure." He slurred his words. "Some had Jenner's vaccine; some didn't. We have tried to separate the sick from the well, but..."

"You worthless toad. I'll do what I can, but be warned. If anything happens to Lady Madeline, I'll kill you...if the pox doesn't."

Back inside the asylum Devlin stood a moment, overwhelmed. Where could he begin to look for Madeline? The asylum, both massive and confusing, imprisoned maybe a hundred patients, but there were far more than a hundred rooms. He dare not waste precious time searching from room to room.

The stench from the sick nauseated him. Devlin leaned against a wall, closing his eyes for a moment, praying for wisdom.

"Here's another one, Doctor. Don't look like she'll last long," called an attendant.

He opened his eyes. His medical duties called, though his heart and body screamed for him to run, to search, to rescue Madeline from this nightmare.

"Put her over here," he directed, and then went to evaluate her condition.

Two keepers lowered a cot with the body of a thin, elderly woman on it. Devlin crouched down and touched her cheek. "She's burning up." The room already held at least ten cots.

He listened to her breathing, then scanned the pustules on her arms. They had broken open and scabbed over. Her breathing was labored; the disease attacked her lungs.

She could lose the battle at this stage in the progression of the disease. Devlin looked in the woman's eyes, but she was unable to focus on anything. The fever had taken over. He stood and gazed down at the frail body. The slight glimmer of a single, silver strand of a necklace caught his eye. Bending to examine it, he gently unraveled it from the cotton blanket. There was something strangely familiar about the locket attached to the chain. Devlin could not keep from opening it.

Time stopped.

Devlin struggled with the enormity of an emotion he thought he'd abandoned years ago. Hope. He sat on the floor next to the woman and stared at two tiny portraits, one of him and his brother and the other of his two sisters.

"It can't be true," he whispered in disbelief. "Mother."

CHAPTER 17

Earth hath no sorrow that Heaven cannot heal.
—THOMAS MOORE,
"COME, YE DISCONSOLATE"

*S*HE DIED...a long time ago. My father told me she was dead." Devlin choked back tears and slowly rose to his knees, then turned the woman's face gently toward him. "Mother?" The past rushed up and hit him with the force of a cannonball. "You can't be my mother."

Elethea Ravensmoore's eyes fluttered open briefly, and she smiled. "Devlin." Her green eyes brightened with joy for a moment and then closed, as if trying to capture and keep the vision of her son. Her labored breathing continued.

Devlin wondered if he'd only imagined his name on her lips. He gently placed her scab-covered hand in his and prayed. "I don't understand. Sweet sanity, how can this be happening? God, don't let her die, not after all this time. Please give her...give us...a second chance." He carefully lowered her hand to her side and placed the locket inside the top of her worn and faded dress. Anger ripped through him like a scalpel slicing flesh. He found it difficult to breathe, or believe. "How could this happen?" He stared at her frail form.

A hand reached out and touched his cheek, interrupting his thoughts. "I will care. I will watch."

"What?" Startled, he looked up. "Amanda." The young girl who'd never spoken a word since killing her father. He understood now how someone might kill his own flesh and blood as Amanda had done. He imagined himself capable of such a gruesome act if his father still lived. *How could he have left Mother here to rot? Why didn't he tell me she was still alive?* Devlin forced himself to push the dark thoughts away, afraid to examine them further, afraid they might destroy him.

"I watch," Amanda repeated softly, her brown eyes full of sympathy and something else, understanding, perhaps.

"You *can* speak." Devlin didn't hesitate. "Amanda, thank you," he said, taking both her hands in his. "Try to keep her as cool as possible. I must go now, but I will return as soon as I can."

Amanda stared at his hands, then gently pulled away and sat next to his mother on the floor. "I care." She applied a damp cloth to Elethea's forehead. Amanda had a better bedside manner than most of the keepers. He hated that word *keeper*, as if these poor patients were no better than animals.

Devlin could not escape the stench of urine and disease as he searched the asylum. The acrid odor filled every corner of the asylum. Devlin's impatience rose. He had to find Madeline. She was here somewhere.

Devlin continued through a long corridor that emptied into yet another room of the sick. Larger than the other rooms, this room held twenty cots arranged in a circle. A kind-faced woman kept vigil over the ill, hovering like a tireless angel of mercy and praying aloud as she ministered to all. He paused a moment, struck by her impossible task.

"I am Dr. Grayson and have only just arrived to assess the situation. How are you managing all these patients, madam?"

The woman wore a gray bonnet and dressed in a plain gray dress covered with a white apron smeared with the grime of the asylum and the filth of sick patients. "I find it easier to care for them like this." She turned within the circle. "They are easy to reach, and I can quickly detect a problem that might otherwise go unnoticed." She placed a cool cloth on the brow of a man whose face, riddled with pustules, resembled so many others.

"So I see."

"May I help you?" The woman's sea green eyes filled with compassion. "Noah told me we'd been blessed with the arrival of a physician. You must be the one."

Devlin nodded, studying the circular arrangement of the cots with interest. "Yes, I am he. What is your name?"

"Mrs. Sharpe. I'm the primary keeper for the women."

Devlin nodded his understanding. "How many keepers are here?"

"Six prayerful women, widows from the village, including myself, assist the female patients, and eight men aid the male patients. The rest fled when they could after the smallpox was discovered. They couldn't be stopped. We have one hundred ten patients, and thirty of them have smallpox. Soon more will be affected."

"I hate to ask more of you, Mrs. Sharpe, but would you look in on those in the far room at the end of the corridor until I get back? There is no attendant."

"I will do so immediately, Doctor. Where are you going? Perhaps I can help you."

"I must find a patient, Lady Madeline Whittington of Richfield. Do you know her?"

"How long has she been here? What is her appearance?"

"She was admitted yesterday and is a pretty young woman with dark curly hair."

Mrs. Sharpe shook her head. "I saw her briefly, when she first arrived. I am surprised they would accept a new patient at such a time. I suspect she's being kept in the area away from the pestilence."

"Can you tell me where that area is?"

He listened as she gave directions. "Thank you." Devlin quickly walked past the circle of infected patients and down another long, dark corridor. Through double doors at the end he found the area filled with inmates that showed no symptoms of smallpox. The staff and patients at the Guardian Gate Hospital were vaccinated against the disease; Dr. Langford made certain of it. Perhaps some of these patients were also protected from the disease.

Devlin wandered into a tiny nook. Nothing. Frustration filled him. *Jesus, help me find her.*

He glanced at the full moon through a high, barred window, a morbid reminder that Madeline didn't belong in this prison of madness.

He tried the door. Locked. Devlin peered through its tiny, dirty window to investigate. He squinted, trying to see beyond the door, but the filthy window hindered his vision. A sudden glimpse of movement caught his eye as he turned away. The abrupt action on the other side of the door left him bewildered. Had he actually seen something, or were his eyes fooling him?

He wiped the windowpane with his hand trying to get a better view. Two dark shapes wrestled in the moonlight on a tiny balcony. A large man harassed his victim.

"Stop!" Devlin gripped the bars.

The man froze and looked at him.

Devlin abandoned the window and put his shoulder to the heavy oak door, trying to force it open. The door refused to budge. *The fool on the balcony probably held the key.*

A huge shadow fell over him. Devlin jerked away, ready to do battle. Recognition flashed. Andrew Wiggins. "Help me."

Wiggins battered the door with several direct kicks. The sound of splintering wood rocked the silence, and the door crashed onto the balcony with a great thud. Wiggins grabbed the man who had retreated from his victim to seek escape and picked him up by the collar, tossing him through the shattered door and into the wall, where he crumpled into a heap.

Devlin hurried to the still form. He gently turned over her limp wet body. Panic seized him. Madeline lay outlined by the light of the moon. "Maddie. What did he do to you?"

Devlin cautiously picked her up in his arms, but the manacle, chained about her wrist, stopped him.

Wiggins did not hesitate. He reached past Devlin and grabbed the chain that held Madeline. Grunting with the effort, he pulled the iron from the wall. Wiggins carried the chain and followed as Devlin carried Madeline inside.

"Hold her," he ordered.

Wiggins took a step back. A look of terror crossed his face.

"Take her. You won't hurt her." Devlin then gently transferred Madeline into Wiggins's hesitant outstretched arms. Devlin removed his coat and spread it on the floor. "Lay her down here, and help me free her wrist."

Wiggins grunted. "I'll be back."

Devlin turned his thoughts and attentions to Madeline. He felt her moist face and neck. She was hot, fevered. From exposure or smallpox? He prayed it was exposure.

Wiggins returned with a hammer and chisel.

"How did you gain access to those?" Devlin asked, both grateful and concerned.

Ignoring the question, Wiggins gently adjusted Madeline's wrist, then went to work. The manacle fell away in moments under his skilled hands.

"What trade did you know on the outside before coming to Ashcroft?" Devlin asked, amazed.

Wiggins gathered the chains and towered over Devlin. "I was a blacksmith." He walked away and disappeared down the corridor. Devlin silently thanked God for Andrew Wiggins.

Madeline groaned.

"Lady Madeline. Maddie. I'm here. I'm going to help you. Can you hear me?" Devlin asked, hoping for a response. None was forthcoming.

He wrapped the coat around her soaked garments and gathered her in his arms, placing a gentle kiss on her fevered brow. "We're going to get through this, Maddie," he whispered into her ear. "We're going to get through this together. God will help us."

Devlin helped Madeline with the aid of one of the female attendants. In the privacy of one of the empty cells, as Devlin waited outside, the keeper removed Madeline's wet clothing, dressed her in a simple gown, and covered her with a moth-eaten blanket.

"It's one of the few decent blankets left in the entire asylum," she informed him. "There's not enough help to do the wash, and even if there were, there are few blankets."

Devlin examined Madeline to determine if she had contracted smallpox. She tossed and turned, calling out for her mother, but her body showed no signs of a rash or blisters. "I don't think the fever is from smallpox." He let out his breath and sat down, relief filling his soul.

"A blessing indeed," said the attendant, who placed a gentle hand on Madeline's head and prayed silently for a moment.

"I must find someone to sit with her, but we need every capable person to assist with those infected." Exhausted, Devlin put his head in his hands.

The woman's hand dropped to his shoulder. "God will provide. I will stay with her until someone else can be found."

Devlin forced himself to stand, secretly wondering if God would provide. It seemed hopeless. "Thank you." He felt Madeline's face and arms again for fever. She remained hot. "Try to keep her cool and continue to pray for her."

"Of course. I will pray for both of you, and I will beg God to deliver us safely from this plague."

Devlin had prayed before entering the world of medicine. He'd prayed for direction and wisdom, for God's guidance. Suddenly he realized how much he'd come to rely on prayer and the peace it usually brought him. But today he found no peace.

He returned to the area where his mother lay ill, afraid a sheet covered her face or that her body burned with the dead in the insatiable funeral pyre outside the asylum.

Why didn't these people have access to Dr. Jenner's smallpox vaccine? This could have been avoided if only the appropriate precautions had been put in place…if only. However, with no physician to look after the patients, and someone like Sullivan managing the asylum, it was a wonder it didn't happen sooner.

"Amanda," he said gently.

The girl pressed a cool rag against his mother's forehead and looked up.

"How is she? Any improvement?" he asked, hope skimming his heart.

"Same." Amanda gently pushed a gray strand of hair behind Elethea's left ear. "Same."

"Thank you for taking care of her. You should rest now. It's been a long day." Devlin pulled out his pocket watch. "Almost midnight. I've been here only a few hours, but it feels like days."

Amanda smiled wanly and gently continued her ministry of a cold cloth to his mother's forehead.

Devlin knelt beside Amanda. His mother's breathing seemed slightly improved. He studied his mother again. Sometimes before a person died, a patient would rally. And just when the family thought the worst had passed, the patient slipped away as though their soul were waiting for the right moment to depart.

"I'll stay. You go rest, Amanda." Devlin raised the young woman off her knees. "I'll call you if I need you."

Amanda nodded and moved off toward a pallet not far away, where she chose to sleep for the night. She knelt and folded her hands in prayer. Devlin wondered what she prayed for and stretched out on the cold floor next to his mother and slept.

He'd felt as though he'd just closed his eyes when someone shook him awake. "What is it?" he asked, confused for a moment. Then he remembered and groaned. Back muscles wrenched in opposition to each other. He sat up, blinking the sleep from his eyes, and discovered Mrs. Sharpe standing over him. "What's wrong?"

"Lady Madeline is awake."

Devlin breathed a sigh of relief. Gathering his thoughts, he looked at his mother. She continued to sleep peacefully.

Two more patients had lost their battles during the night. That made ten dead. How many more would be sick today? They couldn't even cover the bodies for lack of sheets and blankets for the living. Outside, the death fire glowed ominously against the foggy gloom of dawn.

An eerie silence accompanied Devlin as he picked his way around sleeping patients and through the shadows of the corridors to Madeline. The bars on the windows increased his unease. A stone-faced guard let him through the rusting gate. He realized that he'd passed this way before, when he'd treated Wiggins's wounds.

At last Devlin reached Madeline's cell. A female keeper looked up as he entered the tiny cell, and Madeline turned to look at him from where she lay on a cot.

"Lord Ravensmoore." She could hardly believe her eyes. He was here!

Ravensmoore leaned over her and smoothed her hair, combing it away from her face with his fingers, an unconscious, gentle act. He entwined his fingers with hers. "How are you feeling?"

She felt tears spring into her eyes. "Better." She reached out and tenderly touched his cheek in return. "I prayed you would find me. How did you know I was here?"

"Agnes sent Donavan to Lady Gilling to let her know what happened to you. Then Melton and Lady Gilling came to me at Ravensmoore."

Madeline pushed herself to a sitting position. "Is my mother all right?"

"I don't know. Melton is going to investigate."

"Vale is making her sick. Laudanum poisoning, I think. He's trying to kill her."

"Don't worry. We'll find a way to stop him. You're the one I'm concerned about right now." His hand covered her brow. "You still have a fever. I plan to take very good care of you until I'm certain you are well. The first thing we must do is get some decent food in you."

"I'm scared."

"Shhh. I'm here now. No more harm can come to you." He took her hand and pressed it to his lips gently. She shivered, whether in delight or fear, she did not know. Now that she knew the horrors of this place, the agonies of the insane, how could she love him?

"Lord Ravensmoore, I must know something." She paused.

He smiled. "So many questions for one so sick. What's on your mind?"

She blurted out the question. "I must know the truth. Was your mother insane?"

Madeline felt his fingers clench at the words. He cleared his throat, about to say something, then appeared to change his mind. "I must know." She searched his eyes. "Please."

"You don't understand. But how can you? I don't understand

myself," he whispered, turning away from her. "She's here. My mother is *still* here. She's alive...for now."

"Alive?" Her eyes widened with shock. "But I thought she was dead."

"So did I." He raked a hand through his hair. "I discovered her alive only a short time ago, but she is ill. Gravely ill."

Madeline saw in his eyes the pain of the little boy who had lost his mother so long ago. Her heart went out to him. "Look at me."

He turned to her, unshed tears begging for release from his exhausted, unshaven face. The anguish of so many years of pent-up emotion lay bare for her to see. She wrapped her hands around his and could feel the release of his shaky breath.

"I would have visited her if my father had let me. But he didn't, and then he said she died." His voice cracked. "My father arranged the funeral, but I wasn't permitted to see her body. Now I know why."

She gripped his hands, trying to console him. But this revelation was so much bigger than the two of them. She didn't know what else could be done for him. She watched him squeeze his eyes shut, as if trying to block the memory.

"The coffin in the family cemetery must be empty because she's here, alive. All this time she has been buried away in this hellhole. I don't know if she's sane or not."

"I'm so sorry." Madeline gently leaned away and studied him. "It's not your fault. You need rest, or you will make yourself ill."

"I can't sleep. There's too much to be done, and I'm the closest thing they have to a physician." He wiped his face on his shirtsleeve. "Forgive me."

"Why? Because you were done a great injustice as a child? Because you ache for your mother and yourself?"

"Because I didn't tell you about her. Lady Gilling told me how you found out. You must have thought me as deceitful as Lord Vale."

"Shhh. It doesn't matter now." She put her finger to his lips. "I know you would have told me eventually."

He gazed at her, his face solemn. "There's more. You're not yet well, and I don't want to alarm you, but this must be said."

Her heart raced. "You're frightening me. What's wrong?"

Ravensmoore stood and began to pace restlessly. "There's a smallpox epidemic in the asylum. It's inevitable that death will come to many."

Madeline felt sick with dread. Her stomach twisted in knots. "No," she whispered. Her fear of death and disease threatened to strangle her, but she refused to let it, searching instead for strength. "How many are ill?"

"Around thirty out of over a hundred inmates. The keepers are helping the best they can." His tone turned urgent. "Lady Madeline, have you received the vaccine?"

"Yes. Mother had everyone at Richfield vaccinated after my brother and sister fell ill with the dreadful disease. What about you? Were you vaccinated?"

"Of course. Langford made certain all the medical students received Jenner's vaccine."

"I must get out of here soon. Mother must be protected from Vale."

"No one leaves. The guards make sure of that. But as soon as everything is under control, we will go together to get your mother. Even though you have had the vaccine, I don't want you exposed to anyone who may be ill. You are not yet over the fever and must regain your strength."

"Can you get any help?"

"I don't know. I won't leave with so many sick, and I won't leave without you and my mother. Melton knows I'm here to get you out. He might come. I don't want to leave you alone."

"Don't worry about me. Go to your mother, Lord Ravensmoore, and make the most of the time she has left. Perhaps with you here, she will survive. She must be very strong to have survived all this time."

"Yes. But I'm not sure what price her mind and body have paid after all this time. And I am very worried about you too. You've been through so much." He gripped her hand.

"I'll be fine," she said. "Go. Your mother and the others need you."

She watched him leave and felt a strange new strength replenish her spirit. He needed her.

CHAPTER 18

The heart will break, yet brokenly live on.
—LORD BYRON

*T*HE STENCH OF illness filled the air as Devlin found his way back through a maze of interconnecting hallways. Fear and a sense of urgency pumped through his weary body as he thought about what to do next. He felt inadequate to the huge task ahead of him—not only fighting a smallpox epidemic, but also facing the possible second loss of his mother and the danger of rescuing Madeline.

Entering the area where his mother lay, Amanda by her side, he breathed a sigh of relief. Pulling up a short-legged stool, he sat down next to her and Amanda. "How does she fare this morning, Amanda?" He spotted Mrs. Sharpe across the room. "I checked on Lady Madeline. Thank you. Now, I need your help."

She nodded. "What can I do?"

"Do you know where the patient records can be found?"

"They are kept in Mr. Sullivan's office. What you are thinking is very dangerous. He guards those records well, but I know just who can get them for you."

"Good. Let me know when I can see them."

"As soon as possible." She left to seek the assistance she needed.

Devlin turned his attention to Amanda and his mother. "How is she?"

Amanda smiled tentatively. "The same." She wiped his mother's spotted face with a dampened cloth.

Devlin felt his mother's cheeks and neck. "She's still fevered but is a bit improved. Her breathing is not good, though. Amanda, see if you can find another pillow to put under her head. It will make her breathing easier."

Amanda nodded and rose from the floor to search for a pillow. Devlin watched her walk away, her dirty skirt brushing the floor. He wondered again why she'd killed her father.

His mother groaned.

"I'm here, Mother. It's your son, Devlin. How are you feeling?" He gave her hand a gentle squeeze. "Can you hear me?"

She weakly squeezed his hand and tried to speak. Her tongue licked over her cracked lips. "Thirsty."

"I'll get you some water." He walked over to the bucket of water that sat on a small wooden table in the corner of the room. Picking up the well-worn ladle, he poured water into one of the cups, smelled it, and then tasted it. He detected no odor or other sign of impurity.

Devlin squatted next to his mother and put an arm under her shoulders to support her neck. "Sip slowly." Devlin watched her struggle to drink. He didn't think it possible for her to survive. Death now claimed nearby patients, and still she clung to life. Maybe Madeline was right. Maybe she would fight the disease if she knew she had something to look forward to.

"Devlin," his mother whispered. "You are real. I thought you were a vision." She explored her son's face. "How?" The wretched coughing overtook her.

"Drink some more water. You don't have to talk." Devlin struggled with the warring emotions that battled within him. His father's face kept flashing before him. How could the man betray them in such a cruel way?

Elethea recovered with difficulty from the coughing spell. "How did you get here?" She reached up and touched his face with her pox-covered hand. "How did you find me?"

He gave her the simplest answer he could. "I have been studying medicine and was summoned here to help with the smallpox epidemic. I had no idea you were here. What happened the day you were committed, Mother? Do you remember?"

Elethea's eyes focused on the wall in front of her. "I shall never forget."

"Will you tell me about it?"

"It's not pleasant, Devlin. Are you certain you want to hear?"

"I've wondered about it all these years. The girls were too young. And...you are the only one who can tell me."

"The only one? Your father?"

"He died four years ago. You could not have known."

"Your brother?"

"I'm sorry, Mother. Edward was lost at sea, two years ago."

Tears welled in her eyes. "Then you are the earl. You have a right to know the truth." She cleared her throat and haltingly told her story.

"I caught your father in bed with another woman. He was enraged and did not care to take into consideration any feelings I might have on the subject. He defended his mistress as they lay together in my bed! I remember the smile of satisfaction on her face...my deep sense of shock and rage."

She stopped for a moment, a faraway look in her eyes as the past engulfed her, intruding into the present. "I ran from the room, their laughter ringing in my ears. I didn't know what to do. I felt so betrayed, so humiliated, so hurt. I stormed out of the house with no sense of where I was going or what I was going to do. All I knew was that I had to get away from him and the betrayal he'd brought to our marriage bed."

"Where did you go?"

"I walked straight into the woods. I think I wanted to die because, under any other circumstances, I would never have done anything so utterly stupid. Rage is a strange emotion. It was almost dark. A sudden storm hit. I was terrified, and then the wolves came. Two of them."

"Wolves. How did you survive?"

"I almost didn't. It was so dark, except for the fingers of lightning that showed me the path. I picked up a large stick and fought them off as best I could. It was fear that kept me alive."

"How did you get away? Did Father come after you?"

"No," she whispered, the agony of that evening evident in her eyes. "No. Your father never left the house. You see, he was entertaining his mistress while I was nearly devoured by hungry wolves. It was Donavan who saved me. My maid witnessed my husband's betrayal. I remember her calling after me as I fled the house, but I didn't stop. I couldn't face anyone."

"Donavan? The Richfield's groom?" Devlin asked in amazement.

"So that's where he went. He was hotheaded and bold. He saved me from those beasts. My maid went to him and explained what happened. He took a horse from the stable and came after me. If it wasn't for Donavan, I would have died that night."

"He saved you. Donavan saved you. And my father…did nothing."

Seized by another coughing attack, she could not continue. Devlin knew the story had taken its toll. "Rest now. You can tell me how you ended up here later, though I can guess what occurred."

"We will talk," she said weakly, as the coughing subsided. "Later, dear." She nestled under the blanket.

Devlin gently tucked her in. He remembered when she used

to do the same thing for him and how safe it had made him feel. He hoped he'd been able to provide her with just a bit of the same comfort.

Devlin noticed the sun shining through the meager windows in the room. Mrs. Sharpe scurried past him.

"Mrs. Sharpe, a moment please," he said, catching up with her. "I'm hungry. Can you show me to the kitchens?" He fell into step beside her.

"Yes, Doctor. That is exactly where I am going. We all must eat, but we need to inventory what is available. I haven't had time since the pox invaded Ashcroft, but it must be done to see how much food remains. You should also have the medical records soon."

"That should help." Devlin marveled at the woman. She walked so briskly that a woman half her age would be struggling to keep pace with her. "You said there are about one hundred ten patients here at Ashcroft? Do you know how many are new in recent months?"

She frowned. "I'm not exactly certain. Mr. Sullivan tends to lose count periodically when it suits him."

"What do you mean, lose count?" Devlin's stomach growled its discontent.

"It sounds as though we better find you something to eat." Mrs. Sharpe smiled. "Unfortunately, I'm sure it will not be the kind of food you are accustomed to eating."

"You wouldn't be trying to change the subject, would you?" He glanced at her. She studied him.

"Mr. Sullivan loses count when it suits his purse. We may have five to ten patients disappear or gain admittance every so often as Mr. Sullivan's greed dictates. I imagine it's quite a lucrative business for the man and whoever else he may be working with."

They came to a door with a lock on it. Mrs. Sharpe pulled the keys from her pocket. The door opened to the outside. Devlin was taken aback by a gust of air heavy with decay. He tried to hold his breath, desperate not to inhale again. He pulled a handkerchief from his pocket and covered his nose, mirroring the keeper's actions.

"It's usually a relief to step out of the asylum, but not now, not with the bodies burning."

Devlin followed her glance and saw the dying embers of the funeral pyre of the night before. A shoe lay smoking near the edge of the charred remains. Devlin choked back the desire to vomit. "Dear God in heaven, claim those poor souls."

"Poor souls indeed." She removed her handkerchief for a moment. "It's a foul job," she said and wrinkled her nose in disgust. "But you know as well as I that it must be done. Come." She pulled him in the opposite direction. "You must concentrate your efforts on the living."

"I know, but…"

"The asylum is always closed up and stuffy. A horrid place at times," she explained.

Devlin pursued the subject of the asylum and forced the picture of the smoking pile of human remains from his mind. "I thought the asylum was closed up against the rain." He stopped dead. "You mean to tell me they never open the windows?"

"The last doctor that was here said it was unhealthy, that all windows must be closed at all times. He even punished a patient for breaking one. Come, Doctor, we cannot stand here all day. There is much work to be done." Mrs. Sharpe continued toward the kitchen.

"Punished? How?" He fell back in step with her.

"The doctor had many ways of punishing patients, all within the law, of course. The deplorable man called it 'the necessary treatment.'"

"What did he do?"

"He gave them a cold-water bath, more like a drowning if you ask me, and manacled them on one of the many balconies in this mausoleum. Stripped the poor souls of their dignity and sometimes their clothes."

"He what?" Devlin knew perfectly well what she'd said, yet he could not fathom the cruelty of it. "I cannot begin to comprehend the horror."

"I believe you begin to understand." She stopped for a brief moment and looked at him. "It's not easy getting reputable people to help with those that are mad. Unless you know that people are committed to the Lord's work, it's more likely people of the devil's choosing that come looking for employment in places like Ashcroft."

"How can you work in a place like this?"

"I am a widow, sir, with no income of my own. This was the only work I could find. It seems God has called me to minister to these poor souls." She led the way into a large outer building. "The kitchen, sir."

Madeline's stomach growled noisily. She was hungry, a good sign. It was time to find something to eat. She slowly sat up on the narrow cot in the isolated cell and fought off a wave of dizziness. Her legs wobbled but worked well enough.

She slipped on her dry clothes and went out through the open cell and into the corridor where the guard usually stood. He wasn't there. She pushed on the barred gate. It swung open easily. Sun lighted the dust-streaked windows. Madeline longed to get outside.

The morning din reached her ears: moans, laughter, crying, swearing. Hell's cacophony. Madeline sensed someone was behind her. She carefully looked about to see who it was, but no one was there. Then she walked a few more feet and saw something or someone scramble in the gloomy shadows.

"Is that you, Mad Maddie?" croaked a male voice.

Madeline panicked for a moment, wondering if she'd imagined

the voice. Then she heard it again and froze. "Who are you?" She struggled to keep her voice calm.

"Only me." A dwarf with long stringy yellow hair and dancing blue eyes emerged from the shadows to her right. "Mad Maddie, it is you! Shall I play you a song, Mad Maddie?"

Madeline gasped and took a step backward. "Who...who are you? And why do you call me Mad Maddie?"

The dwarf's attire consisted of a dirty white shirt, red vest, and faded brown pants. The shirtsleeves fell below his hands, and the pants had been cut off so he could walk without tripping. The tip of a pair of moldy boots poked out from beneath his trousers. Given his appearance and stance, Madeline did not feel as though she was in any immediate danger.

"My name is Simon. Simon the Dwarf." He bowed gallantly. "I've been watching you since you came to Ashcroft. Simon says your name is Mad Maddie, and so it is!" He pulled a wooden harmonica from his ragged shirt pocket nearly hidden by the buttonless vest and immediately started playing a lively folk tune, spinning about her with amazing agility.

"Simon, you are most amusing." Madeline laughed. "I have not laughed in a very long time."

"I am glad, my lady. It is not often that one hears the sound of happy laughter in this place, mad laughter a plenty, but not truly happy, like yours. Are you no longer mad, Maddie?"

"I was never *mad*, Simon. I don't expect that to make any sense to you, but it's true."

Simon reached up and grabbed her hand. "Follow me."

His hands were cold, dry, and amazingly comforting. "I can't go with you, Simon. I must find something to eat. Do you know the way to the kitchen?"

"There is no way to the kitchen for you. The door is locked, and only the attendants have keys. But you are with Simon, and if Simon says open the door, then it will be opened."

Madeline allowed the dwarf to pull her along. They passed others sitting, sleeping, or pacing the long corridors of Ashcroft. She realized there was a mix of men and women everywhere. "I thought the men were separated from the women, Simon?"

"Don't pay any attention to them, Mad Maddie."

She felt the heat rise in her face. "But—"

"Exactly," Simon said. "Come, now. You must get used to strange sights and happenings in here. It's only normal after all."

"Normal?" Madeline waved her hand in an arc. "You call this normal, Simon?"

"Of course. What's normal in here is bizarre in the outside world, but those in the outside world don't understand or see how bizarre they really are, or someone would put them in here. So…they pretend to be normal."

Madeline looked at Simon and shook her head trying to understand his logic, then laughed. "You must excuse my ignorance, Simon. I have just recuperated from a fever and don't think my power of understanding is quite up to following you yet."

Simon gasped and stepped back. "Fever? You don't have the pox, do you, Mad Maddie?"

"I do not have the pox." She pulled up the sleeves of her gown and showed him that she possessed no rash. "See, there is nothing to fear."

Simon took a step forward and stroked her arm before Madeline realized what was happening. "Your skin is very soft," Simon said and smiled mischievously.

Madeline snatched back her arm. "Simon! You are not permitted to take such liberties."

Simon stuck his nose in the air as if greatly offended and sauntered away. Suddenly he stopped and swiveled around to look at her.

"Well, are you coming or not?" he grumbled. "I thought you were hungry."

The noise of the asylum could be irritating, and Madeline hungered, not only for food but also for silence. "I'm coming."

Simon led her to a door with a large lock on it, but he did not stop at the door. Instead he made a sharp right into what appeared to be a dead end. Then, looking about to be certain no one watched him, he reached up on tiptoe and stuck his hand into a small crevice.

"What are you doing?" Simon may not be as harmless as she first imagined. Perhaps her judgment *was* impaired. Then she heard a scraping sound and was amazed to see the wall begin to shift.

Simon looked up at her and grinned, an incredible yellow, gapped-toothed grin. Then he scampered through the opening, dragging her with him.

Darkness swallowed them. Simon held tight to her hand and led the way, stepping carefully through the secret passage. Her other hand she slid across the damp, cool wall for balance, not daring to think what lay in the spiderwebs she caught as they moved along. She had to stoop in order to hold on to Simon's hand. Something scurried over her shoe and she jumped, stifling a scream, but making enough racket to gain admonishment from Simon.

"Shhh," he said. "We're almost there."

"Get me out of here," Madeline demanded, batting a spiderweb away from her face. Simon's stature did nothing to aid in getting rid of the sticky clinging threads.

Simon stopped, and Madeline nearly fell over him. "What are you doing?" she asked, annoyed. "I don't like confined spaces. I can't breathe." Madeline's breath started coming hard and fast. She knew she'd faint dead away if she didn't get out soon.

"Here, my lady." Simon pulled Madeline from the passage. She breathed a sigh of relief as the sun penetrated her with warm rays. A scraping sound caught Madeline's attention.

"Where are we? What is that dreadful odor?" She looked about, trying to get her bearings.

Simon's impish face sobered instantly. "The dead."

"How awful." Madeline covered her nose with her hand. She quickly examined the outside of Ashcroft, averting her eyes from the smoldering fire. "The poor souls."

Simon scampered off in front of her, then stopped to see if she followed. "Come, come, come. For someone so hungry, you surely are slow. Come now, Mad Maddie, and we shall eat." He held out his hand to her.

"I'm coming." She forced her feet to move away from the horror.

Simon led her across the stone courtyard and toward a low-lying brick outbuilding. They entered through a heavy wooden door, and Madeline came face-to-face with Ravensmoore.

"How did you get out?" Ravensmoore asked, obviously perturbed. "You shouldn't be walking around by yourself. You might be injured or worse."

"But—" Madeline tried to defend herself.

"But nothing. You should...ouch!" Ravensmoore doubled over and grabbed his knee, which Simon had kicked.

Simon purpled with rage. "She's not by herself, dimwit. She's with me!"

"Simon, how rude." Madeline stifled a laugh at the look on Ravensmoore's face. "Lord Ravensmoore, this is Simon. Simon, this is Lord Ravensmoore. He's a doctor."

"How nice." Simon gritted his teeth.

"Dr. Grayson will do for now," Ravensmoore said. "I'd prefer not to use my title in the asylum."

She turned her attention to Ravensmoore. "Simon was kind enough to bring me out in hopes of getting some food. I'm so hungry." Madeline prayed that would cut short their argument.

"The other patients need to eat as well, but there is no sign of food inside."

"Not enough help," said the cook, who had been looking on with amusement. "Too many sick. Simon, what will you be wantin' from me today?"

Simon hopped about. "What's the best you got, Helga?"

The cook looked up at the ceiling, as though in deep thought. "Porridge."

"That's what I'm having then. Porridge! Delicious porridge." Simon looked at Madeline and grinned. "And so is Mad Maddie."

"Simon, stop calling me that," Madeline demanded.

"I think there is one thing we can all agree on, and that is the state of our hunger," Ravensmoore commented. "Let's eat." He put his hand on the small of her back and directed her toward a wooden table that appeared relatively clean.

Madeline settled onto the bench and helped herself to a warm slice of bread. "Perhaps after we eat, I could help distribute food to the patients." She deeply inhaled the aroma of the bread.

Ravensmoore glanced at her and chuckled. "Are you going to eat that thing or just smell it?" He passed her a crock of butter. "Here, smother it with this and enjoy."

Madeline didn't argue. She spread the butter generously over the steaming bread, blew on it gently, and took a bite. "Mmmm, delicious." The butter trickled down the back of her hand. She gasped in surprise when Ravensmoore gently took her hand and wiped the butter away with his thumb, leaving a trail of gooseflesh in its place.

Simon broke the spell by plopping himself next to Madeline. "I will be happy to help you in your efforts," he announced. "I will help Mad Maddie distribute the food while you take care of the sick, Doctor."

"What a generous offer," Helga said, as she settled a huge pot of porridge in front of them. "I know just what a sacrifice that is for you, Simon." She turned from the table and chuckled as she walked to the stove. She returned with a collection of bowls and scooped out generous portions of the hot porridge.

Ravensmoore turned his gaze on Simon. "Can you be trusted to guard her, Simon?"

Simon looked at Ravensmoore and grinned, porridge dripping from his chin. He chuckled. "I will guard her, Doctor. And if you die of the pox, I will ask Mad Maddie to marry me."

Madeline shot a warning glance at Simon. "Not as long as you keep calling me Mad Maddie."

"What shall I call you then?" Simon jumped down from the bench and brushed the bread crumbs from his clothes.

"You may call me Lady Madeline."

Helga looked up, startled. "You are the lady who was teaching the boys, were you not? I never met you, but I heard your name."

Madeline nodded. "How are they? Safely away in London, I hope."

Helga's face sobered. "No, I'm afraid not. They are sick with smallpox."

Madeline gasped. "Not the boys!"

Simon dropped the empty wooden bowl he was taking to the sink. "Jack and Danny?" His fists clenched, and he kicked the bowl across the room. "I hate this place!" He stormed outside in a fit of rage.

Madeline drew herself up. "I will care for them, as I cared for my siblings."

Ravensmoore asked, "Can you show us where they are, Helga?"

"Indeed I will."

Together Madeline and Devlin followed Helga to where the twins were quarantined. The area stood apart from the asylum, an unused building attached to the main home for the patients.

"Danny, Jack!" Madeline rushed to the boys who lay still and unconscious, both in cots next to each other. A sheen of sweat covered their young faces. The wretched markings of smallpox had reached their necks but were not fully emerged. The pustules threatened the smattering of freckles that scattered across their cheeks and noses.

Ravensmoore placed a hand on each boy's forehead. "The fever is raging."

"I will sit with them," Madeline said. "I know how to care for them."

Ravensmoore frowned. "I'd rather you let someone else, Madeline. You are still weak."

"I'm strong enough to care for these two. And you have many others to take care of in the asylum, including your mother. Go to them."

"If you're sure. Keep them as cool as you can. If they have difficulty breathing, they will need to have pillows propped behind them."

"Would the vaccine help at this time?" Madeline asked.

"Once the disease has been contracted, it cannot be turned about by the vaccine. The illness must run its course. The boys are young and strong. They may fare well."

Madeline's eyes grew moist. "And they may not. My brother and sister were young and strong too." She sniffled.

A gentle tapping on the door gained her attention, and the round face of the milkmaid appeared.

"Jenny!" Madeline jumped up.

Jenny tentatively entered the room. "I heard about the twins. Will they be all right?"

"We hope so, Jenny. This is Dr. Grayson." Madeline stared at Jenny's hands and touched Ravensmoore's arm, drawing his attention to them.

"Jenny, how long have you had those spots on your hands?" Ravensmoore asked.

"'Tis the cowpox, doctor. Not smallpox."

Ravensmoore went to her. "May I see?"

She held the pox-riddled hands in front of her. "It's not pretty. Comes from the cows."

"Milkmaids sometimes get the infection from the cows." Ravensmoore turned her hands over. "Jenny, do the twins help you milk the cows?"

"Every morning, sir."

Ravensmoore ran to the boys and opened their shirts. After a moment, he announced triumphantly, "The pustules aren't as big as smallpox. It's cowpox. The boys don't have smallpox, Lady Madeline. They should be fine."

"What are you talking about?" Madeline asked as Jenny went to sit by the boys. "Isn't this dangerous?"

Ravensmoore returned to her side. "Lady Madeline, it's cowpox. This is what Jenner uses as his vaccine against smallpox. The boys and Jenny have received their vaccines from the cows."

Madeline grabbed his hands. "God be praised. Finally, a bit of good news." She squeezed his hands and gazed at him. "I will stay here with them and keep them comfortable. Now go, Ravensmoore, and attend to your mother."

He nodded, gratitude pooling deep in his eyes. "I will come back as soon as I can. Be careful, Lady Madeline."

Their gazes locked for one long moment, then Ravensmoore turned away. Madeline watched as Ravensmoore strode across the brick courtyard heading back to the asylum. Back to the gates of hell.

CHAPTER 19

For I will restore health unto thee, and I will
heal thee of thy wounds, saith the LORD.

—JEREMIAH 30:17

As HE CROSSED the asylum grounds, Devlin watched
thick, black smoke crawl above Ashcroft like charred
skeletal fingers of a bony hand. The gruesome business of burning
bodies continued. He shivered as he entered the asylum and retraced
the maze of hallways to find his mother.

At last he found the small room where she'd spent the night.
"How is she, Amanda?"

Humming a winsome tune, Amanda sat holding Elethea's hand.
"Better," Amanda said, not looking at him. "She's better."

Devlin checked his mother's temperature. "The fever's broken."

"Breathing better." Amanda rocked back and forth on the floor.

Devlin took out his stethoscope and placed it on his mother's
chest. Satisfied with his findings, he breathed a sigh of relief.

"Thank you, Amanda. You might have just saved my mother's
life by sitting with her and keeping her cool."

"You saved her," Amanda whispered. "She's happy now."

Devlin smiled. "Why don't we just say we both helped, and the
good Lord did the rest." He so much wanted his mother to survive.

Amanda chanted. "Lord did the rest, Lord did the rest, Lord did the rest."

"Amanda? Are you all right?"

"Lord did the rest, Lord did the rest, Lord did the rest."

"You've been up too long. Your illness awakes. I want you to go to sleep, Amanda." He led her to her cot. "Lie down now. My mother will be fine, and you both need to sleep."

"Sleep, sleep, sleep," she chanted on, giving him no resistance.

"That's right, sleep." He tucked her in and watched her quickly fall asleep.

Mrs. Sharpe entered the room. "Doctor, we've brought the files we could carry of the patients." Wiggins stood beside her, intimidating and behemoth.

"Thank you, Mrs. Sharpe, Wiggins. You have the list of those who have died?"

"Yes, sir."

"Good. They will tell us who is at risk. We'll separate the inoculated from those less fortunate. Anyone showing symptoms must be quarantined in another area until we are certain it is smallpox. I'll write down the names of those who are well but have not yet received the vaccine. We will make sure the patients stay in the area of the asylum best suited for their needs."

It became clear to Devlin after studying the first few patient records that Sullivan was making a huge personal profit. In one case he admitted a man simply because the man's family said he disturbed them at night. They couldn't sleep with all the noise he made rocking in his chair. Sullivan was paid handsomely to be certain the man never left Ashcroft.

Another patient, a woman, entered the asylum at the whim of her family for talking too much. Another, because she enjoyed bathing, and still another, because she prayed aloud three times a day. There were others who appeared legitimate in their need for safe custody.

Devlin picked up the next record and paused. The name on the outside read *Lady Ravensmoore*. Devlin's hands trembled. His mother told him how she came to be in Ashcroft. He felt suddenly guilty for what he was about to do, but then he mentally kicked the notion aside. He needed to see what was in this record.

He carefully peeled back the yellowed paper. There was a letter on the first page written in a familiar hand, his father's. It read:

> Dear Sir,
>
> I wish to have my wife committed to Ashcroft Asylum. Lord Vale has assured me she will have everything she needs under your supervision.
>
> This is a most delicate matter.
>
> My wife was found in our forest near the manor house, quite distraught. During a storm, my groomsman discovered her fighting off a hungry wolf. She has not been in her right mind since that wretched night.
>
> I expect you will see to her every comfort. In return for your discretion, I will compensate you. Lord Vale guarantees me that you may be trusted.
>
> I will deliver her to you on the fourth day of March. Have all necessary paperwork prepared and at my disposal.
>
> Ravensmoore

Devlin's breath caught. He took in great gulps of air to steady his racing heart. His own father had betrayed him with Vale's help. And now Lady Madeline and her mother were at risk. The monster must be stopped. Devlin would see to it. *God, help me not kill the man with my own hands*, he thought, trying to control his rage.

A glimmer of hope crept into his consciousness—an amazing thread of joy lacing its way amid the fire of anger that bloomed. If his mother was not insane, but merely the pawn of his father's lustful desire for another woman, then he did not carry the seed of insanity. But perhaps his unfaithfulness had already done irreparable harm to her mind. Only time would tell what this place had inflicted on her as well—if she survived.

He shook his head and stood, then went to a basin of water near the doorway and bent over it to splash his face.

"Doctor!" Mrs. Sharpe cried. "Watch out!"

Devlin whirled, and a searing pain sliced through his upper back as the basin clattered to the floor. Looking back, he saw only the dark coat of his assailant as he fled.

Mrs. Sharpe ran to him.

Devlin dropped to his knees. Blood trickled down his back and dripped onto the floor where it mingled with the spilled water, swirling into a macabre painting. The room swam.

"Doctor, lie still." She knelt beside him.

"Check the...wound," he gasped. "Get my topcoat. Use it to...stop bleeding."

Mrs. Sharpe grabbed his topcoat from the floor, balled it up, and pressed it against the wound.

"How...does it look?"

"It's bleeding heavily."

Devlin struggled to speak through a veil of fog. "Get Lady Madeline," he whispered hoarsely, before falling into the dark abyss of unconsciousness.

CHAPTER 20

My God, my God, why hast thou forsaken
me? Why art thou so far from helping me?
—PSALM 22:1

MADELINE WAS JUST wringing out a rag, preparing to place it on Danny's forehead, when Simon appeared in the doorway. "Mad Maddie."

She was about to reprimand him for calling her that dreadful name when she saw the expression on his face. "What's wrong?" Madeline asked, smoothing the cloth across Danny's brow.

"Mrs. Sharpe needs you. Dr. Grayson has been attacked."

Terror gripped Madeline as she followed Simon into the asylum.

Madeline gasped when she reached Devlin. Blood was everywhere, splattered on the floor and soaking through the thick top-coat that Mrs. Sharpe used to staunch the blood. She fell to her knees next to him. "What happened? She picked up his limp hand. "Can you hear me, Dr. Grayson?"

He groaned.

Mrs. Sharpe explained, "Someone stabbed him. I didn't see his face. Just a knife slashing through the air. It happened so fast."

"Is he going to die?" Simon lifted one of Ravensmoore's eyelids. His eyes popped open, and Simon jumped back in surprise.

"I told you before. I am not going to die," Ravensmoore said, his voice hoarse.

Simon crossed his arms over his chest. "I knew you were too stubborn to die."

"Thank God, you're awake," Madeline exclaimed. "Did you see who did this?"

"Don't know. Be...be careful, Lady Madeline."

She sucked in her breath when Ravensmoore struggled to his side and Mrs. Sharpe removed the coat, exposing the wound.

Ravensmoore forced a weak grin. "That bad, is it?"

Her eyes examined a deep slash across the upper back. "I suppose it could be worse." She tried to keep her voice calm and steady. "It is impossible to tell how deep the injury is with all this blood. Simon, can you get us some water to clean the wound?"

Simon scampered away to follow her orders.

Amanda came into the room and stopped, her eyes wide with shock. "Blood everywhere," she exclaimed. "Just like Papa beating Mama. Blood everywhere."

"Amanda! Thank God, you are all right." She hugged the girl close. Ravensmoore turned to look at Amanda and winced. "That's what happened, isn't it, Amanda? You were trying to protect your mother."

Tears streamed down Amanda's pale face, and this time Madeline wiped away the girl's tears. "We won't let anything bad happen to you, Amanda."

Simon returned with a basin of water and set it near Ravensmoore.

"Thank you, Simon," Madeline said. "Keep Amanda with you while Mrs. Sharpe and I help the doctor."

Simon reached for Amanda's hand. He didn't speak a word. He just held her hand.

Ravensmoore struggled to rise. "I think I'm strong enough to sit up."

Madeline laid a hand on his chest. "You must be still, Doctor Grayson. Why is it so hard for a man to take a woman's advice?" Madeline tore her petticoat and used the strip of cloth to wipe away the worst of the blood. Then she tore a larger piece, wadded it into a bandage, and held it against the gash.

Ravensmoore gave her a lopsided grin that turned quickly into a grimace. "You make a fine nurse, Lady Madeline."

"And you, sir, make a difficult patient. Kindly tell me how to stop this bleeding."

"He'll need to be sewn up," Mrs. Sharpe said, examining the wound. "I want everyone out of here, except Lady Madeline."

Simon nodded and led Amanda from the room.

Madeline discarded the blood-soaked cloth, tore another, and held it against the wound for what seemed like forever. "I think it's beginning to slow." Madeline lifted the cloth and looked at the gash. "The bleeding is lessening."

"I will get the necessary instruments from the apothecary. 'Tis just around the corner," Mrs. Sharpe said. "Remove his shirt so I can access the wound."

Madeline stood next to Ravensmoore, alone. Self-consciousness gripped her as she fumbled with his bloodstained cravat. "You are so pale." She gently touched his cheek with the back of her hand.

He placed his hand over hers. "You have gentle fingers."

"And my fingers need to untie your neck cloth. I am not very experienced with such things."

"Would you like me to give you directions?" he teased.

Her cheeks warmed. Steadfastly avoiding his gaze, she bent over him and worked at the intricate configuration. Finally she loosened his cravat, and the knots fell away. She removed the strip of cloth, then unbuttoned his shirt and gently eased it from his shoulders and down his arms. Her breath caught. Never had she been so close to a man. Averting her gaze, she gathered up the torn shirt and pressed it to the wound, holding it in place. Keeping her voice neutral, she asked, "Are you doing all right?"

"Never better." His tone was light, but Madeline could feel the shudders of pain rippling through his back.

Mrs. Sharpe returned with a basket of supplies. First she packed the wound with herbs to prevent infection and then she picked up a needle. "It is time."

A groan escaped Ravensmoore's lips. Madeline bent over him. "Dr. Grayson, how awful is the pain?"

"Don't give me anything," he whispered to her. "I must stay awake in case I'm needed."

"Yes." She rubbed her hands, damp with anxiety, against her skirt and prayed she wouldn't have to guide the needle through his skin. She looked to Mrs. Sharpe for direction.

Mrs. Sharpe touched Madeline's shoulder. "I have done this many times. It's much like the art of needlepoint. Would you like to help?"

"Yes, I would. Dr. Grayson, let me help you sit up."

"A kind offer, but I think I can manage on my own." He swayed to one side and nearly fell over.

"Stubborn man." Madeline prevented his fall. "You have lost too much blood."

"Stubborn? Who tried to walk into her home after falling from her horse?"

Madeline ignored the remark and picked up the black bag that held the medical instruments. "Just tell me what to do."

Mrs. Sharpe explained the procedure while she threaded a needle. "All I need you to do is to hold Dr. Grayson's hands and keep him still so I can stitch properly," Mrs. Sharpe said.

Madeline felt sick as she watched Mrs. Sharpe push the needle into the red swollen skin.

Ravensmoore gasped as the needle completed its first stitch.

"I cannot believe I said not to give me anything," he groaned. "It burns like hell's fire."

"Do quit trying to be so brave," Madeline said. "Take the laudanum." She held the bottle to Ravensmoore's lips. "Sip slowly. I imagine you know how much to swallow."

Ravensmoore took a mouthful and swallowed. In a moment Mrs. Sharpe resumed sewing. Madeline watched in amazement as the woman skillfully sewed the wound together. The gash soon turned into a neat, well-stitched line.

"I am almost finished," Mrs. Sharpe said, "but you must rest. The wound, although not terribly deep, will be uncomfortable. You need time to heal."

Madeline held the bottle of laudanum to his lips again. "It may be best to take one more sip."

He smiled, followed her instructions, then caught and held her gaze. "Thank you." His eyes spoke more than the simple words conveyed.

Tying off the last stitch, Mrs. Sharpe let out a long sigh of satisfaction. "It is done." She bandaged the wound. "Try not to sleep on your back. Now, if you will excuse me, I have other patients that need attention. There is so much yet to do." She left the room.

"Lady Madeline," Devlin said, catching her hand, "you must send for Dr. Langford and Melton."

"Of course," Madeline reassured him. She watched Ravensmoore drift off to exhausted sleep. He looked so vulnerable, not nearly so strong and determined as when he was awake. She must be strong. Very strong, because their lives—and the life of her mother—depended on it.

Madeline left the room and found one of the male keepers. "Have you had the vaccine?" He nodded.

"I want you to go the Guardian Gate Hospital. Ask for Dr. Langford. Tell him of the smallpox epidemic here and of the attack on Dr. Grayson. Tell him to come quickly. And whatever you do, do not be seen, or Dr. Grayson and I may be in danger. If you do this, you will be richly rewarded. Do you understand?"

The keeper nodded again and went his way.

Madeline made her way through the maze of patients. Finally she reached the main door. No guard. She tried the latch. It lifted silently, allowing her access to the corridor. Sullivan's office door was open.

Madeline's heart raced. Perhaps she could find concrete proof of Sullivan's evil doings—proof that would stand up in court. She went to the door and hesitated for just a moment to gather her courage. She stepped into the office. Seeing no one about, she quietly pushed the door closed.

The room was a mess. Dirty dishes covered the desk, and papers were scattered about like straw in a stable. The sun gleamed on a shiny object lying on the floor partially concealed by a piece of paper. She tiptoed to the spot and knelt down.

"Lord help us." She stared at a letter opener covered with dried blood—Ravensmoore's blood! A wave of fear washed over her. She struggled to stand up, her knees wobbly.

Suddenly the door crashed open. Amos Sullivan stood staring at her.

"Ah, here you are!" Sullivan asked. "You appear to be lost, my dear. This is not where you belong."

"It was you. You stabbed Ravensmoore. But why?"

"Because he knows too much. He will ruin everything if he leaves here alive, and I am going to make sure he doesn't." Sullivan's features twisted into a mask of hatred. "And now you also know too much. I'm afraid I cannot ignore that fact."

"What evil do you plot now?"

"I believe you have met my two trusted employees." Two men

stepped into the room—the men who had held her under in the cold bath. Her blood chilled.

Sullivan pointed first to the big man. "Hugh, subdue her." To the smaller man he said, "Thomas, take her to the pit. And make sure she stays there a good long time."

"No! Leave me alone!" She picked up an inkwell and threw it at Hugh. It hit him in the chest, and the black liquid soaked the front of his dirty brown shirt, spreading like the evil that lived in him.

Movement at the window caught her attention. Simon! He ducked beneath the windowsill, but her glance did not go unnoticed by Sullivan.

"Thomas, get the dwarf," Sullivan instructed. "Bring him to me."

Madeline picked up a book and hurled it at Hugh. "Get away from me!" The book bounced off him. She threw another and then another as he stalked her.

He lunged at her. Madeline screamed. She dodged his advance and ran to the door, only to watch it shut, inches in front of her, with a shove from Sullivan. She bit his hand and grabbed the doorknob. Hugh was upon her in a flash.

"Let me go!" Madeline kicked and scratched him, but Hugh was too big and far too strong.

Sullivan laughed. "I will get word to Vale of your disobedience."

Madeline immediately went still. "No! He'll hurt my mother."

"You should have considered that prior to entering my office uninvited."

"Wait! You can't do this." She bit Hugh's hand hard, drawing blood. He swore and twisted her arm behind her back. In desperation, Madeline screamed, a high-pitched shriek, hoping Mrs. Sharpe would hear her. Hugh grabbed her other arm and tied them together at the wrists.

"Get her out of here." Sullivan stuck a gag in her mouth.

Hugh hoisted her over his beefy shoulder as if she were a sack of grain. She stiffened with fear and tried to scream again, but only a muffled sound came from her throat. Blood rushed to her head. Not being able to breathe through her mouth forced her to inhale his loathsome scent. He smelled as though he'd rolled in pig manure.

Hugh strode through a dark, musty passageway.

"You're in no position to argue now, are ye?" Hugh laughed. Madeline thought she would vomit but for the gag in her mouth. She pushed against his shoulder and kicked her legs, hoping to throw him off balance, but he held her tight, his laugh echoing through the narrow passage.

As they descended the stairs, he slowed to maintain his balance in the narrow passage, then stopped. Squeaking hinges and a smell worse than Hugh assaulted her senses. Madeline saw a single torch burning in the room and hastily studied her surroundings.

He dumped her on the ground. She hit against something hard and smooth behind her. Madeline turned to see a bamboo cage, its door hanging open like the mouth of a hungry animal.

"Get up," Hugh commanded, grabbing a handful of her hair and yanking her to her feet.

Tears stung Madeline's eyes. What would happen to Ravensmoore if she couldn't get away? What would happen to all of them if the message didn't reach Dr. Langford?

Hugh untied her hands, and she quickly rubbed them together to lessen the pain of blood filling her numb fingers. She removed the gag from her mouth and thought she would do almost anything for a few drops of water. "Water." The word sounded barely audible to her own ears.

"Get in the cage," Hugh ordered, ignoring her request.

Madeline kicked him hard in the knee. "Never!" She scrambled to her feet and ran toward the passage.

Hugh tackled her to the ground. "You witch!"

Madeline rammed her elbow into his face. "Let me go, you monster!"

Suddenly her head jerked backward. Hugh roared, "I'll let you rot!" He grabbed her arm and dragged her to the cage, throwing her inside.

Madeline fell against the bamboo as though she were a rag doll. The door slammed shut. She winced at the pain in her arm. "Don't do this!"

"I got me orders. I get paid right well to follow them. Hold on tight, *me lady*," he said, sneering at her. "You'll be going for a brief ride." Hugh began turning a hidden lever. The cage jolted into the air, smashing her against the other side of the cage.

"Let me out!" Madeline yelled, hoping he would stop but knowing he would not. She hung suspended in the cage in the middle of the dimly lit, desolate room. Madeline watched as Hugh secured the lever and moved underneath her. "What are you doing? Let me out of here!"

"I will return later. You will beg me to get you out of the pit by then. You will do anything I ask. Anything at all."

She watched in horror as Hugh removed a rusting metal grate beneath her. "You must not do this!" Madeline gripped the bars of the cage and shook the door. "You will not get away with this."

Hugh chuckled. "Welcome to the pit, dearie. We reserve this room for our most special patients." He returned to the lever on the wall and began to lower the cage.

Madeline watched in horror as she descended into the dark abyss.

CHAPTER 21

If it were not for Hopes, the Heart would break.
—THOMAS FULLER, MD,
GNOMOLOGIA, NO. 2689

MADELINE GRITTED HER teeth and tried to rattle open the door of her cage. Her dislike of mice and insects lost to her fear of close spaces. She swallowed hard and tried not to think about what crawled under her neck and over her belly. But for all her effort she found escape impossible. Even if she had been able to escape the cage, she doubted she would be able to scale the walls of the pit.

She stood and brushed furiously at her neck and clothing. Madeline knew that in order to survive, she could not stay here long. The confined space stole her breath; she refused to let it steal her sanity or her life. She had to have food and water. "You can't leave me here!" she yelled, hoping someone would hear her. "Help me!" She fought back a wave of panic and hit the walls with her fists. "Please, Lord. Help me."

Then she surrendered to all the emotions that she'd tried to ward off: fear, anger, and hopelessness. She sobbed and then she prayed. She prayed that God would protect Ravensmoore from those who wished him harm. She prayed that Dr. Langford would drop everything and come quickly. She prayed for her mother. And she prayed for her rescue.

Her tears and melancholia over the last year were nothing compared to this. She was indeed cast into the pit. And the cruel and distant God who'd sent so much trouble her way was now her only hope. She had no choice but to turn to Him.

After hours, or what felt like hours later, the door to her prison in the above room squeaked. *Hugh!*

"Please let me out of here." He was coming back to keep his promises. The thought of him made her skin crawl. *If I can get out, perhaps I can outwit him.* Her heart leaped with the hope. The grate above her scraped back, the sound echoing in the chamber. The lever creaked and strained above her head, and she felt the cage sway as it rose. She surfaced swiftly and hung suspended above the pit. Madeline squinted into the torchlight. "Who's there?" She heard the grate above the hole slide roughly back in place. "Answer me." The cage lowered slowly to the grate. It was not Hugh who awaited her but someone much larger than her captor.

"Who are you?" She forced the words from her throat as the giant drew near. Madeline's hand covered her mouth, stifling a scream. She prayed the end would be quick, for there was no way she could escape this giant of a man. Madeline stared at his bulging eye but refused to cave in to the torrent of emotions that gripped her.

Opening the cage, he reached inside for Madeline and gently pulled her out.

"I will not harm you. Come." He gestured, and she followed, stumbling behind, as he led her away from the pit and up a staircase to a secluded room.

"You rest," he commanded, and disappeared through the door.

She sat on the floor, forcing herself to be calm, and breathed in great gulps of air that didn't smell of the pit. She had no idea where she was or who it was who had carried her away from her prison, but she was grateful. "Thank You, God. Thank You for sending this man."

Madeline pushed herself off the floor. Her legs trembled, but she leaned against the wall for support until she felt steady. Looking around the small room, she noticed a tiny window, through which she spotted a red-streaked sky. So it must be evening.

She crept out of the secluded room into the silent hallway. Moving through it she found herself near the cold baths where Hugh and Thomas had nearly drowned her. "Ravensmoore," she whispered aloud. She headed in the direction of the makeshift infirmary, watching and praying that Hugh and Thomas were not around the next corner waiting to capture her and return her to the pit.

Fortunately Madeline spied Mrs. Sharpe. Suddenly the strain of her ordeal overwhelmed her, and she began to weep.

Mrs. Sharpe hurried toward her. "What is it, my dear? What's happened?"

Madeline struggled to gain control of her emotions, but the tears continued to flow. Mrs. Sharpe put a comforting arm around her and led her to a chair in a small room away from the stares and the voices of the insane. Pulling a rumpled handkerchief from her skirt pocket, she offered it to Madeline.

"I went to Sullivan's office," Madeline said, forcing herself to concentrate and not fall apart. "He's the one who stabbed Dr. Grayson. He ordered Thomas to confine me to the pit, and that is where I have been."

"Lord protect us," Mrs. Sharpe whispered. "I knew he wasn't trustworthy, and I've heard rumors, but I never thought he would stoop so low as to dance with the devil himself. How did you get out?"

"A horribly disfigured giant rescued me. He must be one of the patients."

Mrs. Sharpe nodded. "I know exactly who it was. His name is Andrew Wiggins. You're fortunate. You might still be in that horrid place if not for him. And thankfully I saw Hugh, Thomas, and Sullivan leave not too long ago, so you are safe for now."

Madeline wiped at her eyes and looked at Mrs. Sharpe. "How is Dr. Grayson? Is he bleeding again?"

"No. The stitches are holding well. He has been sleeping, but I am sure he will ask for you as soon as he awakes."

"I must get back to him, Mrs. Sharpe. He will tell us what to do next."

She nodded. "I will go with you."

Devlin woke at the sound of voices. "Here he is, Dr. Langford."

"Thank you, Mrs. Sharpe. You may leave us now."

Devlin blinked and rubbed his eyes, breathing a sigh of relief at the sight of his teacher, lantern in hand, staring down at him over his spectacles. "Dr. Langford, thank God."

"Ravensmoore, what kind of trouble have you gotten yourself into now? Let me take a look at you."

Langford motioned for Devlin to turn over so he could check his wound. He removed the bandages and traced his finger along the stitching. "Nice stitching," he observed, wrapping the wound once again. "Be sure you rest easy at least another day. We'll have to watch for infection, and you're certain to be stiff and sore for quite a while." He motioned for Devlin to lie back, then pulled up a stool next to the bed.

"I have brought the law," he said simply. "First Mr. Melton tells me that Lady Madeline Whittington was brought here against her will, and then one of the keepers shows up with word that you've been stabbed. They are looking for Sullivan now."

"But what of the epidemic?" Devlin asked. "Will you be able to stay and help? I must help—there are too many ill."

Langford interrupted. "Better to work when you gain a bit of strength tomorrow than to collapse tonight. I will take over now, and we'll reassess your situation in the morning. Try not to break the stitches open."

Devlin sighed. "I have never seen so much death in one place." He raised himself up to a sitting position and winced.

Langford pushed his glasses up on his nose and rested his gaze on Devlin. "Death is never easy. Watching someone die is heartbreaking, unless you can do something to ease their pain. A simple touch of the hand is sometimes a better cure than all that medicine has to offer."

He folded his arms, regarding Devlin with something akin to curiosity.

"So, are you going to tell me why you left the profession? You were my best student, Ravensmoore. I can tell from your work here that you were paying attention." Langford looked at him over those infernal glasses, waiting for an answer.

Devlin looked away. "I had other more pressing issues. Personal issues. I thought I would lose the woman I loved if I didn't give up my work." He squeezed his right hand into a fist. "I had doubts. I've been wrestling with God and my calling. Or at least what I thought was my calling."

"And now?" Langford repeated, pressing for more.

"I have much to consider, Dr. Langford. For one thing, I have just discovered my mother alive in this wretched place, held against her will for ten years." He quickly filled Langford in on the story, then asked, "Will you check on her for me? She is quite ill."

Langford's face had turned stormy as Devlin told his story. "I always thought there was something wrong with Sullivan," he muttered. "Of course I will look after your mother."

"She's at the west end of the asylum with the others who are infected."

Just then Devlin heard footsteps hurrying down the hallway.

Madeline and Mrs. Sharpe came into the room, and Madeline went straight to Devlin's side. "How are you?"

"Better." Feasting his eyes on her, he noticed new rips in her clothing and fresh tear streaks against a dirty face. What new horrors had she endured while he'd been sleeping?

She turned to his teacher. "Dr. Langford! I am so glad to see you. We are in desperate need of your help." Quickly she told her story—of confronting Sullivan, of being captured and taken to the pit.

Devlin listened intently. Rage claimed his heart with each detail she revealed. "Where are the cowards?" he demanded. "They must be stopped and confined until the authorities can lock them up."

"I saw all three of them leaving Ashcroft not too long ago," Mrs. Sharpe said.

Dr. Langford cleared his throat. "They must have heard that the law was coming. And their escape could mean the epidemic will spread wherever they go. Does anyone know if they were vaccinated?" He peered over his glasses at the assembled group.

Devlin leaned forward and winced again when the stitches grabbed him. "If Sullivan had the nerve to come into the asylum and stab me, then he must be very desperate. When I arrived here, he was terrified of being exposed. He said he had not been vaccinated."

Madeline nodded in agreement and then turned her attention to Mrs. Sharpe. "Do you have any idea how long Hugh and Thomas have been employed here?"

"Not more than a year."

Simon entered the room. "Yes, yes, not more than a year. The louts." He made a fist and punched the air.

"Chances are they were never vaccinated," Langford said. "We must assume the worst. I will notify the authorities to be on the lookout for them." He looked at the dwarf with interest, then turned to Mrs. Sharpe. "Is there anyone here we could trust to help with the search—someone who could identify these men?"

Simon jumped up and down, waving his hand. "Me! Me! Oh, send me!"

Mrs. Sharpe gave him a wry look then turned to Langford. "Simon has his quirks, but I do think he could be of help to a search party."

"Simon." Madeline knelt and held her hands out to him.

"Yes, Mad Maddie?" Simon glanced at Devlin, pleased with the attention.

Devlin smiled in spite of the situation and the pain in his arm. Simon was obviously smitten with Maddie.

"What you are doing is very brave. Thank you." She gave him a gentle kiss on the cheek. A deep shade of crimson inched up his neck and face. "Thank you, Mad Maddie," he said, holding his hand to his cheek as if to keep the memory of her kiss with him. He turned to Dr. Langford. "I'll go now!"

Langford nodded. "Devlin, I'll be back once I've talked to the authorities. Stay here and rest for the night." He left the room, Simon skipping in his wake and Mrs. Sharpe following behind.

Devlin watched them depart. He was glad that Langford had arrived, but he was anxious to have Madeline alone. He turned to her and took her hand, his head bowed. "You could have been killed, and I was useless. Forgive me."

Looking up, he saw pain cross her face before she clamped down on her emotions. "I am safe now. The Lord provided escape through Andrew Wiggins."

"I would have preferred he had sent me." Devlin searched her face, saw an awakening there, but something else...doubt? Fear? Reluctantly he dropped her hand.

She turned slightly, saying briskly, "Lord Ravensmoore, I must go to Richfield. My mother is in danger. I must get her away from Vale."

"You can't do anything this time of night." He made sure to talk sensibly, reasonably. If he ordered her about, she would be sure to defy him. "Let's get you something to eat," he said, changing the subject. "Then, you will sleep."

"How can I sleep? I must get home!" Urgency spoke through her words, sparked in her eyes.

"Lady Madeline, be reasonable. We have both been through a terrible trauma, but for now we are safe, and the best thing we can do is sleep and regain our strength so we can take up the fight tomorrow. We will discuss what to do next in the morning, after we hear from the authorities. I do not want you in harm's way again, especially when I am not equipped to protect you."

Madeline heard him out, her face conflicted. Just then Amanda peeked in the room.

Devlin beckoned to her. "Lady Madeline, I want you and Amanda to get something to eat. Then keep Amanda with you. Ask Mrs. Sharpe to have Wiggins remain on guard outside your room and get some sleep. Both of you." He turned toward Madeline. "Please, Lady Madeline, do as I say."

She nodded reluctantly. He watched, his heart in his throat, as she left the room with Amanda holding Madeline's hand. He cursed Sullivan for the wound that had kept him from protecting her as he should.

CHAPTER 22

Decisions can take you out of God's
will but never out of His reach.

—ANONYMOUS

*G*OOD HEAVENS, WHAT a nightmare!" Madeline awoke
with a start to discover herself tangled in the bedsheets.
She shuddered and tried to ward off unwanted images.

She heard the sound of scurrying and an insistent rapping. "Are
you well, Lady Madeline?" Mrs. Sharpe called from the other side
of the door. "Is anything amiss?"

"Just a moment. I'm fine." She looked down at Amanda, who lay
on a mattress on the floor. "Let her in, will you?"

Amanda hurried to the door and let Mrs. Sharpe inside.

"I just had a bad dream and must have called out in my sleep,"
Madeline explained as she untangled the sheets.

"Very good. I am relieved. I thought there was trouble, and I
just sent Wiggins away." Mrs. Sharpe looked her over. "It looks as
though you were wrestling with demons in your sleep."

"You could say that." Gloom fell over her, and she wondered
when Ravensmoore would take her away from Ashcroft. "How is
Dr. Grayson this morning?"

"Improved and overdoing it already."

"Thank God." Her nerves were taut as a bow ready to release its arrow. The dream loomed vividly in her mind. "I dreamed I was back in the pit."

"'Tis understandable. I will take Amanda with me so you can dress. She can sit with Dr. Grayson's mother. Come, Amanda."

Madeline hugged Amanda before she left with Mrs. Sharpe. "Take good care of Lady Ravensmoore, Amanda. I will see you later." They left, closing the door behind them.

Madeline stood barefoot on the hard cold floor, shivering in her chemise. She looked at her clothes lying in a heap where she'd discarded them. How could she get access to a clean set of clothing? She longed for a warm bath.

She shivered again, not from the cold, but from the nightmare. The closed windows, shutting out the fresh air, increased her sense of panic. The pit haunted her.

Refusing to dwell on the dream any longer, she surveyed the room for possibilities and spied her trunk sitting in the corner. An answered prayer, she thought, gratefully. Perhaps Mrs. Sharpe was responsible for this blessing. Daisy had packed the trunk, but this was the first time she'd seen it since entering Ashcroft. She knew that many of the patients never received their personal items or clothing. *Sullivan probably sold them for his own gain.*

Madeline noticed the broken latch. She moved toward the chest and opened the lid. "Oh no." Someone had pillaged the trunk, leaving only a few undergarments and two day dresses. She touched the soft material, so different from the coarse fabric that most of the patients wore at Ashcroft. Holding it to her nose she breathed in the clean scent of lavender that reminded her of home.

"Now, if I only had a place to bathe." She looked at the pitcher and basin on the small chest of drawers and wished them a tub filled with steaming water. But memories of the frigid bath she'd endured under Thomas and Hugh suddenly made the basin and pitcher appear inviting. She poured the cold water into the bowl and picked up a thin cloth. Soaking it through, she made quick work of washing herself.

Donning the clean undergarments, Madeline peered into the trunk at her choice of dresses. "Blue or green?" She gazed at one muslin garment and then the other, holding them against her one at a time. "Green it is."

Brushing back her hair, which was in desperate need of washing, she flinched when a tiny spider spilled from one tendril, dangling by an invisible thread. Her first instinct was to bat it away, but something stopped her.

The spider was no danger to her. And in this place where sanity and insanity blurred together, she felt sympathy for the tiny, vulnerable creature. She floated the spider to the floor on the invisible thread and watched it scurry under the door.

Feeling better, she followed the spider's lead. Madeline opened the door just a crack and peered out into the empty hallway.

"Lady Madeline, you are awake!" Ravensmoore strode down the hall, a smile lighting his face. Someone had supplied him with a fresh shirt open at the collar. Despite the circumstances, a pleasant thrill of excitement raced through her. He looked rakishly handsome even in this hellhole.

"Good morning, Dr. Grayson." She returned his smile, then dropped her eyes, afraid he might see more in them than she was willing to share at this point.

"Are you all right?" Ravensmoore asked.

She raised her eyes, regarding him. "Yes, but I must get home as soon as possible. Will you help me?"

His eyes darkened. "You cannot leave. I know this is hard for you, but it is far too dangerous for you to return to Richfield."

"Why?" Now that she was rested and recovered, her first priority must be her mother. Why could he not understand that?

"If you were to go to your mother now and Vale discovered you there, God knows what might happen. I don't think he will harm her in the next few days. His plan is probably for a slow decline."

"You don't know that for certain, do you?" She moved forward and gripped his arm. "Please. Surely, you don't think I need to remain here."

"Of course, you don't *need* to stay here, but you *need* to be careful." He pulled Madeline back into her room and gently tilted her chin up to look her in the eyes. "Listen to me. I can't have you running off to Richfield without me. I'm needed here. Langford cannot take care of all these sick people by himself."

"I know. I'm just so worried. I cannot help but feel something is terribly wrong. Vale promised that if I made trouble, he would punish my mother."

"I doubt Sullivan has told Vale what happened yesterday. He was just trying to save his own neck by getting out of here as soon as possible. We will go together to Richfield, just as soon as possible. I promise."

"Dr. Grayson." Mrs. Sharpe rushed toward them. "It's your mother. She's taken a turn for the worse. Come quickly."

Ravensmoore glanced at Madeline, unable to conceal his concern. "We'll talk later. Stay here," he ordered. "I'll send Wiggins."

Madeline watched Ravensmoore disappear from sight. Returning to her room, she paced restlessly up and down. She couldn't stay here. She just couldn't.

She made up her mind, no matter the consequences. Scrawling out a quick note, she let Ravensmoore know where she'd gone. Then she stepped outside the room, determined to make her escape.

Elethea gasped for breath. Devlin knelt next to her, Dr. Langford opposite him. "Mother, I'm here." He took her hand and felt her squeeze it in response, but she could not speak, only cling to every breath, curled in a ball on her side.

"What else can be done?" he asked Langford.

"I don't think there is anything we can do except pray. It is out of our hands. She will either survive this attack or succumb to it."

"I won't let that happen." Anger and helplessness overwhelmed him. "There must be something." Devlin looked around the room. "There *is* something." He reached a chair in two long strides and dragged it to his mother's cot.

He looked at Langford's doubtful expression and thought he might throttle his teacher. "Just help me." Devlin felt the pull of stitches in his back and silently groaned as he and Langford assisted Elethea into the chair.

"Sitting up may help you breathe easier, Mother. I'll be right here with you. Now close your eyes. I'll get you through this." Devlin bowed his head in silent prayer. He held his mother's hand and willed air into her fragile lungs. God must have a plan if He'd brought them together after all these years of separation. To lose her now would be unbearable. He tried to quell the anger that welled inside him against his father. The man had never been tender and he'd always been closer to Edward, but that was only natural, wasn't it? Edward was the heir, or should have been the heir. The title suited him to perfection.

His thoughts drifted to Madeline and her mother and all that family had endured. He couldn't expect Madeline not to go to Richfield when the opportunity presented itself—her mother was the only family Madeline had left. He'd been near ready to lock her in a cell just to keep her here, but then that would have destroyed any sense of trust he'd been able to engender.

He'd do everything he could to help her as soon as he knew his mother was out of danger.

Madeline looked over her shoulder. A sense of relief mingled with encroaching guilt gripped her heart as Ashcroft Asylum disappeared from sight. She didn't enjoy deceiving Ravensmoore, but she felt she had no choice. She had to help her mother. She'd waited too long already.

She'd encountered Wiggins when she'd entered the barn looking for a horse. He knew of a couple old mules kept in a remote shed away from the barn. The two of them rode through woods and fields heavy with the green of spring. "There it is, Wiggins. Richfield." The midmorning sun shone down on the rambling manor house and grounds, bestowing them with a warm glow. She could not believe how much she had missed home, but most of all she had missed her mother. She'd taken both for granted.

Madeline kicked the old mule forward, anxious to be home.

As they approached the stables, Madeline spotted a familiar figure. Donavan looked up from his work and wiped his grimy hands on his work trousers. "Lady Madeline! You're back!" A smile of relief spread over his face but quickly faded when he caught site of Wiggins. "Is this man dangerous?" He helped her dismount all the while she watched him watching Wiggins.

"Thank you, Donavan. I'm glad to be home. This is Andrew Wiggins from the asylum. He aided me in his escape."

Donavan nodded. "Are you all right, my lady? I sent word to Countess Gilling soon as I could."

"You and Agnes saved my life, Donavan. Lady Gilling notified Lord Ravensmoore, and he came to help me. I am indebted to Mr. Wiggins also. Is Lord Vale here?"

"No, Lady Madeline. Lord Vale left yesterday."

"Thank God. Do you know where he went and when he will return?"

"No, my lady. He's as tight-lipped as a corpse."

"How is my mother?"

Donavan's face turned stony with sorrow. "The same," he reported. "Agnes is with her now."

"I must go to her immediately. Thank you, Donavan. You and Mr. Wiggins have something in common. I will let you get acquainted."

Madeline hurried past the stables and the gardens blooming on this side of the estate. How could such beauty hide such terror behind its walls? The daffodils and tulips in all the colors of the rainbow brightened their walk. If only Mother could regain her strength. What if Vale had done irreparable harm? *Lord, show me a way to defeat him.*

She entered through the kitchen, catching Cook by surprise so that she spilled the flour she'd been measuring out. "Lady Madeline!" she shrieked. "God be praised, you're back!" Cook tried to wipe some flour from her face but only succeeded in making it worse.

"Cook, where is my mother?"

"In her room, my lady. She isn't well. Agnes is with her."

Although Cook tried to control her expression, Madeline could tell that the situation had worsened since she'd been taken to the asylum three days ago. Fear wrapped its long tentacles around her. Giving way at last to her alarm, Madeline lifted her skirt and raced from the room and up the stairs to her mother's room.

Suddenly the door flew open. There stood Agnes.

"Lady Madeline. Praise God." Agnes threw her arms around Madeline and began to sob.

Madeline gently stepped back and studied the old woman, noting the black circles under her eyes and the way she wrung her hands, a nervous habit she'd never seen Agnes exhibit before.

"Agnes, Cook says Mother remains ill." Madeline stepped forward to enter the room but Agnes blocked her way, reached behind her, and pulled the door closed.

"Agnes, I wish to see my mother." Madeline desperately fought off the wave of panic that threatened to overtake her.

"Prepare yourself, Lady Madeline. Your mother never got a bit better after ye were taken away. She's worse."

"Agnes." Madeline fell into the old servant's arms. She needed comforting, perhaps even more than she'd been aware of the need. "I must see her."

"I know, dear." Agnes gently pushed Madeline back. "Your mother is very sick. It's as though she's willed herself to die. Perhaps seeing ye will be the best medicine she could receive, but ye must prepare yourself."

Madeline nodded.

Agnes turned and opened the door, waiting for Madeline to enter. Madeline's feet felt heavy. Maybe she wasn't as prepared as she'd first thought.

Grace was in bed, apparently sleeping, but as Madeline drew closer, she could see that she was awake and staring out the window.

"Mother?"

Grace did not move.

"Mother? It is I, Madeline. I'm home." She reached for her mother's hand lying outside the coverlet.

As her mother turned toward her, Madeline fought to hide her alarm. Her mother looked as though she'd been fighting off death.

"Ma–Ma–Maddie." Her mother struggled to say her name.

"Keep talking to her, Lady Madeline," Agnes cried in surprise. "'Tis the first word she's said in days. Look at her eyes. Why, they're shining with life!"

Her mother's reaction to her, and Agnes's words, bolstered Madeline's courage. "Mother, I'm here now. I'm going to help get you well."

Fear filled her mother's eyes. She tried to sit up but was far too weak. She gripped Madeline's hand with amazing strength. "No. Danger here. Go." She collapsed. Her courageous attempt to rally—gone.

Madeline pulled the coverlet up and tucked it in around her. "I'm not leaving you, Mother. No matter what." Madeline removed herself from the bed and motioned to Agnes to meet her in the hallway.

"When was the last time a physician saw my mother, Agnes?"

"She's not seen a physician. Lord Vale forbids it."

"She's not been examined? He forbids it? That's outrageous! Vale will pay for this. And in his absence, I'll just see what can be done to remedy that situation." She felt better already at having some recourse to take for her mother. "Agnes, do you know when Lord Vale will return? I spoke with Donavan in the stable, but he had no idea."

"It's hard to tell with that one. Wherever he is, I'd say he's up to no good."

"Indeed, Agnes. And I intend to do something about it."

Madeline ran to the stables. "Donavan, I need you to ride into York. Find a physician who will come and examine my mother. I want to get her out of here as soon as I know she can travel."

Donavan nodded. "I will leave immediately. Is there a special doctor you want?"

Indeed, there is a special doctor, Madeline thought, wishing Ravensmoore was present. Guilt ate at her for going against his wishes. "Yes, go to the Guardian Gate Hospital. Dr. Melton is there. Tell him it is urgent. Ride Samson." Donavan disappeared into the stables.

She turned to Wiggins. "Stay here, Mr. Wiggins. You may familiarize yourself with the stables."

He nodded.

"And Mr. Wiggins, stay alert."

Madeline went back inside. "Agnes, I want you to help me move Mother and anything she may need to a guestroom in the east wing of the house."

"Yes, Lady Madeline. But why move your mother?"

Madeline wearily sank into a chair. Thoughts of Vale and fear for her mother continued unabated. "Because Lord Vale will return."

CHAPTER 23

Be not afraid, only believe.

—MARK 5:36

*D*EVLIN FOUGHT OFF the demons in his dreams, easily slaying each one. Then a vision of his mother appeared before him; he tried to heal her, using all of his ability and knowledge. The vision began to shimmer and fade.

He awoke with a start. The morning sun had gone behind the clouds, deepening the gloom in the already shadowy room. "Mother." He looked at her and feared the worst. *Was the dream a premonition, or have I already lost her?*

Elethea sat in the chair, her head forward, resting on her chest. They had loosely tied her to the chair to keep her upright, and her body hung weakly against the restricting band.

"Mother?" Devlin repeated, and gently touched her shoulder. "Mother?" He held his fingers against her neck searching for the heartbeat.

"Devlin," she said, slowly raising her head and looking at him. "My son."

Tears flooded his eyes, and he dropped to his knees. She was alive. His mother was alive!

Her hand rested on his head as he gave way to years of pent-up emotion, shaking with grief and anger and exhaustion. "Mother," he said again and again. "Mother."

At last the crying subsided. Wiping his eyes, he lifted his gaze to her and found her watching him, weak yet calm.

"My back hurts, son. Can you help me out of this awful chair?"

Devlin scrambled to his feet, and with his good side he helped her out of the chair and back into her cot. Elethea sighed and turned her head toward him. "I believe I could eat something."

Devlin smiled with joy. "You *are* better!" He looked about for an attendant to send to the kitchen, but none was in sight. "I'll see what food I can find," he told her. "Rest, and I will return as soon as I can."

Devlin went straight to the kitchen and ordered that some broth and a pot of tea be taken to his mother. He then made his way to Madeline's room.

Strange—the door to Madeline's room stood open. Where did she go? He forced himself to remain calm. The room was empty.

"Now what?" he mumbled to himself. Then he spotted the piece of paper on her bed. Crossing quickly, he opened the paper and read it.

Forgive me, Lord Ravensmoore. I couldn't just sit here and do nothing to help my own mother while you so diligently attended to your mother. You know how tenacious I can be. I will be safe. Do not worry.

She must have left soon after he saw her last. Of course Madeline would be desperate to save her mother—as desperate as he'd been to save his own.

"Blast it all!" Anger and frustration boiled within him as he returned to the infirmary, where he found Langford attending a patient.

"Lady Madeline has gone to her mother," he explained to

Langford. "I've got to go after her. But Lord knows where I'll find a serviceable horse at such short notice."

"Perhaps I can be of service, Ravensmoore." Charles Melton stepped into the room, a cocky grin on his face.

"Melton," chorused Devlin and Langford.

"Where did you come from?" Devlin asked, relief spreading through him. "How did you get here?"

"I rode my horse. That is a common means of transportation these days." He strode forward, gripped Devlin's hand firmly, and then greeted Langford. "I told you I would return to check on you. It sounds as though Lady Madeline has escaped you yet again. I suggest you borrow my horse and go after her."

"I owe you a debt, Melton; thank you. Dr. Langford will fill you in on what needs doing. And about a special patient who needs your attention." He gazed meaningfully at Langford, who nodded his understanding.

"I'll take excellent care of your patients, Ravensmoore. Now go, before you lose more time."

Madeline picked up the brush and comb on her mother's dressing table. She hadn't thought she'd relax at all, wondering when Vale might return and discover his wife missing, but the familiarity of the surroundings somehow put her at ease. After moving her mother, she ate a few bites of toast and sipped a strong cup of tea.

Agnes rapped on the door and entered. "I'm sorry to say, Lady Madeline, that Donavan returned without Dr. Melton. Apparently he is at Ashcroft as well, and no one could return with him to help the countess."

"Oh, no." Madeline allowed herself one moment of despair, then rallied. "Agnes, stay here with Mother." She returned to her mother's room on the other side of the house to gather a few more essentials and think out her next steps.

Catching her appearance in the mirror, she sat down at the dressing table and pulled the brush through her hair, smoothing it into a tight knot at the back of her head, then securing it with pins. She thought it wise that she and Agnes had moved her mother out of this room to the east wing. She did not want her mother easily available for Vale's abuse when he returned.

A door slammed below. *Vale!* Madeline dropped the brush and held her breath. Where were Donavan and Wiggins?

Measured footsteps on the stairs panicked Madeline. *He is here already*, she thought. *Lord, help me to be strong.* Slowly, she stood, bracing herself.

Vale entered the room, still wearing his greatcoat and hat, and the moment he spotted her, his face reddened with anger. "What the deuce do you think you're doing? How did you get out of Ashcroft? And where is my wife?"

"Where you can no longer hurt her," Madeline snapped.

Vale reached her in two long strides and grabbed Madeline's shoulders, shaking her. "You tell me where she is right this moment."

"Let go of me." Madeline struggled against him. "You're hurting me."

"Release her at once!" It was Ravensmoore's voice, cold as steel and razor sharp. "You will be the only one leaving, Vale," he said. "And it's straight to prison you'll be going."

Vale dropped his hands from Madeline's shoulders and whirled around. "Ravensmoore. I should have guessed you'd be skulking about." Vale glared at him with unmistakable loathing. "However, it makes no difference."

Ravensmoore stepped forward. "I know what you have been doing, Vale, and you will pay for your crimes."

"You have no proof of anything. You're more the lunatic than the ones behind the bars of Ashcroft." Vale tried to walk past Ravensmoore.

Ravensmoore grabbed his arm. "You sound very sure of yourself. Why is that?"

Madeline watched a thin muscle in the side of Vale's neck pulsate and tense. *He's nervous*, she thought, glad to think that maybe he was beginning to squirm.

"Get your hand off of me!"

"Not until you agree to leave. And if you think Sullivan or those two apes he's with are going to help you, you are sadly mistaken."

Vale's mouth twisted into a strange, absurd grin. "I don't know what you're talking about." He pulled away from Ravensmoore and straightened his coat. "I don't need anyone's help. I have nothing to hide. Get out of my way."

Ravensmoore's eyes blazed like green steel. "I'm on to your game, Vale."

Madeline watched a dark river of red creep just above Vale's cravat. *He is guilty, I know it, and he is slipping away.* She battled for control of the anger that swept through her like the fires of hell itself. She said fiercely, "I will see to it that you go to prison. You are trying to kill my mother. I know you are feeding her laudanum."

Vale threw her a mocking look. "I would never kill Grace. In any event, your mother cannot do or say anything against me." Vale took a step toward her. "A wife cannot testify against her husband. Or did the two of you forget that fact?" He grinned an evil, knowing smirk.

Madeline held her ground, not wanting to show her fear. "Maybe she can't testify, but I can. It is just a matter of time."

"You stupid witch!" Vale moved toward her, but again Ravensmoore intervened.

"Stay away from her." He pulled a pistol from his coat and aimed it at Vale, whose eyes widened just slightly, then narrowed in anger.

"Now get out of here." Ravensmoore gestured with the pistol, forcing Vale out of the room. Together they descended the winding staircase, Vale with his arms raised, Ravensmoore following behind.

Madeline held her breath, watching from the top of the stairs as Ravensmoore guided Vale through the foyer. Phineas stood like a sentry by the door, a gapped-tooth grin on his usually solemn features. He opened the door wide for the two men.

Vale descended the front steps, then turned. "I'm coming back. This is my home, and Grace is my wife. There is nothing you can do to change that." He stomped off to the stables, and Phineas closed the door after him.

Ravensmoore replaced his gun in his coat as she came down the stairs. "I can't believe you came!" she cried. "Thank you, Ravensmoore." She reached him and held out her hands for him to take.

He bent over them and kissed each hand. "After I found your note, I came as quickly as possible. I knew you might need help." He raised his head, and for the first time she noticed the exhausted circles around his eyes.

"Are you all right? What about your wound? And your mother?"

"Not to worry. I'll be fine. And my mother is on the way to recovery. Now I need to check your mother's condition. He will come back, Lady Madeline. We have to get her out of here."

Madeline's mind raced, but the confusion and fear of the last few minutes had her rattled. "Where will we take her?"

"To Ravensmoore."

While Ravensmoore examined Grace, Madeline and Agnes quickly packed a small valise of Grace's belongings. Then Donavan came to carry Grace down to the carriage.

Madeline tucked a blanket tenderly around Grace, who lay

half-conscious against the cushions. "Good-bye, Mother. Agnes, you'll take good care of her, I know. Devlin and I will follow as soon as we can." She kissed Grace then climbed from the carriage to stand beside Ravensmoore.

Together they watched as Donavan took up the reins and urged on the horses. The carriage pulled away, heading down a lane of dappled afternoon sun.

"I pray she will be safe." Madeline clenched her fists. "That man is a monster."

Ravensmoore touched her arm gently. "It's going to work out, Lady Madeline. I know this is happening fast, but we must be smarter than Vale. If he returns, we will be able to delay him and prevent his finding your mother. It is too late now, but tomorrow we will go to the authorities, and you can press charges against him."

Ravensmoore slept while Madeline spent the time resting in her room and praying. Late in the afternoon there was a quick knock on the door, and Daisy entered, a silver tray set with dinner balanced in her hands.

"Lord Ravensmoore said I was to serve ye dinner, Lady Madeline."

"That is not necessary." Madeline smiled. "It is nice, though. Thank you, Daisy. Where is Ravensmoore? Vale has not returned yet?"

"Do ye think it would be this quiet if he was?" Daisy set the tray down on a bedside table. "Now, ye just get comfy." She pulled the pillows behind Madeline, fluffing them as she did so.

"Mmm. That smells wonderful."

Daisy set the tray across Madeline's lap and removed the lid to reveal fresh ham, potatoes, beans, bread and butter, and a steaming cup of tea.

"Why, there's enough food here to feed five people. Daisy, really. You know that I never eat anywhere near—"

"You've had an awful few days. It won't hurt to spoil ye just a bit."

Madeline was nearly finished with her food when she suddenly realized she'd been duped. "Daisy. You didn't answer my question a moment ago." Madeline studied her maid. "Where is Ravensmoore?"

"Yer food is getting cold. It is important that you eat and keep up your strength with all ye've been through. Lord Ravensmoore asked me to be sure that you had a very nice dinner before I told you." Daisy started straightening the room.

"Daisy! What are you hiding from me? Where is he?"

"I promised. I promised that you would eat yer dinner and not get all excited."

Madeline gave Daisy a look that brooked no further hesitation. "Get excited about what?"

Daisy took a deep breath. "The carriage was attacked an hour into their trip, and your mother was taken. Donavan escaped to tell Lord Ravensmoore. He believes your mother is being taken to Vale House and has gone after him in pursuit."

"Mother!" Apprehension tore through Madeline. "When did he leave, Daisy?"

"Not more than an hour ago."

"Help me get dressed in my riding costume. I'm going after him."

CHAPTER 24

Malice drinketh up the greater
part of its own poison.

—SOCRATES

*M*ADELINE AND DONAVAN rode north through thickening clouds, leaving Wiggins behind to guard Richfield. She was pleased that Ravensmoore had insisted the groom remain behind to guard her. Now she had help. Ravensmoore was certain to have something to say about her plans when she caught up with him. She just didn't want to hear it.

"I really think we should go back, Lady Madeline. 'Tis not safe. Lord Ravensmoore is bound to hang me from the nearest tree for allowin' you to leave Richfield."

"It was not your decision to make. You were just following my instructions."

"Somehow I don't think his lordship will be seein' it that way."

"I imagine you're right." Madeline smiled. "I will deal with him."

Vale House sat in a shadowed valley, dark and foreboding against the stormy evening sky. "Perfectly fitting for a man like Vale," Madeline said as she and Donavan watched from a distant hill.

Donavan grunted. "The house needs care; the fields are overgrown. 'Tis rotten. Just like Vale."

"So it is."

"What are you plannin' to do after we get to the house?" Donavan asked, his voice edgy. "This is not a good idea. If Vale doesn't kill me, Lord Ravensmoore will."

Shakespeare whinnied and pranced anxiously. A brisk wind picked up, and the rustle of leaves heightened Madeline's senses. "A storm is coming."

"And the only place of shelter is down there," Donavan said, pointing toward Devil's Backbone. "We better get movin' before it hits."

Madeline felt a tiny splash upon her face, then another and another. "Here it comes."

Madeline and Donavan circled around to the back of the stables to avoid detection. The place seemed deserted. "I have the distinct feeling that Vale doesn't keep many servants." The stable door creaked loudly, and Donavan poked his head inside.

"What do ye see?" Madeline asked as she tried to peer around him. "Is anyone in there?"

"I don't believe so." He gave her an uneasy glance. "Stay here. I'll be right back." He disappeared into the stable before she could object.

The wind moaned. Madeline grew more nervous with every second that Donavan did not return. She poked her head inside. "Donavan? Where are you?"

"'Tis safe," he finally said. "No one is here. Just a couple of horses."

Madeline let out a sigh of relief and stepped inside. "We can't leave our horses outside. It's too dangerous."

"I'll get them."

He retrieved their horses and led them into the dark stable, the storm raging overhead. The musty smell of wet hay permeated the rickety barn. "I got as close to the house as possible before gettin' the horses; didn't see a soul."

"You did what?" Madeline's hand flew to her throat. "Have you lost your senses? You could have been killed. We don't know where Sullivan or Vale are, and it doesn't look like Ravensmoore has arrived."

Donavan led the horses into empty stalls. The other horses stomped and whinnied as thunder shook the barn. "This place is scary. I don't like being scared."

"I don't either," Madeline said, thinking that perhaps her plan might have a few flaws in it.

"What now?" Donavan asked, distraught.

"With the noise of the storm," Madeline said, her brow creased in thought, "and the probability that Vale doesn't retain many servants, let's see if we can make our way into the house."

"No disrespect, Lady Madeline, but if there was any doubt in my mind that you belonged at Ashcroft, it has now vanished. You have surely lost all reason if you think for one moment that you are goin' into that devil's home. Ravensmoore would never forgive me for puttin' you in such danger. And your father would curse me from his grave, may he rest in peace."

"Can you live with yourself if anything happens to my mother? We cannot wait for Ravensmoore."

"All right. Blast me for a fool. But if we do find a way in, I will go, and you will come back here. If I do not return within a few minutes, you must hide here until Ravensmoore arrives."

"No," Madeline said, tossing her loose wet hair back over her shoulder. "I will not leave you!"

Donavan shook his head. "Females! They will be my undoin'." He extended his arm. "After you, Lady Madeline. And if you see Vale comin' this way, run like the wind."

"If I see Vale coming this way"—she stopped and looked about the stable then grabbed a shovel—"I'll hit him with this." She waved the tool in the air, barely missing Donavan's face.

"The thought does not encourage me. Put that thing down." He took the shovel and leaned it against the wall. "Now, let us go."

Madeline's heart hammered against her chest like a surly beast hoping for escape from its cage. The rain battered her face until she was certain she'd be black and blue from the stinging daggers.

Madeline and Donavan edged their way along the side of the manor. "No matter what happens," she said, breathing hard, "we stay together. Let's see if we can discern anything from the windows on the rear porch." Madeline pointed to the windows. "Over there."

Three of the six tall windows were pushed open, allowing fresh air to enter into the rooms. Fortunately it allowed them entrance as well. Donavan slipped through the third window at the same time Madeline slipped through the second.

"What now?" Donavan whispered behind her. "'Tis gloomy as a graveyard."

"Gloomy indeed," Madeline agreed, her eyes quickly assessing the sparsely furnished drawing room.

"Let's get out of here." Donavan turned back toward the windows.

Madeline grabbed his hand. "This may be our only chance to rescue them."

Donavan turned back to her. "But where are they? This place is huge."

"You stay here, Donavan. I'll explore."

Donavan shook his head. "No. If anyone goes, I will. 'Tis too dangerous."

"You worry like an old woman, Donavan," Madeline said, keeping her voice low. "I must find my mother!"

"You won't be able to help your mother if ye get caught, now, will ye?"

"Agreed. I will wait here, but come right back. Don't go far, and tell me what you find," she insisted.

"I will." Donavan disappeared into the hallway.

The moment Donavan left, she became frightened for him. *What if he becomes lost or captured?* she thought. Tentatively she moved down the hallway.

A black-gloved hand appeared in front of her face. A handkerchief smothered her nose and mouth. She stumbled backward and fear gripped her heart.

"Blast it!" From a nearby hillside Devlin watched two shapes run from the stable toward the house. The rain nearly obscured his view, but he was close enough to know it was Madeline and Donavan.

The fools! What do they think they're doing? I told Donavan to protect her, and he's leading her into the lion's den.

Dressed in black from head to toe, Devlin blended in well with the storm. He had been circling around the estate for over an hour, watching for movement within and trying to make a plan of attack. Now Madeline had forced him into action.

He led his horse into an old shed, not wanting to get too close to the house. He studied the surrounding area to be certain he was alone. The fierceness of the storm covered normal sound, and it would be unwise to consider himself safe. Vale could be anywhere.

A tree limb broke behind him. He turned and came face-to-face with Amos Sullivan...and a loaded pistol. Wrapped in a black cloak, his hat streaming rain, the man presented a formidable figure.

"So you're still alive," Sullivan said. "More's the pity. Now toss me your gun, and carefully," he ordered. "I don't trust desperate men."

Devlin raised his hands. "I'm hardly desperate, Sullivan. Seems to me that you're the one that's been running scared. Where are you going to hide?"

"None of your business. Now lay down your gun. You've wasted enough of my time."

Devlin removed his gun from his coat and laid it on the ground. "And why did you enter the asylum to stab me? Why take that risk? I thought you were afraid of smallpox."

"I had the vaccine," Sullivan said, scooping up the gun. "'Twas a convenient excuse to stay as far away from the lunatics as possible during the epidemic." He waved his pistol. "Start walking. I've had enough of this rain, and as I said, I don't trust desperate men."

"And I told you, Sullivan," Devlin growled. "I'm not the one who's desperate."

"You will be."

A clap of thunder echoed through the black sky in ominous warning. Devlin prayed for wisdom. The real storm was about to break loose.

Madeline's head ached as though someone had taken a mallet to it. Her eyelids—so heavy. Suddenly she remembered the black glove, the acrid smell, the difficulty breathing. She felt her confinement. *He's tied me to a chair. Well, I won't give him the satisfaction of seeing my fear. He must be close. Think, girl, think. God, what should I do?*

"I know you're awake. You can't fool me, sweet Madeline."

Vale's voice forced her heart into her throat. She steeled herself for the battle to come and prayed that God would give her courage. Raising her head, she slowly opened her eyes to meet her captor's.

"Vale." She tested her bonds. They held firmly. "You coward." Her head ached. "How dare you take my mother!"

"She's my wife. I can do as I please."

"Where is she? I want to see her now!"

"What's this? You remain a she-cat? How disappointing, my dear." He walked toward her, his black boots quiet on the wooden planks. "I assume you are not happy to see me." He moved behind her. "I, on the other hand, am very happy to see you." He combed through her dark wet tresses with his long fingers.

Madeline shuddered at his touch. *God, give me strength.*

"What have you done with my mother and Agnes?" she demanded, trying to ignore the pounding in her head. "They'd better be unharmed, or you will pay dearly."

"You are in no position to demand anything. Perhaps you should adjust your tone to something more respectful." His fingers came around to cup her chin as he moved in front of her. He tilted her face up. "Mayhap I should have married you, instead."

"You vulgar, good-for-nothing, evil, thieving—"

Vale stuffed a rag in her mouth, cutting off her torrent of venomous words. "You really must learn to use more appropriate language, my sweet." He bent and whispered in her ear. "I must insist upon it."

His foul breath wafted across her face, causing her to wrinkle her nose. He ran his finger down her cheek, a lingering, tormenting warning of what he was capable of doing.

Show no fear. The words echoed in her brain, a reminder of her intent. Again she tested her bonds, hoping to find them weakened. They held tight. *Where had Donavan disappeared to?*

"I must leave you for a while. I am expecting more company." He patted her head as though she were a child of no significance and left her.

How could I have been so foolish? As he headed down the hillside toward the gloomy estate, head down against the driving rain, Devlin mentally ticked off his options, but none seemed feasible. He couldn't turn on the man out here without being shot. His mind raced ahead. "Where are you taking me?"

"To Vale, of course. He will pay a pretty penny to watch you tortured and shot." Sullivan pushed Devlin ahead of him toward the stable, a half mile away.

An agonizing ten minutes later they arrived at the stable doors. "Open them," Sullivan commanded.

Devlin pulled open the heavy wooden doors. As they entered, a cat jumped off a ledge and darted in front of them.

Seizing the opportunity, Devlin turned and lunged at Sullivan. They wrestled to the ground fighting for the gun. It exploded, the bullet barely missing Devlin's face. He scrambled for the weapon. Sullivan gained his footing and tried to kick the pistol away.

"No, you don't," Devlin roared. He grabbed Sullivan's foot. The man went sprawling to the ground. Devlin leveled the gun at Sullivan. "Don't move," he warned from where he knelt on the floor. He felt a warm trickle of blood soak through his shirt where his stitches had ripped open.

"Where are they?"

Sullivan went pale. "I don't know."

"I will give you to the count of three, and then I will pull the trigger. One. Two."

A gunshot blast thundered through the stable, competing with the storm outside. Sullivan looked past Devlin with dead eyes, a hole through his head. He slumped forward.

"Three." Vale concluded. "I should have done that a long time ago. You may drop the gun, Ravensmoore, and say your prayers. I will not fail."

"So you're finally doing your own dirty work, Vale." Devlin seethed with anger. "Where is Madeline?"

"If you wish to see your sweet Madeline again, Ravensmoore, throw down the gun."

Devlin weighed his options.

"I said, throw it away."

Devlin gritted his teeth and laid the gun on the floor.

Vale picked it up and stood over him, studying the red stain spreading across Devlin's shirt. "So Sullivan shot you. That should make things easier. I'll just let you bleed to death. Then I'll set my next plan in motion. But first, I must take care of a few details."

"You are insane."

"I disagree with your diagnosis, Doctor. All will work to my advantage. It always does. Now get down on the floor."

Vale brought his heel down on Devlin's back. "Is it this side? No? Then it must be this side."

Devlin groaned his agony when the remaining stitches gave way and blood coursed down his back, soaking his shirt.

Vale sneered. "I win."

Devlin blinked, trying to clear his vision. When he lifted his head, there seemed to be two of Vale. "You will not win. Never."

"You're dead already, Ravensmoore." Vale stomped on his back again.

A jolt of excruciating pain burst through his skin. Devlin thought of Madeline at the mercy of this madman. And then all thought that loomed in his mind went black.

Madeline worked at the knots in the rope that tied her wrists. Sweat seeped through her clothes, and her fingers burned as she labored against the rope. A hand closed over hers.

"Shhh." Donavan put a finger to his lips as if he didn't see the gag in Madeline's mouth.

Madeline couldn't believe her eyes. *Thank You, Lord!* Then frustration simmered while Donavan worked on her bonds, failing to remove the gag. As soon as the ropes fell, Madeline yanked out the gag and grabbed him by the shoulders. "Donavan." She breathed hard. "Did you find my mother?"

"Not yet. I've been keeping watch over you," Donavan whispered.

"Vale will come to the house soon. I must get you out of here." He jerked her toward the door.

"Wait!" She looked out the window and froze. "God protect us. Vale is coming."

She turned and nearly collided with Donavan. "Hurry. We must get out of here. He's coming!"

She ran ahead, Donavan following, and they made it to the first floor and ran through drawing room where they had entered the house.

The front door slammed shut. "Vale," she whispered. "He'll find us."

Donavan grabbed her hand. "This way." They slipped through a window that led outside, and within moments they were running toward the stables. They reached the shelter of the barn, and Donavan pulled her inside. "I must return to the house. I'll find your mother and Agnes. Make not a sound, and you'll be safe here." He turned and disappeared into the deepening gloom.

The storm raged fierce and strong, and the stable was so thick with darkness that Madeline could barely see. Her eyes now adjusted to the dark, she looked up and saw Sullivan's body, slumped in the corner, a bullet hole in his head. Her blood ran cold.

Tentatively she stepped farther into the barn. Then she heard a sound. A groan. She followed the sound and spotted a dark form slumped at the base of a horse's stall. She crept nearer. "Devlin!"

She ran to him, kneeling at his side. Her hands slipped under his coat and closed around his back. A sticky wetness covered her fingers. He shuddered and seemed to awake to her presence. "Madeline!" His eyes widened with alarm. She pulled back.

"Ravensmoore, you're bleeding. Let me help you."

"Madeline, you must leave. Now!"

Suddenly the stable door blew open, and Vale entered like a giant bird of prey, his cloak billowing around him, a lantern in his hand. He drew his pistol. "What a pretty little reunion," he sneered. "Aren't you dead yet, Ravensmoore?"

Ravensmoore struggled to sit up, pulling Madeline behind him. "You'll never get away with killing us," he said.

Vale laughed. "Oh, that will be easy enough. I'll blame it all on Sullivan. You rescued Madeline from the asylum, discovered the fraudulent workings of Sullivan, and threatened to turn him in. He followed you here and killed Madeline before turning the gun on you. Unfortunately, he did not mortally wound you, so you were able to take the gun from him and kill him. But this is a deserted place, and you died of your gunshot wound before help could arrive. It's a bit complicated, but I think I can lie well enough that the authorities will believe me." He smiled and raised his gun.

Suddenly Donavan appeared from behind and tackled Vale. The gun went off, and for a few moments all Madeline could hear was the sickening sound of flesh against flesh as the large groom pummeled Vale into submission.

The pistol spun in their direction, and Ravensmoore reached to pick it up. "I've got the gun, Donavan."

Donavan sent one more blow to Vale's jaw for good measure before standing up and dusting himself off. Then he hauled Vale to his feet, where he stood glaring at them, blood dripping from his nose. Undaunted, he sneered, "Grace is still my wife. You cannot change that."

Ravensmoore struggled to stand, and Madeline wound her arm around his waist to help. Lightning flashed, and they could see Vale's exposed skin through a rip in his shirt. Madeline gasped. The markings on Vale's chest and neck were unmistakable.

Ravensmoore pointed. "I don't think you'll be up to any husbandly duties for some time. You've got smallpox."

"Liar!" Vale jerked back as though an invisible hand had reached out and slapped him. He pulled his shirt apart and stared at the pustules on his torso. "No! This isn't possible!"

"You're sick, Vale. You must return to the asylum and wait this out with the others. If you survive, you can go to the gallows."

Vale fell to his knees. In a shocked whisper he said, "This cannot be."

"Tie him up, Donavan." He put an arm around Madeline. "Let's go find your mother. And then let's go home."

"My home or yours?" Madeline asked.

He smiled wanly. "Whichever you choose."

She pressed closer, fearful that he would fall without her support. "I choose Ravensmoore."

Chapter 25

For by grace are ye saved through faith; and
that not of yourselves: it is the gift of God.
—Ephesians 2:8

*I*N THE DAYS following, Devlin succeeded in persuading Madeline and her mother to stay with him at Ravensmoore until the situation with Vale could be fully resolved. He sent for his mother as well and carefully saw to the healing of both women, rejoicing as they slowly returned to full health. He too recovered from the ordeal—Langford's expertise made certain of that, as well as days of rest and respite, where he was coddled by his sisters and comforted by the presence of Madeline and his mother.

Two weeks after the tumultuous events, word came of Vale's death from smallpox, and just days later came a message from the constable in York. Alone in the library, Devlin scanned the letter quickly.

> Dear Lord Ravensmoore,
> The following information is most sensitive in nature. I thought it best that you should disclose this knowledge when and as you see fit. I hate to add to your burdens, as you have been through much of late, but I rest in the assurance that you will relay this troublesome bit of news to the countess at the appropriate time.

It appears that Vale was a very busy man. We have discovered that he was legally married to another woman, and that after staging her own "death," she schemed with him to attain the countess's fortune. Vale's marriage to the countess is therefore null and void.

As you know, in addition to this abomination, Vale and Sullivan found another avenue for gaining riches through the unnecessary and undeserved incarceration of innocents to the madhouse at Ashcroft. This included the unfortunate imprisonment of your mother and many others. Typically, young girls and married women were victims of his schemes. We are currently engaged in investigating possible victims and securing their release. Simon Cox has agreed to help us in this investigation since he has firsthand knowledge of the schemes that Sullivan and Vale employed.

Sincerely,

Constable Barton

Devlin mulled over the letter, frowned, and asked Hummel to have Madeline brought to the library. Meanwhile he read another letter, smiling at the very different news he read there.

A moment later Madeline appeared, and he set that letter aside. His eyes roamed over her, and he marveled at the difference in her from the time he met her on the hunt field till now. Today she was dressed in a lilac silk gown that made her eyes sparkle. "You are beautiful, Lady Madeline."

Madeline blushed. "Thank you, my lord."

He led her to a chair. "It appears we must trouble your mother further. And though you intuited Vale's character from the beginning, this will be a shock."

"What's wrong?" Madeline furrowed her brow.

Devlin handed her the letter from Constable Barton. Watching the array of emotions that crossed Madeline's face, he wished he could have spared her this latest insult. She had been through so much already, and he had held back these two weeks, watching her carefully to be sure she did not slip back into depression. Knowing that they all needed time to recover from the trauma of recent events, he had not yet declared his feelings but instead treated her with brotherly gentleness.

"The bigamous thief!" Madeline jumped up from the chair and paced the room with the letter in her hand. "How could he get away with such horrible crimes? To think how close my mother came to dying. And your mother. Look at all she's lost. It is so very sad. Why does God allow these dreadful things to happen?"

Devlin shook his head. "There are many mysteries we will never be able to understand, yet God has a plan. All we can do is trust."

"You're right. I know you are, but still it is difficult." She turned from him. "I must share this with my mother immediately."

He followed as she led him down the hallway toward the drawing room.

"We have more news—about Vale, Mother," Madeline said, as she and Devlin entered the room.

"What have you heard?" Grace rose from her place at the pianoforte.

"You both look so serious. Is something wrong?" Elethea asked from the sofa where she sat reading. She adjusted the veil that covered the smallpox scars upon her face. Miraculously, in spite of the years of suffering, her mind was less scarred than her face. Her stability of mind amazed them all and relieved Devlin of the fear he'd harbored of carrying the seed of madness.

Hally and Melton had joined them for the afternoon. Both brought joy and laughter into the house and were a comfort to them all. Hally caught Madeline's hand, and Devlin heard her whisper,

"Isn't that the lilac silk gown your father bought for you? The one you promised to wear only for a special occasion?"

"It is." Madeline smiled. "I thought it time."

Devlin rejoiced at this sign of Madeline's progress. Perhaps today *was* the day…

Madeline squeezed Hally's hand then continued to the pianoforte, where Grace had been playing for their entertainment. She held out her hand, leading her mother to a settee. Devlin waited as they settled themselves, hands entwined.

"I've received a letter that will explain it all," Devlin said, and then he read it aloud.

Grace gasped. "How could I have been so blind to his nature? You were right, Madeline. You were right from the beginning." Grace dabbed at her eyes with an embroidered handkerchief. "Why didn't I listen to you?"

"We all have our blind spots, Mother."

"But I was so certain that he loved me. How could I have been so wrong?"

"Perhaps he did, Mother, in his own distorted way. However, his love of self and his obsessive greed were stronger. I am so sorry."

"God's love is greater, Countess Richfield," Elethea said gently. "He will heal your broken heart, and in His time you may yet love another man."

"I do not believe I will ever trust another man," Grace said sadly, "much less love one."

Hally spoke up. "Lady Ravensmoore is right. When I lost James, I too felt that I could never care for another man. But then God sent Mr. Melton." She smiled. "I mean Dr. Melton." She pressed his hand and gazed into his eyes.

Elethea smiled and turned back to Grace. "Give it time, my dear. If God could keep me sane in a prison of insanity and despair, He is mighty enough to heal your heart as well."

Leaving their mothers behind to comfort each other, Madeline allowed Ravensmoore to lead her into the gardens. "It's been a difficult day, my dear. But I don't want you to go to sleep tonight with bad memories." Ravensmoore took her hand and led her deeper into the maze of flowering plants and blooms the colors of the rainbow.

Stopping under a shaded trellis drooping with trumpet vine, he smiled. "I have another surprise for you. A good one this time."

"What is it?" She eyed him curiously. "I can't imagine."

Ravensmoore's eyes twinkled. "I have received good news today from Dr. Langford. He has declared me competent to practice medicine. He will provide the highest recommendations regarding my expertise in surgery and that of general practitioner. I am finally and officially a qualified physician."

"Congratulations!" Madeline smiled up at him. "You are truly gifted, my lord. Never doubt that God has called you to this work. After observing your efforts over the last few weeks, both within the asylum and with our mothers, I cannot begrudge your calling in medicine."

Ravensmoore shrugged. "Granted, I am not a typical physician. Society will say I serve below my station, but I serve only God."

"I'm very proud of your accomplishment." Madeline beamed.

"There's more. I've hired Wiggins as a blacksmith. And I've made inquiries about purchasing Ashcroft Asylum. Melton has agreed to run the place for me so I can attend to my duties here at Ravensmoore and still do hands-on work for the patients in need. I want to do all I can to help the poor souls at the asylum as I expand my medical knowledge. It is the only thing I could think to do."

Madeline looked up at him, letting her pride in him fill her gaze. "I think that is a marvelous idea. It will mean so much for so many."

Seemingly encouraged by her words, he went on. "I've decided on a new name for the asylum. *Safe Haven*. We will put the bad memories of Ashcroft behind us. I will do everything possible to make it a true shelter for those who suffer. Then patients like Amanda can get the help they need. Mrs. Sharpe and the others will want for nothing to help those in their care."

Madeline nodded. "No one will be there who doesn't need to be there. You and Melton will not allow those dreadful 'treatments' to continue."

"I was hoping you'd see it that way."

Silence fell, and Ravensmoore stepped closer, taking her hands into his. "I have been waiting to talk to you, Madeline. Waiting to see if you have suffered any lasting effects from all you have endured."

She shuddered slightly. "Thank God, that is all behind us now."

"You weren't made to carry your burdens alone, Maddie."

She glanced up at him, pleased by his use of her name. "I know that now. I mourned my family members' deaths for far too long and nearly lost my mind because of it. But God rescued me from the pit, Devlin. I will never forget that. I know now that He loves me and watches over me. And no matter what happens, I'll never separate myself from Him again."

"He holds us both, Madeline," Ravensmoore murmured. "He holds us both." He pressed a kiss to the tips of her fingers, then pulled her still closer. "I wonder..." he murmured.

She held still, waiting.

"Could you marry a man like me, Madeline? A physician and a surgeon and possibly a doctor of the mind? The *ton* will snub us. We will not be able to lead a conventional, fashionable life. And I will be a constant reminder to you of illness, insanity, even death." His face darkened at the thought. "I wish I could offer nothing but sunshine and flowers, but God has called me to battle the demons of suffering. Are you able to join me in that battle and be my countess?"

"Of course I will." Her eyes held his. "When I staunched your bleeding in the asylum, I knew the panic you encountered with my father. I know now that his death was not your fault. I simply could not face it at that time because I wanted someone to blame. We've come through this fiery trial for a reason. I trust you, Devlin, and I trust God, who brought us together."

She raised her lips to his and lost herself in a sweet storm of delight. When their lips parted, he breathed her name as though it would be on his lips forever, as his kiss would forever be on hers.

"My Maddie."

Devlin pulled her close in the protection of his warm embrace and whispered in her ear. "Together God will guide us on this journey, Maddie, for He alone is the safe haven of our souls. But you, my love, are the refuge for my heart."

A Note From the Author

Dear Reader,

I am grateful that you chose this book, *Secrets of the Heart*, to read from all the other books calling to you from brick and mortar bookstore shelves and those in cyberspace. I love that you spent your time escaping into the past with me to explore the world of Regency England and the characters I populated it with who struggle with their own flaws and challenges, much as we do.

I pray that you enjoyed this story and that in some small way it does give you encouragement for the future. I hope you look forward to my next book, *Chameleon*, which will make its appearance in 2012.

The history of mental illness and its treatment is a long and complicated battle for sanity often filled with misunderstanding. Even with today's modern treatments and therapies many patients still face difficulty and stigma both within and outside of the church. Families and loved ones pray for relief of those affected by depression, anxiety disorders, and the many other mental health disorders that prevent quality living and a life passionately filled with purpose.

It is my greatest hope that someday the secrets of the brain and mind that harbor illness will be unlocked so that true peace of mind can be experienced by everyone.

Remember 2 Timothy 1:7: "For God hath not given us the spirit of fear; but of power, and of love, and of a sound mind."

Gratefully,
Jillian Kent

COMING IN 2012—

BOOK TWO OF
THE RAVENSMOORE CHRONICLES:

Chameleon

CHAPTER ONE

London 1818

"An adventure at last." Victoria stared in unabashed awe at the sea of activity that surrounded them as their coach merged with others making its way through the muddy, rutted streets. The crowded sidewalks teemed with people of all classes. Women in brilliant gowns of color swirled past street urchins and beggars, meshing into an ever-shifting tapestry of humanity.

She'd stepped into a world bigger than York, a world she'd only dreamed about. Victoria leaned back against the banquette and sighed. "London is simply wonderful."

Nora, her servant and traveling companion, nudged her. "Ye might need to see your brother for more reasons than simply visiting him, Lady Victoria. Me thinks the trip has been over hard on ye noggin, and ye may need a wee bit of the medicinal herbs."

She looked at Nora in confusion for a moment and then smiled. "You jest, of course."

Nora sighed. "Of course."

Victoria and her best friend, Lazarus, a behemoth of a mastiff, vied for the window when a group of young boys chased a dog down the street. Lazarus barked and strained against the coach door in hopes of joining them, but he only succeeded in pushing Victoria out of the way.

"Such a window hound you are, Lazarus," Victoria said, rubbing a hand over his big, sleek head while she turned and looked out the opposite side of the coach. Men and women hawking wares called to them in hopes of making a profit.

The busy streets gave way to quieter and more prestigious avenues as they made their way to Grosvenor Square and her brother's London townhome. The quality of the air improved as they moved farther from the central streets of town and into the areas of the upper crust. The coach slowed and then pulled to a halt in front of number three, Devlin's home.

"I cannot wait another moment." Grabbing the handle of the coach door, Victoria stepped out onto the curb. Lazarus bounded onto the street.

"Good heavens, it's a bear," an elderly passerby said, clinging to her equally astonished husband. "What will become of us?"

Victoria smothered a grin. "He's quite harmless."

Lazarus barked, and the couple hurried their steps. Nora bolted out of the coach and grabbed the dog by the collar before he chased the unsuspecting couple down the street. "Thank you, Nora. Just in time."

Victoria gathered her blue velvet traveling skirt and ran up the five steps to the entrance. She desperately wanted to open the door and race inside. She forced herself to reach for the gilded knocker, hesitated, and then grabbed the doorknob with her gloved hand when the door swung open, pulling her with it. She collided with a body that knocked the breath from her. Strong hands captured her before she tumbled down the steps.

"Dash it! I could have killed you, woman."

Gulping for air, Victoria regained her balance and her nearly lost blue-feathered bonnet. Lazarus leaped on the man, knocking him down and pinning him to the ground.

"Get this drooling beast off of me!" the man yelled, lying half in and half out of the doorway entrance. "Now!"

"You, sir, are not my brother."

"Indeed." A sheen of sweat showed on the man's brow. "I dislike dogs. Call him off."

"Stay, Lazarus." Devlin laughed and patted the dog's head as he slid past them and wrapped his sister in his arms. "Are you unharmed, my little Snoop?"

"I believe so." Victoria burrowed deep into his warm, comforting embrace. "I've missed you, Dev," she whispered into his chest and squeezed him tight. "I've missed you so much."

"And I you." Devlin held her back at arm's length. "It's good to see you. Now, come in and tell me all about your journey and how my wife is doing at home without me."

"Have you forgotten? We have company," she said.

"In that case, allow me to introduce you to Jonathon Denning, Lord Witt."

"A pleasure to meet you, Lord Witt," Victoria said, bending over to see him. "Do you always go about knocking down unsuspecting women?"

Witt groaned under the weight of the dog. "Ravensmoore, I do not find this amusing."

"Answer my sister's question, Witt. Are you in the habit of such ungentlemanly behavior?"

"Only when female newcomers appear."

Victoria grinned. "He shows a sense of humor."

Devlin's butler appeared and stood over Lazarus and Witt. "May I be of assistance, your lordship?"

"Thank you, Henry." Devlin patted the dog. "It's all right, Lazarus. Go take Henry for a walk."

Lazarus stepped off of Witt. "Good boy, Lazarus. Good boy," praised Victoria. The dog turned and nuzzled Victoria's hand for the treat that awaited him.

Lord Witt sat up in the doorway and ran his hands through disheveled black hair. "I could do with a brandy."

"Lady Victoria." Henry straightened his already straight back. "Welcome to London." He executed a most noble bow and assisted Lord Witt to his feet.

"Henry!" Victoria said. "It is good to see you. Do you mind taking Lazarus? He adores you."

"For you I would take Lazarus and one of his friends." The butler smiled, turning his serious face into cheerful amiability. "Come along, old friend." He accepted a leash from Nora. "Welcome to London, Nora. Would you care to accompany me?"

Nora nodded. "It will help me find my balance again after a long journey."

Devlin turned to the butler. "Henry, feed the beast when you return, and then bring him to Victoria."

"Feed him, sir? And just who should be the sacrifice? Lazarus has a shine to his eyes, and I'm thinking it is for me."

"Get creative, man. Start with Cook."

"Now, there's a right smart answer. Cook will faint dead away."

Devlin grinned, a wicked glint in his eye. "There's your answer. If Cook has the nerve to faint, let Lazarus eat her."

"Devlin!" Victoria feigned horror. "What an outlandish thing to say." She covered a grin. "That would bring her around faster than smelling salts."

Lord Witt leaned against the doorjamb, listening to their banter. "I could use some smelling salts myself." He grabbed a handkerchief from his coat pocket and wiped at his forehead. "Forgive me, but I've never shared the passion that some do for dogs. Did I introduce myself?"

Victoria turned toward him. "No, but my brother introduced you. Don't you remember?"

"All I remember is your dog drooling on me." Lord Witt shook out the handkerchief and wiped at the wetness on his coat sleeves after wiping the sweat from his face. Victoria mentally weighed his first movement. He'd been unnerved. He was trying to hide that now, but he'd been taken quite off guard by Lazarus. Lord Witt tucked the handkerchief away and turned his gaze on Victoria. "May I ask if you visit London often, Lady Victoria?"

His gray eyes swept over her form with such intensity that she shivered. He studied her in the same open manner she'd seen men study women during the country assemblies in Yorkshire. Those gentlemen were besotted by a lady's beauty, but his perusal added a hint more of the rogue. Isolated as she had been, she had learned to depend far more on her powers of observation and deduction than on feminine beauty and the ability to flatter. But before she could recover from his scrutiny and utter a response, Devlin stepped between them.

"I believe you were leaving before my sister arrived, Witt. I suggest you not delay."

Victoria looked from her brother to Lord Witt. Interesting. They didn't like each other.

Lord Witt appeared to mentally calculate the situation. "I bid you good day, Ravensmoore. Lady Victoria, this is a day I will not forget." He picked up his hat and left.

Devlin said, "Let us go inside, Snoop. I want to show you the house. And I insist that you take a nap."

Victoria stopped and looked behind her before going through the door. She sensed the gentleman's eyes on her, yet she could not see him. Her intuition told her life was about to change in ways she couldn't imagine. She turned her back on the street and felt a thrill of excitement race through her as she stepped into her brother's home.

Witt watched from across the street. So she was Ravensmoore's sister. Seeing her again would take some doing since Ravensmoore and he were not on the best of terms. Still, there were ways to get what one wanted, when one wanted badly enough. What exactly did he want? He'd just met her. So why did he feel as though he'd just looked into the eyes of his future?

He knew that Ravensmoore had just come from Parliament. The House of Lords session for the day had ended, and there were several issues being discussed. He was certain that the Lord Doctor, as Ravensmoore had been dubbed, was not at all happy with the direction the last discussion had taken related to reforms of the mental asylums. It was bound to make his life even more controversial than it already was at the moment.

A page from the palace approached him. "Lord Witt? I was asked to give this to you." The boy put the note in his hand and disappeared before he could offer a coin. Witt scanned the note and frowned. Returning to the street, he looked for his coach and signaled his driver.

The team of horses moved onto the muddy street just as rain splashed gently across his face. Witt jumped into the interior of the coach.

"Where to, sir?" called the driver.

"Carlton House, Denton."

After a short ride Witt entered the home of the Prince Regent. Grand chandeliers, marble floors that went on forever, and ceilings painted with scenes of myths and legends greeted him—a wonderful place to visit, but not his kind of purposeful, long-term living. He much preferred the country. What could be so urgent that Prinny would send for him so soon after their recent conversation?

A young page approached him, a serious expression clouding his young features.

"Lord Witt, His Royal Highness awaits you. Follow me, please."

Witt smiled. "Thomas, you're far too serious this day. Why the frown? I enjoy the sound of your laughter much better than the stern look you wear."

"You will know soon enough, and you will understand."

An edge of uneasiness rippled down his back as he followed the boy in the direction of the royal guestrooms. As one of the preferred spies for the Crown during the war, he'd never lost the senses he'd honed from that time. But those days were past, and he enjoyed his quiet life in the country now.

The page knocked on a door and bowed out of the way as the door swung open. A dozen men occupied the chamber. All wore serious expressions.

"What has happened?"

"Stone has been attacked," said the Regent, stepping from the circle of men who surrounded a large four-poster bed with drapes drawn.

"How? What happened to him?"

"We are not entirely sure…that's why I sent for you. When word gets out of what has happened…" Prinny threw his arms in the air. "What must be done? This is unacceptable! His family must be informed, and that will create chaos if not outright panic."

The look of fear on everyone's faces said much. "Tell me what happened."

Lord Whitby came forward. "Take a look for yourself." He pulled the drapes back from the bed.

Witt thought he had seen every manner of injury during the war, but this, this was hideous. "That's Stone?" The slashing of the face and neck appeared to be the work of something with sharp claws.

"Has the royal physician seen him?" Witt swallowed hard as he studied the ghastly features of Lord Stone.

Prinny looked to Witt for direction. "We must decide the best course of action, and soon. Never has anyone dared to attack a member of Parliament since Bellingham assassinated Prime Minister Spencer Perceval, and that was six years ago. Stone is near death, and his wife and eldest son have been summoned. It won't be for long that we can keep this flagrant attack quiet." Prinny slammed both fists on the desk.

Witt took charge. "We must proceed with caution. I suggest we pull Lord Ravensmoore into this conversation immediately. It may be that having a physician who is a peer proves to be most helpful."

The Regent paced and mumbled to himself, seemingly in a struggle to make a decision. Finally he declared, "Send for him."

"Well, my dear sister. What did you think of your trip?" Devlin cut into a juicy piece of beef but kept his eyes on her.

"The trip was an adventure and a delight, though I doubt that Nora saw it that way. You would not believe how overprotective she's become. She hovers about like a bee on a tulip."

Devlin imagined that Snoop had lived up to her name throughout the trip and been more than difficult to keep track of at every stop along the way.

"You look healthy. A nice glow in your cheeks and the usual mischievousness in your eyes assures me that you are quite well."

"And you, brother, look as though you haven't slept for days. There are dark circles under your eyes, and I gather you have been busy caring for someone quite ill."

"That's why I'm a doctor, Snoop." He never could fool his sister; she'd always had an uncanny sense of knowing how people felt, probably because she'd fought her own sickness for most of her life.

"I do hope you have arranged to take some time off while I'm here so you can show me about and not leave that to someone else." She accepted more rosemary potatoes from the server and ate with a hearty appetite. "Mmm, how wonderful these are." She sighed her enjoyment. "I'm surprised you're not fat, brother. The food is most enjoyable."

Cook brought the dessert in herself. "He's rarely home to eat his food, Lady Victoria. He's far too busy a man. Perhaps he will be makin' himself more at home now that he's got your company. I hope you'll be enjoyin' this puddin'. 'Tis special for tonight."

Cook set a bowl of bread pudding between them with clotted cream to accompany the decadent dessert. Beside the dish she added a small bowl of mixed fruit.

"Cook, you've outdone yourself. Thank you. I can see from the sparkle in my sister's eyes that she is most grateful." He grinned and raised his glass in a toast. "To health."

Victoria did likewise. "To health and to adventure. May this visit prove to be the beginning of many more adventures."

Henry appeared. "Your lordship, a message." He held a silver tray with a note upon it, which in itself meant nothing until Devlin saw the seal.

"Interesting. It's from His Royal Highness."

"The Prince Regent?" Victoria leaned close to her brother. "What does it say?"

"If you let me open it, then I shall know." He ripped the missive open and read, "You are needed at the palace. Come at once."

"May I come with you, Devlin?" Victoria pleaded, her eyes wide with interest. "Please."

Devlin wondered what this could possibly be about. The Prince Regent had his own physician. What could he possibly want?

"Dev, please. It would be a wonderful way to begin my adventure in London."

He pinched her cheek gently. "No."

"But why not?"

"Because I don't know what's going on and you've not been summoned. It's me that must go. You must rest from your long journey and settle into your room. I think you'll like your room. I've left you a surprise under your pillow."

"Drat, I'd much rather go with you than stay in my room. That's what I'm trying to escape, if you remember."

"And so you have."

"Ravensmoore." Witt greeted Lord Ravensmoore instead of sending Thomas. He'd wanted to escape the chamber upstairs and have some time to think about what had happened. He was certain there was more to this story, but Prinny had made it clear that he wanted Ravensmoore on hand before the conversation proceeded further.

"Witt. I didn't expect to see you again so soon."

"Nor I you, but as fate would have it, the Prince Regent asked me to fill you in on events. Follow me."

"Follow you where, and what events?"

"Upstairs. You have a patient who needs tending."

"A patient?" Ravensmoore raised an inquisitive brow.

Witt nodded, admiring the man's ability to refrain from asking who. "Follow me." Ravensmoore had made it clear when he allowed that monster of a dog to remain on top of him that it was his idea of getting even for the interrogation, at Prinny's behest, of working as a physician and a peer. Witt had no doubt that if he hadn't caught Lady Victoria, Ravensmoore would probably have encouraged the dog to finish him off. A razor-sharp ache gnawed up his back. He flinched.

"You all right?" Ravensmoore asked.

He'd already caused enough upheaval for one day. "Yes. Just an old war injury."

"I understand that you prefer to live in the country since the war."

"You aren't listening to rumors, I hope."

"Rumors sometimes hold a grain of truth, Witt. I'm just curious."

"Curious why I'm here and not in the country? I'm sure you are wishing I'd remained in the country."

"The thought had crossed my mind."

"Lord Stone was attacked. He has been seen by the royal physician and is sedated with laudanum, but it's complicated. Everything you are about to hear must be kept in the utmost confidence. Do you understand?"

"Of course." Devlin stopped as they were climbing the steps. "What kind of attack?"

"He's been slashed about the face. But we don't know how or why. He'll not likely survive. But there's more. You have been called in out of desperation because you're a doctor and a peer."

"What can I do?"

"That's what the Regent wants to know, I believe." Witt opened the door to a meeting room this time, just as Thomas had opened it for him less than an hour ago at the chamber where Stone lay.

The Prince Regent, known for his frivolous lifestyle, appeared to Witt as though he might fall into an apoplectic fit. This was in contrast to his usual jovial manner. He rushed to meet Ravensmoore when they entered the room. "Thank you for coming so quickly. We need to treat this situation with the utmost of care."

Prinny's hair and clothing were disheveled, and that in itself showed just how out of sorts the Regent was this day. He would not want to fall below the standard that Beau Brummel set for the *ton*.

Ravensmoore bowed slightly. "Of course, Your Royal Highness. Whatever I can do. But I suggest you sit down before you fall ill."

The other lords in the room nodded. Some paced with their hands behind their backs. Two looked out the windows to the gardens below. Others sat in chairs with exhausted expressions on their faces.

"Yes. Yes, you're right," said the Regent. "Please make your own assessment of Lord Stone." He slid to a chair and took a deep breath. "Witt has told you what has happened?"

"Just that Stone has been attacked. Disfigured?"

"Yes, yes. But there's more. A message."

"What sort of message, sir?" Devlin asked.

The Prince Regent looked to Witt and nodded.

"A note was found on Stone's person." Witt produced it from his coat pocket and read, "You have been found guilty of conspiring with sinful men for sinful purposes. I will now handle the situation as I see fit."

"This sounds like Stone did something that someone else did not approve."

"There's more," said Witt. "Underneath the scrawled name was writing in Stone's blood. It reads, 'He is only the first. Repent and guard your lives for you won't have them long.' And it's signed, 'Lord Talon.'"

Witt studied Ravensmoore as he absorbed the implications of this information. Shock, surprise, and then anger swooped over his features.

"Who would do such a thing?" Ravensmoore asked. "Why? And who is Lord Talon?"

"My thoughts as well." Witt handed him the scribbled note that had been found on Stone's body. "His penmanship lacks the benefit of practice. Perhaps he's not a learned man, or perhaps he's trying to disguise the fact."

"Whatever the case may be," the Prince Regent said, "he must be found immediately. God knows what havoc this Lord Talon fellow could cause within the House of Lords." He leaned toward the two of them. "I need your help, Ravensmoore."

"I'll do whatever I can, but what can be done? You have the royal physician at your disposal; surely he can be counted on for his discretion and talents."

"The royal physician has grown soft and is not exposed to injuries like these. We need someone like you."

Witt explained, "You are unique, Ravensmoore. You are both physician and nobleman. You can work with the royal physician, but you also have an ear close to the common man and may hear or see things on the street that others may not. A convenience, indeed."

"Witt here also possesses talents from his years in my service, and he has agreed to do all in his power to locate this demon and stop him." Prinny mopped the sweat from his brow.

"I'd like to see Lord Stone, sir. Where is he?"

"Witt, show Ravensmoore to the suite of rooms I've assigned to Stone. I'm keeping him well protected in case the madman who did this decides to try and finish him off. I've dispatched messengers to every member of Parliament to convene early tomorrow morning and to be aware of the danger."

Witt and Ravensmoore stood and bowed.

As soon as they'd left the Regent's chambers, Witt heard Ravensmoore take a deep breath. "This is unbelievable. An attack on a member of the House of Lords and a threat to the others. What if he can't be found?"

"I'll find him," Witt said easily. "The difficulty will be stopping him before someone is murdered."

FREE NEWSLETTERS
TO HELP EMPOWER YOUR LIFE

Why subscribe today?

❑ **DELIVERED DIRECTLY TO YOU.** All you have to do is open your inbox and read.

❑ **EXCLUSIVE CONTENT.** We cover the news overlooked by the mainstream press.

❑ **STAY CURRENT.** Find the latest court rulings, revivals, and cultural trends.

❑ **UPDATE OTHERS.** Easy to forward to friends and family with the click of your mouse.

CHOOSE THE E-NEWSLETTER THAT INTERESTS YOU MOST:

- Christian news
- Daily devotionals
- Spiritual empowerment
- And much, much more

SIGN UP AT: **http://freenewsletters.charismamag.com**

8178